In Too
DEEP

JADE CHURCH

Also by Jade Church

Temper the Flame

This Never Happened

Get Even (Sun City #1)

Coming Soon

The Lingering Dark

Fall Hard (Sun City #2)

About the Author

Jade Church is an avid reader and writer of spicy romance. She loves sweet and swoony love interests who aren't scared to smack your ass and bold female leads. Jade currently lives in the U.K. and spends the majority of her time reading and writing books, as well as binge re-watching *The Vampire Diaries*.

Contents

Content Warning

In Too Deep contains themes and content that some readers may find triggering, this includes: *references to anxiety and panic attacks, alcohol use, stalking and threat, gun/gunshot, knife/knife wound, death of an animal (brief, mostly off-page), hospitals and car accident.*

To everyone who thinks they're prepared for what life might throw at them... Surprise.

Chapter One

S ometimes, Rose really couldn't remember why she was friends with Samantha. She'd arrived back in Cincinnati from New York a few minutes ago and had checked her phone once she'd landed, finding a slew of texts and messages that were mostly from her overexcited mother.

Then there was Samantha.

Rose could almost picture the slight wrinkle between Sam's eyebrows, the way she'd pucker her mouth and nod her head slowly and condescendingly while Rose talked. They'd gone to college together, so she supposed it had been a friendship of convenience, but the truth was that Samantha made Rose feel small. The month she'd spent with Sam in New York had felt a lot longer than four weeks, and as terrible as the thought was, it had only really driven home just how much Rose missed Maia. Sam and Maia, Rose's best friend, had only met a handful of times and couldn't be more different. Where Maia chased love, romance, and adventure, Samantha's biggest ambition in life was to be

1

married with at least three children before the age of thirty-five. While there was nothing wrong with that in itself, the way that Samantha sneered at the thought of doing anything else was more than a little aggravating, especially for someone like Rose whose mother constantly badgered her about 'settling down'.

Rose had only been free of Sam for the duration of the plane ride and she was already pestering her, though thankfully she knew that Sam would likely have forgotten all about her by the time evening rolled around and Samantha remembered all her other snooty, judgy friends. Rose was no stranger to snooty, but Samantha's girl group was on another level.

Deciding to check the messages from Sam and her mom once she was actually off the plane, Rose stepped back onto the tarmac and froze at the well-coiffed woman waiting next to a blacked-out town car, beaming. So much for a peaceful ride home.

"Mother," she said, resuming her walk as she moved towards her. "How did you know what time my flight got in?" Because Rose *definitely* hadn't told her.

"Samantha let me know." Her mom's lips puckered when Rose didn't immediately hug her and she sighed, putting her case down by the car door and letting her mom wrap her into a heavily perfumed embrace. "Though I would rather have heard it from my daughter," she whispered reproachfully in Rose's ear and Rose bit back her sigh. "I take it you haven't seen the messages?"

Rose disentangled herself and pulled open the door with a quick nod to her driver as he stowed her luggage in the trunk. "Gosh, Mom. I landed two seconds ago, so no, I've not checked anything yet." Her irritation rising with every moment that passed, Rose tugged her phone back out of her purse again as her mom climbed in the car.

Sam's latest text message did little to assuage the feeling of irritation. The whole time she'd been in the city Sam had been pestering her about dating. Of course, *Sam* had been seeing a nice, bland, corporate man for the past two years and was certain he was about to pop 'the question' any day. This, naturally, prompted the conversation of 'and who are *you* seeing, Rose?' To which the answer was simple: nobody. She was in the city to work, not to speed date, regardless of how many eligible bachelors Sam had thrust under her nose at surprise lunches or drinks in the evening.

Samantha, much like Rose's mother, felt that Rose needed to 'put herself out there more'. So she didn't do casual sex? It wasn't for everyone! So she hadn't been on a date in… crap, had it really been over a year? Well, that wasn't her fault – dating as a DuLoe was practically impossible between the people more interested in her parents' businesses and money than her and the others who only liked her family name.

Rose was an events coordinator, one in fairly high demand because she didn't strictly *need* to work – so she only took on the projects that genuinely interested her. Take New York for example, she'd been there to organize a masquerade ball that doubled as a fashion show for an upcoming designer. Now *that* was interesting – listening to Samantha ramble about how big her engagement ring would be, on the other hand, was not.

Worse, Sam knew her mother. They'd met at the graduation party her mother had put together for Rose and they had clicked in a way that had been wholly horrifying. If it was just Samantha in the text chain, Rose might have been able to blow off the date Sam had arranged without consulting her. Unfortunately...

ANNABEL DuLoe: A blind date! Oh how fun, you must bring him by *The Hummingbird,* darling. What a fabulous idea Samantha!

ROSE GROANED but quickly smothered the sound as her mom gracefully sank into the seat next to her. Dating just didn't excite her anymore, and why did she *need* a man anyway? She was successful, rich, attractive, educated, and well-traveled. What could a man really add to any of that? And bringing him to *The Hummingbird* was just asking for trouble. It was one of the many establishments her family owned and ran, though it was by far the newest, and as such it held her mother's attention a lot more than the chain of hotels she'd bought and renovated several years ago. Going on a blind date was bad enough, but doing it in front of her mother...?

Rose loved her mom, really, but they were very different people.

"So how was your flight? How was New York? It must have been so nice for you to catch up with Samantha. You two don't get to see each other nearly enough."

Rose let her mom ramble on, after all, she didn't pause for breath and clearly wasn't looking for an actual conversation. Instead, she nodded in the right places and made sympathetic sounds whenever there was a slight silence as her attention drifted.

It was only a short drive to the apartment suite at *The*

Hart but with traffic and her mother in the seat next to her, she knew this drive could easily double as torture. At the very least, they had the AC.

Her mother's next words caught her drifting attention and she blew out a harsh breath as she tuned back in, wrinkling her nose and hoping she'd misheard.

"I'm sorry, what?"

The frown she gave Rose had her forcing out a polite smile and her mom sniffed as the car finally began to move again. "I *said* don't forget we have dinner with the Blakes next week. Grace has been dying to see you."

A bitter feeling crawled its way up her throat until Rose had to swallow, biting her tongue against her next question because she wasn't sure she wanted the answer.

Back in town for barely any time at all and her mother had already corralled her into dinner with the Blakes as well as this blind date. Grace was her mother's best friend, though their friendship was something of a mystery considering they were polar opposites. If it were just dinner with her, Rose wouldn't have minded too much. But her mother had said *Blakes* – as in, plural. Combined with the fact that her mother was constantly trying to set her up, Rose had an unfortunate suspicion that she knew who else would be at that dinner. David.

David Blake was charming, sexy (if the recent press photos she'd seen were to be believed) and stinking rich. Rose also hated him with pretty much every fiber of her being.

They had been forced together a lot as kids because their families were close and, at first, Rose had always wanted to hang out with Blake and his slightly older group of friends. But naturally she was younger and therefore uncool, yet in the quiet moments she'd resented Blake less – like when he'd snuck her extra dessert, or held her hand all the way home after she'd fallen over into the sea at the beach party her parents had been hosting.

Unfortunately, the unpleasant memories fully outranked any small acts of kindness David Blake had seen fit to send her way. Especially once they both had become older. The dinners and parties and lunches and cocktail meetups had become unbearable, partially due to the fact that Blake had become handsome and knew it and the rest was down to Rose's mother's unabashed hope that Rose and Blake might... date. Of course, eventually Rose had simply begun to decline the invitations. It was for the best really. Blake got under her skin in a way that made it hard for her to keep her mouth shut and her thoughts to herself, he seemed to make it his personal mission to annoy her whenever they saw each other. So far, she'd managed to successfully avoid him for about five years which was no mean feat considering her mother's proclivity for setting them up.

"I've texted you the details," her mom continued when Rose stayed silent. "It'll be nice to have the gang together."

"Will Dad be there?"

"Oh, well, you know how busy your father gets."

She did. In a lot of ways, Rose took after her father more so than her mother. "Of course." Talking to her mom was always hard. At least with her dad, the silences were comfortable. Often with her mother, the silences felt... stifling. Rose was young and accomplished but, somehow without saying anything at all, her mom made her feel like she wasn't enough.

"You didn't have to meet me at the airport," she said at last and her mom shrugged, a slip of white-blonde hair falling free across her cheekbone.

"I wanted to," Annabel said and Rose found herself out of words again. It was ironic really, how alike she and her mother looked. They both had the same slim nose and long blonde hair, but Rose had her father's eyes. If not for them she would look like a carbon-copy of her mother, and when she'd been younger she'd loved that. They'd dressed up in the same costumes at Halloween and done mother-daughter piano duets at Christmas, but at some point Rose had grown up and realized she didn't know who she was. Of course, that was the same feeling most college students had, but it was strange to realize that she'd spent so long being her mother's mini-me that she didn't know who *she* was or what styles *she* liked. Sometimes their relationship was a loss she mourned, despite it still being right there.

The sounds of the city here were so different from New York, more like a comfortable hum of background noise rather than the roar that New York seemed to operate on constantly. By the time they pulled up to *The Hart* the silence had become permanent and her heartbeat had slowed to a gradual calm.

Rose waved her mother off as she slipped off her seatbelt and leaned in, pressing a kiss to her cheek. "No, no, stay here. The driver will take you wherever you want to go, I'm just going to head inside and relax."

"Don't forget about your date!" her mom called as Rose grabbed her suitcase with a smile of thanks to the driver.

"I wish," she muttered before waving as the car drove away and then headed inside. Luckily, she'd been dropped off right outside the entrance to the hotel because already a few people seemed to have taken note of her arrival. Rose ignored them as she pushed through the doors and into the lobby.

These days she didn't even try to keep up with her social media notifications, but she was certain that now she'd been spotted arriving back into Cincy she would have been tagged in half a dozen photos already. It was a vaguely nauseating feeling, knowing someone was always watching.

Rose only had the small carry-on suitcase to roll up to her suite on the top floor, thankfully. Most of the clothes she'd worn in the city had been one-time pieces that she'd left in the closet at *The Phoenix & The Dove,* one of her family's hotels in New York. For someone like her, re-wearing an outfit was a statement and she didn't feel the need to make it. Instead, the gorgeous dress she'd worn to the masquerade would stay in the private penthouse at the hotel until she ever decided to break it out again. The penthouse was closed to the public – much like the suite at *The Hart* that served as her primary residence.

Her case was a shimmery baby pink color that matched her nails and caught the light as she made her way through the hotel lobby to the elevator, humming idly as it took her up to the penthouse that was accessible only with the special key card she carried.

The suite was a sight for sore eyes. Rose traveled a fair amount for work, planning various events and attending them too, but she couldn't say she always enjoyed it. The travel was stressful even if you were in first class and, while she normally stayed in hotels that her family owned, there was always a sense of the unfamiliar that set her on edge.

Life for a DuLoe was constantly in the limelight and most of the time she didn't mind it so much. Her parents both came from old money and decided to build a business portfolio so large that it was unlikely any of their grandchildren would ever have to work. But Rose, much like her parents, enjoyed it. Having a busy mind suited her, idle hands made her antsy.

But having every move cataloged and analyzed and critiqued came with its own set of anxieties and made keeping secrets and dating a little more difficult, plus god forbid she gained a few pounds or ever went out without make-up – the tabloids would be screaming that she was pregnant or dying. There were definitely a few things about having a high profile that she would change if she could.

The elevator doors opened and the soothing beiges and baby pinks of her lounge area made her shoulders drop as she took in the familiar gold accents with a small smile. Maia had helped decorate this place to be both luxe and soothing, so it was no surprise that she was in such high demand for her services these days when her interiors came out like this.

A card sat atop the marble countertops, propped up by a wooden fruit bowl that one of the maids had likely replenished for her. The staff at *The Hart* were amazing – of course, it helped that the DuLoes owned the place.

Rose left her suitcase by the elevator doors, nudged off her cream heels and sighed at the feel of the thick cream carpet beneath her toes as she padded her way over to the cream fabric sofa with the card in hand. It had a simple red heart on the front and the paper was thick, likely expensive. Rose smiled softly as she opened it and read the typed message inside. *I missed you.* Maia had likely arrived back home before Rose had and left this for her. The note wasn't signed, but it was exactly the sort of thoughtful thing Rose's sometimes-roommate and always-best-friend would do.

For a moment, Rose just held the note to her chest. She'd missed Maia a lot and above all else, was glad to be home. She was a creature of comfort, that was for sure, and her least favorite part about traveling was living out of a bag and how much it affected her everyday routine. But she was home now and had a couple of hours to unpack and get ready before the date Samantha and her mom had arranged for her later tonight.

Rose looked longingly down the hallway to where she knew her sinfully large bathtub waited and thought once again that she really needed to gently cut things off with Sam. If not for her, Rose could be enjoying a long soak right now instead of having a quick shower and getting dressed up for a date she didn't even particularly want to go on. Rose could only hope that her date would remain ignorant of who exactly she was, despite going to *The Hummingbird,* otherwise it became impossible to work out whether they liked *her* or her name. To have any possibility of that happening she would need to call the bar while she got dressed and just pray she could get there at a time that her mother was not. Though now her mom knew about the blind date, the chances of that happening were slim. The bar was her mom's baby so she was there most nights, but hopefully luck would be on Rose's side and her date would never have to know he was there with the heir to the DuLoe fortune.

Chapter Two

At first, she'd thought the date had been going surprisingly okay. He'd arrived on time, had dressed-up, and opened her car door for her. A good start. Great, even. She'd tried her best in the car to convince him to go to another restaurant or bar, but there weren't many people who would pass up the chance to go to *The Hummingbird...* including her date. It wasn't an exclusive bar, but it was high-end and often booked out weeks in advance unless, like Rose, you knew the right people.

Uneasily, she'd settled back into the car ride, nodding in the appropriate places as her date spoke to her about his work in the private security sector – not something that Rose really had much expertise in so there wasn't much she could say. This seemed to suit her date just fine though and Rose ignored the unease running through her the closer they came to the bar and the more her date spoke – chances were that this guy shared Sam's views on marriage and kids and a woman's 'place'.

She couldn't climb out of the car fast enough when they arrived, but her eagerness faded as she spotted a familiar dark-blonde head inside. David Blake. Better known as the bed-warmer of most of the women in Cincinnati, he was currently seated at a table with three other women that Rose paid very little attention to as Blake looked up like he could feel her gaze. Rose clenched her jaw and turned away sharply, only to run right into an even bigger disaster as a shockingly tall, blonde woman strode over to her with her arms held wide.

"*Darling!* I'm so glad I caught you. I decided to cover for Lola tonight." Annabel DuLoe patted non-existent stray hairs back into place before pulling her daughter into a bone-crushing hug and Rose wanted to scowl at the theatricality of it all. She knew her mother had likely been lying in wait and had rushed out as soon as she'd spotted them come in.

"Yes, well, I–"

"Your father's upstairs, if you wait just a second, I can go and get him and he can meet this lovely young man!"

Her mom looked like she was seconds away from sprinting towards the office upstairs when her date took her hand in his and pressed a bold kiss to the back. At first Rose was relieved, she didn't need any more spectacle surrounding this car-wreck, but when the guy's lips lingered for too long to really be appropriate Rose wanted to gag and only barely resisted the urge.

"Oh my, what a... gentleman," her mother said at last, retrieving her hand and looking almost sorry that she'd covered for Lola, the Maitre'd who was *supposed* to be greeting her and...Tim? Was that her date's name?

But of course, Cal wouldn't have told her when Rose had called that her mother was covering for Lola – not when it would be more amusing for him to watch Rose rock up with a date and get snared by her mom. Rose shot a narrowed eye look at her cousin and he smirked at her from behind the bar. She couldn't be too annoyed with him really though. With the prospect of Rose's dating life in the mix, there had been no way her mom was going to miss this.

"I'm sure Dad's busy. We're just going to head to the bar." Rose cast a furtive look at her date and held back a groan as Tim (*Tom? Todd?*) stared around with appreciative eyes, clearly aware that not only was he in *the* most up-and-coming bar in Cincinnati, he was on a date with the DuLoe heir. It was something she usually waited until the fourth or fifth date to drop into conversation, though it wasn't often that Rose got to that point as the gossip columns or the paparazzi usually did the honors for her. Plus, she was a workaholic and everyone knew it, more likely to be out for business than pleasure. A dark smile twisted her mouth as she caught a glimpse of David Blake out the corner of her eye again. *He definitely couldn't say the same.*

The last time she'd been within five feet of David Blake was her ill-fated graduation celebration. By this point, Rose had begun to feel that perhaps her and Samantha weren't well suited to a friendship given that Sam had beamed up at her after Rose had walked across the stage and said, "Well, you were bound to do well. Only an idiot could fail Fashion and Events Coordination." But to make matters worse, Sam's eyes had fixed immediately onto Blake once they'd arrived at the party and Blake, man-slut that he was even back then, had obviously noticed. His smile had been big and toothy and Samantha had blushed so hard Rose had wondered if she was having an aneurysm. Sam had been attached to Blake all night, stirring a sense of nausea in Rose's stomach every time she saw Samantha laugh because *ew*, it was *David Blake*.

So Rose had ignored them for most of the night, other than shooting the occasional glare Blake's way, and instead opted to chat with Blake's undeniably cute friend Christopher. She'd actually harbored a small crush on both Chris and Blake when she'd been about eight. Of course, then she grew up and realized Blake was a dick. Case in point, the unfortunate ending of that night – Blake had spouted off some garbage about Rose's taste in classy friends as well as some other things.To be honest, she'd been deep into several glasses of champagne and couldn't remember what specifically he'd said... only her reaction. She'd been absolutely enraged that Blake had hijacked her friend – even if she didn't like her very much – and that Sam had let herself be taken. Then he'd wound her up further and Rose had reached behind her for the crystal bowl full of bright pink punch and assorted fruit before promptly dumping it over his head.

And that had been the last time she'd been in spitting distance of Blake, which was generally how she preferred it.

Wiping her damp palms discreetly on her pale pink slip dress, Rose raised a haughty pale blonde eyebrow when she turned and caught Blake unabashedly staring her way. God, the man had no subtlety. *Three women at his table and he was still looking over here?* Her eyes had no trouble picking him out in the early evening crowd, which was slightly unnerving but was likely just because he was a familiar face.

"Let's head to the bar, Todd."

"Tom."

"Right, yes, sorry."

Tom's arm hooked through her own tightly and she

delicately coughed at the overpowering minty aftershave he seemed to have bathed in. Where had Samantha found this guy? Cal smiled politely, but Rose could see the humor in his eyes as he pushed away from the back counter behind the bar and towards them.

"Good to see you, Rose, lots of familiar faces in tonight." His dark eyes shifted to Tom, who was still ogling her mother, and a slight curl of Cal's lip betrayed his disapproval even as he teased her. Callum had also been at her now-infamous graduation party and while he hadn't been around as much when she was a child to see her grow up with Blake, he knew enough stories to know Blake's presence would be riling her up.

She straightened her shoulders and stopped herself from rolling her eyes with a great deal of effort, simply muttering, "Blind date," while Tim remained distracted.

"What can I get you tonight?"

Rose opened her mouth, but before she could say anything Tim's hand patted her arm and he said, "I can take care of this, honey. She'll have wine, a merlot if you have it. I'll take a beer, easy on the foam." Cal shot her a mocking look and she grit her teeth. Cal knew she couldn't stand red wine and Tad's behavior made her want to throw it straight in his face. She was going to kill Samantha. This date already sucked and they hadn't even made it to dinner yet. She would happily take being called 'uptight' if it meant avoiding painful experiences like this. Tom pulled out one of the dark-wood barstools and steered her into it by the arm, and she wasn't sure if it was because he thought she was incapable or to stop her from running away.

"You know, I'm actually not a big fan of red wine," she

15

said hesitantly and Tom blinked muddy gray-brown eyes at her as he settled into his chair.

"Don't be ridiculous." He smiled at her and she honestly didn't know what to say. "Girls like you love red wine."

Girls like her? What did that even mean?

"Look, Tim, I don't think–"

"Ohmygosh, *Rose!* Is that you?"

She let out a long breath, the voice triggering a slew of happy memories that instinctively made her body relax even as Cal set the red wine down in front of her with a wink. What was it he'd said? *Lots* of familiar faces, god, she'd been so wrapped up in her annoying date and Blake being there that she hadn't even noticed her old college roommate in the crowd.

Rose gratefully spun around and gave a delighted squeal when she confirmed that it was exactly who she'd thought. "Katie! You're here, oh my god, *how* are you here? I feel like it was forever ago that I saw you at that party." Katie was one of the few people Rose actually missed from college but they both led busy lives, often traveling, and before you knew it, you fell out of touch.

Katie was gorgeous, her deeply tanned skin perfectly off-set her blood-red dress and dark wavy hair and she had more curves than most people knew what to do with. Her piercing crystal-blue eyes shone brilliantly and crinkled at the corners when she laughed, which was often, and Rose was usually one of the people laughing with her. "No! Has it really been that long? Why don't you come and join me? We can catch up."

"I'd love to!" Freezing, she realized she'd forgotten about Tim. "I'm sorry, Tim, but this wasn't working out. Your drink is on me – feel free to have the red too."

Tim spluttered, and Cal coughed to hide a laugh when her date's face turned an unpleasant shade of purple synonymous with the plush velvet stool tops. "I-What? You're leaving? I thought..."

"Mmm... enjoy your night though." Maybe next time he was on a date he wouldn't act like a condescending prick. Life was too short to sit through miserable dates.

Katie gave a low whistle as Rose followed her back to her table, struggling to keep up with Katie's pace in the three-inch silver strappy heels she'd worn. At five-eight, Rose was already relatively tall, but with the heels on she felt downright leggy.

"I see you're still breaking hearts then."

Rose snorted delicately. "He was an ass, and it was only a first date. If he was in-love with anything, it was my name." Katie winced sympathetically but Rose's heart started to thud a little quicker as she realized exactly which table Katie was seated at. No. Surely not. "Besides, you can talk. You look absolutely amazing, I bet every girl in here is dying for your number."

Katie had spent a long time trying to make it in the fashion industry before giving up and moving onto interior design. The fashion industry was not so quick to change – especially when it came to being plus sized. They actually used to see each other a lot at various fashion events before Katie changed careers, and Rose knew Katie still had a big platform in the body positivity community on social media. Whenever they'd done posts together in the past they'd blown up a ridiculous amount – though admittedly not all of the attention had been so good. Despite Katie's undeniable gorgeousness and style, being fat still came with a lot of stigma in the fashion world.

"Rose, this is David Blake, Meredith, and Cara, David's younger sister and my date. Though, I believe you guys are already acquainted?" Katie smiled and extended a perfectly manicured hand to the dark, leather-backed chair she'd seemingly pulled from nowhere. Rose knew Katie wouldn't be smiling if she knew the strange and dramatic history between her and Blake, but there was a time and a place and Rose *definitely* didn't want to go back and sit with Tim again.

Cara slowly stood and looked at Rose from head to toe. She knew exactly what Cara must be seeing, slightly too-flushed cheeks, brown doe eyes that had been coated in a generous layer of mascara, and the blonde hair that had been painstakingly coaxed into heavy, full curls to fall against her cheek. Cara's hair was darker than her brother's, sitting on the edge of brunette, and Rose knew instantly that she and Katie were probably stunning when they entered a room together.

"Delighted to *finally* meet you, my brother's told me so much about you... and Katie has too, of course!" Cara said, pulling her in for an unexpected hug. "Please let me borrow those shoes!" she whispered into her ear and Rose laughed, the friendly welcome not entirely unexpected because of their family's connection. Cara had traveled almost as much as Rose, even attending school abroad, so they hadn't really met at any functions, though she felt almost like she knew her already from all the stories she'd heard.

"The elusive youngest Blake," Rose teased. "I already like you more than your brother." The redheaded woman sitting next to Blake seemed to choke on her drink, but Cara just grinned.

Rose's eyes drifted to Blake as she took in his reaction to her words and fought off a wave of nervousness. A lot had changed in five years. His familiar baby blues were already on her, a slight smile of amusement curving his full mouth as he dragged his eyes up over her legs. His eyes were where Rose's familiarity ended. Sure, she'd seen press photos, but they hadn't really done him justice. David Blake had always been heartbreakingly, annoyingly, gorgeous, but somehow he had become even more so since she'd last seen him – more man than boy and more rugged than beautiful. Blake and his best friend Christopher were just a couple of years older than her at twenty-eight and tended to run in the same social circles. Old money had a way of sticking together. Christopher had always been the nice one. Blake had always been an ass.

Blake brushed dark blonde hair from his eyes and gently reached out and grasped her hand, brushing his lips against it and sending an unexpected and unwanted tingle through her whole body. *No*, she sternly told herself. She would *not* be attracted to David Blake. She knew better. Blake didn't do relationships and *she* didn't find egotistical asshats hot.

"A pleasure as always, princess." His eyes said they knew exactly the sort of reaction he usually elicited, and his smirk said he liked it. Or, more likely, that he liked annoying her. If not for the annoying childhood nickname, she might have even been charmed. Rose couldn't remember if he'd always had this raw magnetism surrounding him, but she was certain she wanted nothing to do with it. Or him. As usual, the only thing David Blake did to her was piss her off. Meredith, presumably Blake's date, was unsurprisingly a little frostier having just watched her date coaxingly accost another woman's hand.

"Yes. A pleasure." Her green eyes said she found Rose anything but, and her thin red lips curled as if she smelt something unpleasant. Rose pulled her hand out of Blake's with a sharp tug. "Well, do sit down, Rose. Tell us, how exactly do you know Katie?"

She ignored the hostile undercurrent to Meredith's words and gave her a warm smile. "We went to college together, didn't we, Kate? God, I can't believe how long it's been. I actually just got back from an event in New York, so I spent some time with Sam." Katie winced sympathetically and Rose smiled slightly. Katie and Samantha had never really got on. They had very different ideas about what 'made' a woman – plus, Katie was very *very* gay and had no interest in Sam's lectures on how to properly please a man. "How did you and Cara meet?" Fully determined to ignore Blake completely, she was surprised when he chipped in, drawing her gaze back to him.

"Oh, I introduced them, of course. Katie works with me over at *Horizons* now. They met at the staff Christmas party." There was absolutely nothing sexual about his words, and yet he made it seem like they were the only two at the table. His voice dripped honey as his eyes focused absolutely and intensely on her. A bead of sweat slid down her spine at the heat in his gaze and it suddenly became clear to her how this infuriating man had seemingly bedded half the women in Cincinnati.

"Of *course*," Rose said, flustered, reduced to childish taunts in an effort to ignore the way his eyes felt as he watched her.

Katie nodded, clearly not sensing the tension. "Yes, we hit it off straight away! I mean, how could we not? We're ridiculously alike." Katie smiled, clearly infatuated, and by the look in Cara's faded-denim eyes, she was just as in love.

Rose smiled back at her. "I'm glad you're doing well. It's such a small world."

"Well," Katie said, slyly smiling, "not that small. I *had* heard this place was owned by the DuLoes and I hoped I might run into you here. I've been out of the country for a few months on a job for David, but I wanted to catch up now that I'm back."

"I'm flattered." Rose grinned, but her smile dropped as Blake's gaze continued to burn into her and she shot him a glare. "Is there something on my face?"

Blake leaned forward in his chair, a grin edging around his mouth as he brushed his thumb over her lips. "There. Much better."

"I didn't see any—" Meredith frowned, and her words cut-off as Cara pulled her into a conversation with Katie.

Rose's skin tingled where Blake had touched her, and she let all pretenses drop as she glared at him flatly before dismissing him entirely and looking back towards Katie beside her. "Well, we should definitely meet up again. Maybe we could go shopping or something. Cara could join us?"

"Oh! That'd be wonderful," Katie said as Cara squealed her delight. "Do you have to be somewhere right now though? I *did* rescue you from your date after all," she teased, sensing Rose's unspoken hint of immediate absence.

She gave Katie an apologetic smile and nodded towards the bar. "I want to get out of here before my date finds the courage to come over and attempt to retrieve me." Katie laughed as the table all looked to Tim. His eyes were darting between her and Blake, his face pale and his hand clenched around his red wine. "Your tab is on me though. Let me know when's good for you guys to go out." Rose stood and smiled, deliberately not looking Blake's way even as she felt those stupidly-blue eyes on her face.

Katie waved her off, hands flapping in a gracefully theatrical movement that only she could pull off. "Gah, say no more, darling, you'd better run. Lovely seeing you again. I'll be in touch."

Air kisses dotted the air as Cara and Katie said their goodbyes. Meredith remained noticeably frosty and acted as if she were oblivious to the whole fanfare. Rose stood, her chair scraping against the wooden floor, but what made her wince was Blake's words and not the shrill noise. "I'll walk you out."

Before she could protest or shoot Katie so much as a *please help me* look, his hand was on the small of her back and escorting her to the door. Meredith's face was white with fury and Rose couldn't help but feel a little bad for her. Sure, Meredith reeked of knock-off *Chanel* and she had been noticeably bothered by Rose's presence, but her behavior hadn't been entirely undeserved due to Blake's unwanted attention. Cal raised his brows with a taunting quirk to his mouth as she caught his eye on her way out. Damn it. She just knew her mother was going to get wind of this. Annabel DuLoe was absolutely *desperate* for grandbabies ("But *darling!* Think of the tiny outfits and accessories!") and she wasn't above playing matchmaker to fulfill her wish. Her mother would have bona fide kittens *and* probably arrange their marriage before Rose could say so much as *hell no* if she saw them voluntarily together right now.

Rose listened intently for the slightest *click clack* of the tell-tale sound of her mother's approaching heels as they neared the doors. The coast was clear. She all but dragged Blake out the front door, his blue eyes watching her with a wry humor as if he knew exactly what she was hoping to avoid. Well, she supposed he probably would, being one of the city's most elite families came with familiar territory. He probably had to sneak his female companions around all the time to avoid scrutiny. With the ugly thought of Blake's conquests in mind, she quickly stepped out of *The Hummingbird*'s alcove entrance into the warm night air and consequently away from the hand that seemed to burn against the small of her back.

"Thank you for walking me out. I'm not sure why you felt the need, but I'm fine from here." She raised her hand for her driver, giving Blake her most disinterested stare as she did so.

He smirked. "Oh, you're welcome. I mostly figured I should try and be nice to you, seeing as we're going to be working so closely together for the next few weeks."

Her raised arm seemed to turn to lead. "I–*what?*"

That infernal smirk stayed in place as he slowly wet his lips and blinked innocently at her. "Your parents didn't tell you? They've offered your services for a fundraiser I'm hosting, what with our families being so close and all."

Her mother certainly hadn't mentioned *that*. "I–that is, they didn't–"

"Well, I'll happily catch you up," he said disdainfully, like it was the biggest inconvenience of his life. "I'm throwing a gala on behalf of *Horizons,* most eligible bachelors auction, the proceeds go to charity, of course."

"Of course," she muttered, only slightly sneering.

He raised a cool eyebrow. "If you don't want the job, that's not my problem. It's out of my hands – you know how it is. I don't want this any more than you do."

Drawing her pale pink shawl around her tightly, Rose

stuck her chin into the air and glared. She didn't want to work with him at all, but hearing him say he didn't want this either? It rankled her, annoyingly so. He'd caught her off-guard at first, but if he thought she was just going to *sit* and *stay* like a good little girl he had another thing coming. "I got back into Cincy less than twenty-four hours ago, so I'm not all caught up yet. If you're that desperate to work with another planner, then go for it. I've got plenty of people who'd kill to be in your position."

He rolled his eyes and she ground her teeth. "Easy, princess," he said and she breathed slowly, trying to bite her tongue even though he *knew* how much she hated that nickname. He'd first said it to her when she cried about getting the wrong ice cream flavor – she'd been seven and, yes, maybe a bit spoiled, but once Blake saw how much she hated the name, it was all he'd call her. *"When you stop being a brat I'll stop calling you princess, but you're a brat all the time."*

"I see some things don't change. It's all for a good cause and everything has been arranged. Even if I wanted to, I don't have time to find anyone else now. I can tell the next few weeks are going to be... interesting." He paused and there was a look in his eyes she hadn't seen before. Sure, he was a flirt, but he only did it because he knew she hated it. Yet tonight felt different somehow. "I'll have my people send over the details."

Shocked at how quickly this had escalated and not trusting herself to not cuss him out if she opened her mouth, she just glared. The truth was, as much as her mom's meddling irritated her – because it could have been nobody else, Rose was certain her dad had no idea about any of this – *Horizons'* charity galas were legendary. Rose had been out of town for pretty much all of them, and generally she was happy to avoid Blake so she didn't mind. But if doing this would get her mom off her back about this botched date *and* she'd get to not only attend but *run* a *Horizons* benefit...

Blake nodded at her like he could see her thoughts all over her face. "Good. I'm glad we could sort this out. I'll see you tomorrow for our first meeting. Don't be late." He spun around to go back inside, but instead completed the turn and swept her hand into a light kiss that she felt all the way to her toes despite the cheesy move. He gave her a lazy grin before heading back inside and Rose felt queasy, like being at the height of a rollercoaster and waiting for the drop. Working for David Blake? *I'm going to kill my mother.*

Chapter Three

David Blake was rich. Obviously, he came from a wealthy family, but the gorgeousness of his house surpassed even his parent's old money. It was ostentatious enough to intimidate almost anyone. Almost.

Brickwork marked a large boundary around what could only be described as an estate, blocking off the press – how they'd known she was going to be there today was baffling. It wasn't like she had someone watching her twenty-four-seven to tip them off.

Gone was her pink slip from yesterday evening's tragic mimicry of a date. Instead, Rose was dressed for battle in a matching two-piece suit in a bright, vibrant red that matched the color of her lips. White heels complimented her white shirt and her blonde hair fell in heavy waves to the center of her back. She looked damned good, and she knew it. By the time she left this house, everyone else would know it too, thanks to the paparazzi skulking outside of the enormous black security gate that sat between the bricks. The world (including her parents) would know that she was here in no time, probably driving the gossip columns rabid as the most eligible bachelorette in Cincy visited its most eligible bachelor.

Cameras flashed as she stepped out of her car and Rose did her best to ignore them, even as reporters buzzed about, calling out questions about why she was there – though thankfully nobody approached. Often the clamor of lights and the sounds of several people all calling her name made her head spin, her stomach dipping at the prospect of facing the vultures until she remembered that she was *Rose DuLoe* and no damned reporter was going to make her hands shake. You couldn't tell from looking at her that she'd been up late researching *Horizons* and David Blake, nor could you see the dread that was making its way through her. She'd lain in bed a full ten minutes after her alarm had gone off – unprecedented for her – just to delay this meeting a little longer.

She made it through the tight security at the front gate, bemused at the little security guard booth that allowed visitors to be buzzed through or turned away. Blake clearly took his safety seriously. Rose was pleased that they'd been expecting her but pissed that she didn't have an excuse to go home, and then felt down-right despairing as she took in the long approach between the guard box and the entryway to Blake's home, covered in swaths of unstable gravel. Why hadn't they allowed her driver in? Her heels were going to be the death of her.

Rose flicked a glance back at the burly security guard and found him staring impassively at her, though his lips did twitch when she placed one heeled foot delicately onto the stones and wobbled. At this rate she was going to be late and knowing Blake, he'd likely lord it over her. Bastard.

Rose stepped out carefully onto the gravel and resolutely made her way down, jaw clenched and hands wide spread low at her side for some semblance of dignified balance.

It wasn't lost on her that things had felt different between her and Blake when she'd seen him at dinner. He was as annoying as ever, but he'd grown more handsome too, which only heightened Rose's irritation. Five years could change a lot, but David Blake was still a douchebag. Of that, she was certain.

She made it onto smoother paving without breaking an ankle and strode calmly over to the large white door and rang the bell. It was opened almost immediately by a friendly-looking red-headed girl. "Hi, I'm Rose DuLoe. I understand there's a meeting here today?"

The girl looked slightly puzzled but opened the door fully and gestured her inside. "If you'll follow me, Ms. DuLoe."

Rose followed the girl, who identified herself as Lacy, through the bright white corridors of Blake's impossibly large house. The place even had a ballroom that they'd be using for the gala. The wooden stairs seemed to wind on and on and the walls were bare but for large pieces of colorful art that seemed to add an open cheer to the place she hadn't been expecting. Admittedly, she'd been expecting leather and lots of red velvet, maybe even strippers. Perhaps she'd misjudged David Blake. Or he had an excellent interior designer. *God knows he could afford one.*

Lacy led her through an open doorway into a room with plush cream carpets and a relatively small glass table, as well as a waiting David Blake.

"You're late," was his only greeting.

She rolled her eyes. "I was here on time, no thanks to the walk to the front door and endless staircases. Perhaps you should consider installing a lift. Maybe then your business associates would get here quicker."

He seemed to ignore her sarcastic tone and scrubbed a thoughtful hand over a slight tracing of stubble. "Hmm, yes, maybe I could gut the second dining room and convert that. Would that meet your expectations, princess?" He finally looked up from the tablet in his hands and his eyes appeared to get stuck somewhere around mid-thigh until they lowered to her high heels and he smirked. "You did surprisingly well in the driveway."

Had he done that on purpose? It had definitely seemed odd to not let her driver in and instead make her walk the rest of the way. For what? To test her stubbornness against the uneven ground? So he could have a good laugh if the paparazzi had managed to get a photo of her falling on her ass from their places behind the gate? Or maybe he'd thought she would live up to her princess nickname and demand a car be brought around to drive her to the door. "You're lucky I didn't break my neck!"

Blake shrugged. "You look fine to me."

"Is there a reason I had to walk when I'm presuming your clients are usually escorted to the door?" It definitely explained his housekeeper's odd reaction. She had probably expected there to be a car.

"I wanted to see what you would do, princess," he said simply, placing the tablet onto the table and relaxing into his chair with one leg bent on top of the other.

Bastard. She glared at him but otherwise resolved to ignore his words as she walked to the table and sank into a cushioned chair opposite him. Yet, as often happened whenever she was around David Blake, the words snuck free, her tongue refusing to be blunted for a mere moment in his presence. "I'm not twelve anymore, so don't call me that. I suppose I should have expected you to be unprofessional, but I had hoped you might have grown up a little in the last five years." Blake looked like he was trying not to laugh and it only stoked her temper further, her words clipped and short as she pulled out a notebook. "Let's get on with this. Where's everyone else? I thought we were having a meeting."

"Oh, *we* are." He cleared his throat lightly and blinked as he seemed to relax further, clearly not in any rush to get started. "Can I get you anything? Tea? Coffee? Charming walk down memory lane?"

Rose rolled her eyes. "Sure, how about the time you convinced me Santa's magic came from the brandy we set out for him every year and I ended up having my stomach pumped on Christmas day?"

Blake's lip twitched, but he stifled any other traces of humor as he raised an eyebrow. "Hmm, can't recall. How about the time I heroically rescued you from the sea?"

"Oh yeah, I mean, I don't know who possibly could have left me out there alone to begin with," Rose growled, crossing her arms over her chest and flushing when Blake's gaze dropped half an inch. "Or how about the time you paid my date to stand me up before prom?"

A scowl rolled over Blake's face, and she was surprised that out of everything she'd just said *that* had been the thing that got a reaction. "You didn't hear what that little asshole was saying–" Blake pinched the bridge of his nose and let his foot fall to the ground with a small *thump* that startled her.

"Never mind. You were out of town before? What were you doing?"

"Things," Rose said sharply. Discussing the past was one thing, encouraging chit chat about her present was another. "Tell me what you were going to say before."

"No," Blake said, blue eyes steady on hers as his jaw clenched, making one of the dimples in his cheek pop out. Rose's teeth ground together and she bit her tongue, absolutely refusing to keep up this childish back and forth. She was here for a job, as a favor to her parents and Blake's. Nothing more. The past needed to stay as just that.

When she stayed silent, Blake stroked a thoughtful hand over his jaw, like he was trying to conjure up new ways to torture her.

"What about Cara?" she asked, trying to steer them back onto less irritating topics.

"What about her?"

"Is she involved in the gala? The company?"

David shrugged, and she ignored how the fabric tugged at his broad shoulders. "No. The company's mine."

Rose nodded absently. "You throw these things often. Why? Good tax break?"

He rolled his eyes. "Sure, princess. You know, it's so refreshing being around you. Most people actually like me, you see. So it's nice to mix things up a bit."

She shook her head and he laughed, enjoying making her uncomfortable, relishing getting under her skin in any way he could. *This* was why he ended up with bowls of punch dumped over his head.

"Are you single?" he said, startling her out of her thoughts and leaving her gaping for a second as her heart seemed to jump a little in her chest, heat instantly rising to her cheeks, and Rose wanted to scream at her traitorous body for giving away her embarrassment.

"Married to my work," she said a beat too late, smiling sweetly and opting to ignore her flushed skin. "Do you have a guestlist yet? Or a theme?"

"Black tie, open to anyone with enough money to donate. I hear your specialty is for creating something fresh and unique, so the theme should really be your thing, right?" Rose half-nodded, half-shrugged. It was true that she kept her events interesting, enough so that half the appeal was that the guests wanted to know just what she might have created this time. "Don't you want to know if I'm single too?" Blake leaned forward a little, his forearms resting against the table as he looked at her, looked and looked until she felt dizzy.

"I'm afraid I'd have to care about the answer in order to ask," she bit out, willing her hands to remain steady as those blue eyes attempted to work their charm on her. "Besides, I'm no stranger to the gossip columns. We all know you don't date, Blake."

"David," he said, mouth forming his name almost sinfully slowly, pink tongue sneaking out to wet his bottom lip, and Rose was scared by how attentively she watched. Eyes deepening to warm pools, he smiled slowly as he leaned forward in his chair, placing his forearms on his knees and emphasizing the muscles in his arms. "Don't you think it's high time we got to know each other better, Rose?"

She couldn't remember the last time he'd said her name rather than *DuLoe* or *princess* and half-wished she could go back in time to undo ever having heard the way his mouth moved around the syllables. "I already know you far better than I ever could have wanted to, Blake. Dream on."

A silent laugh seemed to ripple through him as he sat back again. "Don't worry, I will."

Rose scowled. Was he like this with everyone or did he just take particular pleasure in winding her up? She didn't think for one second that David Blake was actually interested in her. Maybe he wouldn't be opposed to sex, but that's because he was Blake, not because she was Rose. "I think we're done here. Email me the relevant details and a brief. I already have someone in mind to help me with the décor. I'll brief them and let you know what they come up with. I'll update you on any final decisions."

"Of course," he said, annoyingly handsome face smooth and impassive. "I'll walk you out."

"I'd decline, but I think I'd get lost."

He laughed as he stood, and it truly was a crime that someone so irritating could fill out a suit as well as he did. "I wanted to have plenty of room to work with when I designed this place."

She was genuinely surprised that he'd designed the whole place, given its bright and homey feel. "Did you decorate it too?"

"With Cara's help, yeah. She lives here too. We have separate floors." Rose tried, and failed, to hide her surprise. He laughed. "I know it's shocking that I'm more than just a pretty face, but what did you expect? *Horizons* is an interior design company after all."

She shrugged. "I actually didn't know that before yesterday." She had never cared enough to look into what Blake's company was or did, had known nothing about it beyond their yearly charity gala. But she had been begrudgingly impressed by all the companies *Horizons* was affiliated with – office design sounded fairly boring to Rose, but to be *the* go-to for workspace design for such big clients was a real accomplishment.

They walked in silence until they came to the end of the winding staircase and she turned to shake his hand. She could and *would* be completely professional. Her hand still in his grip, Blake pulled her slightly closer and unthinkingly she angled her head to better position their lips, watching his as he spoke.

"Interesting," he murmured, his eyes flicking across her face, and anger was a warm flush in Rose's chest as she quickly took a large step back. Blake smiled smugly, those dimples popping out. "Working with you is so much fun, princess. Can't wait to hear all those ideas in your pretty little head." He released her abruptly and began walking back the way they came, and Rose could only stare. *David Blake thought she was pretty?* A hand gripped her elbow and she almost jumped out of her skin.

"Jesus, Cara!" Her hand splayed on her chest as she stared at the petite woman for a second. "You completely startled me."

"Yeah, you did seem a little... distracted," Cara said with a grin as she nodded in the direction of Blake's retreating figure. Rose winced, belatedly realizing what it looked like she'd been watching as Blake strode away.

Rose sighed. "He's a very distracting man."

Despite that, she'd made it through the meeting without killing *or* kissing David Blake. She was calling it a win.

WHEN WORK DIDN'T TAKE her outside of Cincy, Rose spent the majority of her time at one of the DuLoe's hotel complexes. The penthouse at *The Hart* belonged to her for as long as she wanted it, off-limits to the public. The DuLoes owned a lot of property, but none felt quite as much like home to her as *The Hart*.

There was an unfamiliar bustle to the hotel when Rose walked through the glass doors later that day, something about it setting her on edge as she watched the hotel manager, Louis, grimacing at the phone while he sat behind the large wooden front desk.

Rose called a greeting and Louis looked up, his auburn hair tousled and his angular face a little red from scrubbing his hands across his stubbled jaw. He hung up the phone as she walked over, and concern made her brows furrow as she leaned against the edge of the chest-height counter.

"Rose! Good to see you back, how are you?" Louis always struck her as too young to be managing a hotel as big as *The Hart,* but he'd proved over and over that he was more than capable. For anything to be rattling him it had to be big.

"I'm well, thanks. Is everything okay? Things seem a little... off." A sigh slipped free from him and real worry began to drive at her.

"I'm sure it's probably nothing, but you know we take the safety of our customers very seriously here and, well, it's just *odd*."

"What is?" she asked, drumming her fingers anxiously against the wood in front of her before stilling her hand with a frown.

"Somebody pressed the alarm inside the elevator today." Louis spoke like he'd eaten something sour, nose wrinkled as his eyes darted around to check that nobody could hear what he said next. "But once we got inside to see who was trapped... it was empty."

"Empty?" Rose's brow furrowed as she took in Louis' agitation. "Was it a system fault or something? Maybe there was never anybody inside?"

"We have several witnesses who are certain they saw someone go in." Louis shook his head and an uneasy feeling settled around Rose's shoulders as it became clear that whatever this was, it had Louis rattled. "The system seems to be working. The lift stopped at floor eleven. The alarm was pulled, but when we called the lift back down it was empty and everything seemed fine. We've got a technician double-checking it now, but it doesn't look like there's a fault."

"So you think someone stopped the lift intentionally?" Rose gasped, pressing delicate fingers to her mouth as Louis shook his head in worry rather than negation. "But why?"

"We don't know, we're reviewing the video footage from inside the elevator now, but I don't like the thought that someone might be able to access your private floor without a key card by stopping the lift and climbing up the shaft." Louis sank back against a fancy desk chair but immediately sat up straight again as a security guard made their way over. Rose's head reeled. Had someone been trying to access her suite? "Any news?"

"Someone was definitely in there," the man said, his face betraying no emotion and his deep voice even. "They kept their hood up and face turned away from the cameras, but when it stopped it *does* appear that they opened the access in the roof to slip out of the elevator. My guys are doing a sweep inside the access shaft now, and we will have extra bodies coming in and placed on every floor for tighter security."

"What's your name, sir?" Rose asked as she offered her hand and the man assessed her with cool, green eyes as he slowly took it and shook once, firmly.

"Noah Greene. I'm the new head of security. You're the owner?" His face remained pleasant and calm, but a shrewd look in his eyes told her that he thought she was too young to call herself the owner of anything, let alone an entire hotel.

"Greene," she said with a wry smile, "like your eyes." Noah looked slightly startled, and Rose cleared her throat as she mentally shook herself. It had been a strange day, and now with the thought of her personal safety compromised or, worse, targeted... "Yes," she said curtly a moment later, trying to forget the unsettling thought. "One of the owners, anyway." Rose glanced at Louis and bit her lip on a smile as he gazed dreamily at Noah. "Please do keep me updated on your findings. I'd rather handle this in-house, and security is my top priority."

"Of course," Louis said and Noah nodded, still watching her intently.

"The sweep will be done within the hour," Noah assured her and Rose smiled, beginning to walk away towards the elevator when Louis called out to her again.

"I'm sorry, Rose, but the elevator is out of order until we've got this cleared up."

She grimaced, for once seeing the downside to living all the way up on the top floor. "You mean I have to take the stairs?"

"Afraid so." Louis grimaced and Rose groaned, wrinkling her nose in distaste and making her way over to the sweeping marble staircase before nudging off her heels. There was no way she'd make it to the top while wearing them.

"I'll escort you," Noah called out, jogging towards her, and Rose nodded her thanks. He set a brisk pace up the stairs that had her nearly panting within moments, though he seemed unfazed. She supposed she could only be grateful that he wasn't attempting to also make small talk too.

"Shouldn't we pace ourselves?" Rose gasped a few minutes later, sweat pouring off her as they reached floor four, and she began to regret wearing the heavy blazer to Blake's earlier.

"Sorry," Noah said, a touch of amusement in his voice, "do you need to slow down?"

Rose's back straightened, and she forcefully got control of her breathing. Twelve floors. It was only twelve floors. Eight to go. "No," she growled. "I could do this in my sleep."

"Good to know," Noah replied, speeding up a little more and turning his face to hide the smile skating across it as she stomped up the stairs faster, trying not to slip in her own sweat on the gold-veined marble. "So how come you live in the hotel?"

Crap. Now he wanted to make conversation? "Travel a lot," Rose said curtly, trying to maintain her breaths. "Like it here."

Noah coughed to hide a snort and Rose glared.

By the time they made it to the top floor stairway, she was covered in a fine layer of moisture and was panting. Annoyingly, Noah looked like he'd barely broken a sweat. Rose shot him a narrow-eyed look and he smirked as he waved away her key card, instead reaching for his own to access the corridor outside of her suite. It was going to be a novelty coming in this way, she hardly ever saw her front door because the elevator opened up straight into the lounge when she used her card.

"After you," he said politely, like they hadn't just been through something harrowing together, and Rose snorted as her legs wobbled with every step she took. There was no way she'd be able to get her heels back on, but she also didn't want to walk her dirty feet on her lush, cream carpet when she got inside, so she would have to settle for tiptoeing and cringing as she moved while her feet muscles spasmed.

Noah pressed a hand to her arm, preventing her from walking too far from the door they'd just exited. "I just want to take another quick look around here, okay?"

Nervousness coiled in her stomach as she nodded, remembering her own worries of the suite being targeted and smoothing the lapels on her blazer to soothe herself as Noah walked the short distance to where the corridor ended and checked the supply closet. Locked. A slow breath eased its way out of her and Noah gave her a smile as he walked back and ran a critical eye over the door to her suite. Apparently deeming it untampered with, he beeped his way inside and ignored Rose's protests as his heavy boots left footprints across the pristine floor.

Rose brushed past the large potted plant in the corridor that stood nearly opposite her suite before standing awkwardly in her own doorway and fixating on the dark smudges across the floor.

"Does everything look as you left it?" Noah asked and she bit her lip, looking away from the carpet and thinking back to her hasty exit this morning, eyes resting on the plant outside the suite door for a second.

"I think so." Rose generally kept things tidy. She only let the hotel staff into the suite infrequently to clean or to maintain the suite while she was away at work. "I don't know how long that plant's been there but I'm guessing Louis bought it. I usually take the elevator."

"How often do you stay here?" Noah poked his head

around the doorway that led to the bathroom before glancing back at her.

"It's pretty much my permanent residence, except for when I leave town for work."

Noah eyed the lack of clutter with a raised eyebrow. "Seriously?"

Rose folded her arms across her chest and winced as the material stuck unpleasantly to her still-slick skin. "Yes." Mess made her anxious and she liked to keep things in a particular state. It was just better for everyone if they let her get on with tidying and cleaning. If she let the staff in to clean, she usually only ended up re-doing things the way she liked them anyway.

"Okay," Noah said, wrinkling his nose and stretching the word out like he didn't believe her. "Well, if there's nothing amiss to you then everything looks fine to me."

"Thanks for walking me up," she said primly and Noah bit his lip on what looked like a laugh, likely remembering how he'd run her ragged on the stairs, slowly increasing his pace until they were near running by floor ten and Rose had been cursing through her panted breaths.

"Here's my card. If you notice anything odd, then give me a call, or the front desk."

Rose smirked. It was sweet of him to say, but she owned this place. He reported to *her*.

"Thanks, I'll expect a report on your findings by the morning."

Noah scowled as he moved toward the door and Rose chuckled. Payback was a bitch.

The elevator dinged, the sound unexpected and jarring, and Rose spun toward the noise with a gasp. Noah's gun was in his hand in a flash, pointed unwaveringly at the glossy doors as they parted.

He opened his mouth just as a young black woman stepped out, her hair a riot of Afro curls and a decorative orange scarf fluttering through the air behind her. A breath of relief mixed with laughter fell from Rose as she waved Noah off.

Maia's eyes were wide as they found the gun that was still in Noah's hand, her shoulders relaxing fractionally when he flicked the safety back on and slid it away into his side holster.

"Sorry ma'am." Noah scratched the side of his head bashfully and then raised his hands as he backed away a little.

Maia watched him warily for a moment before becoming distracted as Rose launched herself at the other woman, engulfing her in a hug. It had been at least a month since she'd seen Maia in person thanks to them both being out of the country, and she couldn't wait to make cocktails and catch up with her sometimes-roommate.

Maia laughed, her long arms coming around Rose and gripping her tightly. Rose pulled back, staring into the open elevator behind Maia.

"I can't believe they let you get the elevator up!" Rose glared accusingly at Noah, and he shrugged as if to say it hadn't been his call.

"I guess they're done processing it," he said innocently, and a vein in Rose's head started to pulse.

"You mean I could have just waited for twenty minutes and avoided death-by-twelve-flights?" Her hands clenched at her sides, fingernails digging in as Noah feigned thoughtfulness.

"Well, I suppose so, but I thought the stairs were a breeze?"

Rose growled and Noah laughed, shooting both women smiles before leaving the way they'd come in with a wave goodbye.

Maia tutted at the footprints on the carpet and Rose groaned, "It's okay. I'll clean it up."

"You'd better, the last thing I want to do right now is vacuum." Maia grinned broadly, and Rose squealed again as she hugged her best friend, loving the familiar sight of her smile. "Did you really walk up all those stairs?"

Rose groaned as she pulled away and grabbed the vacuum out from the cupboard and plugged it in. "Walk? No. Practically run full tilt? Yes. God, I need a bath." Maia laughed and the sound made Rose smile. The suite felt much more like home now that she was here. "Are you staying here tonight?"

The suite was as much Maia's as it was Rose's – Maia often called it home in between trips away and whirlwind romances. It was the place Rose wanted Maia to always rely on.

"Yeah, if that's alright. I need a break from Thierre."

Rose shot her a look. "Of course it's alright. You know where your room is. Where have you been this time?"

"France." Maia sighed dreamily and fingered a simple, gold locket that hung around her neck and looked to be new.

"Something you picked up in... Paris?" Rose guessed and nodded to it as she put the vacuum away, already daydreaming about the long soak she was going to have.

"Thierre got it for me." Maia grinned as Rose cooed over it, clasping it delicately in her fingers as she inspected it.

"The same Thierre you need a break from?" She grabbed

a pair of slippers from near the couch and slid them on to prevent any more dirty footprints on the floor. They were only the hotel branded ones so she knew she could replace them in a heartbeat... unlike her carpet.

"Oh," Maia waggled her eyebrows, the pale green gemstone in her nose glittering wildly as she shook her head, "no, it's not him I need a break from. I need a *break.* Sexually."

Rose snorted. "Good to know you were properly amorous in the city of love."

"When in Paris," Maia said in a thick faux French accent and they laughed together for a few moments as Rose shucked off her blazer and moved into the kitchen, pulling out the ingredients for cocktails as Maia grabbed the glasses.

"What was going on downstairs?" Maia asked once they'd settled onto the couch and queued up the Kardashians.

Rose shrugged, trying not to let her worry get to her. "They think someone intentionally stopped the elevator to get out somewhere they shouldn't be."

"Like the suite?" Maia's brown eyes were wide, and Rose winced as she nodded. It was the only floor that was keycard restricted, so it had to have been where the mystery person was heading – buy why? It was true that Rose lived a seemingly glamorous life, but she didn't have much worth stealing unless they were interested in designer handbags – she'd made her ambivalence to expensive jewelry known in the press enough times that nobody would bother coming here looking for that. But if not for theft, what else could they have wanted?

"They've got extra security coming in and watching all the floors. We're probably even safer now than we were before," Rose eventually replied, and Maia's full lips pursed as Rose avoided the real question before Maia decided to let it go.

If theft wasn't the goal and the suite hadn't been tampered with... what was someone looking for on the top floor?

Chapter Four

"**M**om," Rose complained, trying to interrupt the steady stream of chatter Annabel DuLoe had kept up ever since Rose had answered the phone twenty minutes ago. She blew out an annoyed breath as her mom rambled on about the *nice young man* she'd gone on a date with two nights ago and Rose was close to pulling her hair out. Conversations with her mother were always the same: Rose being spoken at and over for the majority of the time and then grilled incessantly towards the end of the conversation about her love life, her job, and whatever else her mother could think up. It was why she normally checked who was calling before she answered, but she'd been distracted this morning.

"*Please* tell me you are tapping that fine piece of interior design ass." Maia's voice cut through her mother's rambling and Rose looked up sharply from her perch at the breakfast bar to the large TV that Maia was watching across the room.

David Blake's wide grin took up most of the screen as the paparazzi grilled him outside of his estate. The topic of conversation? Her. "What was the nature of your meeting with Ms. DuLoe yesterday, David?"

Rose opened her mouth for a denial once her friend's words sank in, but Maia shook her head. "Uh-uh, it is *everywhere* right now that you strolled into his house. That *suit*! That *hair*! God, I fucking *died*, Ro. It was like art. No – poetry! In motion!"

She couldn't help the laugh that escaped her as she strode over and wrapped Maia in a hug while her mom chattered away, not realizing her daughter's attention was elsewhere. Thank god the photographers seemed to have lost interest in her quickly and not captured her awkward walk up Blake's driveway.

Maia grinned and her teeth were a perfect white against her dark skin. "For real, what is going on with you and Blake? You could tell me about the horrible blind date Sam set up, but you *conveniently* leave out these deets?"

Just then Blake's voice caught her attention. His voice was deep and might even have been relaxing if it wasn't accompanied by his smug face and hateful personality. "Well, you know me, gentleman. I don't kiss and tell." Then he winked. *Winked.* Like a damn Bond villain or something, and she could feel her molars grinding as she thought about the fervor his words were undoubtedly going to ignite among the press. *Fuck.* Next thing they knew, she and Blake were going to have a ship name. There was no way she was going to let herself – let *them* – become DuBlake. No way.

"Mom, I'm going to have to call you back," Rose cut off the call in the midst of her mother's squawking protests, and Maia let out a low whistle as she saw the expression on her face. "That *bastard*."

Maia settled back against the sofa and sighed. "You've got some explaining to do, girl."

"There's nothing to say! It's just *him* trying to piss me off. He knows I can't stand it when the press butts into my life." Rose spun towards the door as someone knocked and thanked the security guard standing at the door holding a large bouquet of pink roses as she took them inside and checked the note. *I liked you better in pink.* Was Blake for real? Why on Earth would he – Rose glanced back at the TV and fought back a growl. David fucking Blake got on every single one of her nerves. Riling her up was one thing, but riling up the press to piss her off on his behalf?

Maia stood and peeked at the note over her shoulder, snorting as Rose crumpled it up. "Nothing to say, huh?"

"Nothing! I don't care if David Blake likes me better in gods-damned pink! His opinion means nothing to me. He's an arrogant, pig-headed, cocky–"

"Gorgeous," Maia cut in as she sat back down again, and Rose glared as she threw the flowers in the trash. God, if the press got wind of those... Generally she could trust the staff at *The Hart* to be discreet, but it only took one slip-up and she would be the talk of the town. Not that it would make much difference if Blake kept up with those interviews.

"Nothing happened between us, and nothing ever will. He's just riling the press up because he knows it'll piss me off." Rose folded her arms across her chest as she scowled at the handsome face on the TV, annoyed that he knew her well enough to know what buttons to push. Already there was a sub-headline running beneath his chin that questioned whether the Blakes and DuLoes might be about to *formally unite* – wow, they'd blown right past dating and headed straight for marriage. *Over my dead body would I ever marry David Blake.*

Knowing Maia was going to need more information than that, Rose flopped down onto the sofa next to her friend and groaned. "My parents have got me working a job with him, that's all. If you're free, I was hoping you could be my consult for the décor?"

Maia clapped her hands together as she jumped up and down on the seat in a show of excitement that had her bright red gauzy scarf drifting about in the air. "Hell *yes*! That sounds amazing!"

Possibly her favorite thing about Maia was her unending enthusiasm. She was the kind of person who always wanted to try new things and make the most of everything. She was also one of the most fashionable people Rose knew. It was what made her such an excellent designer, both interior and otherwise.

"God, this would be perfect. Maybe he'll let me consult for *Horizons* if I do a good job."

Rose blinked in surprise. "*Horizons*? I had no idea you were even interested in working there. I thought they designed office spaces?"

Maia shrugged. "They do a lot of different work, but even their office spaces are ridiculously chic, Ro. They're not exactly gray cubicles and fake plants. We're talking designer CEO suites."

"Huh." She'd honestly had no idea what Blake's company did despite the quick research she'd done a few nights ago. In the past, she'd made it a general rule to ignore any articles or mentions of her childhood enemy. "Why didn't you mention this to me sooner? You know I can set that up easily for you. You're practically family."

Maia smiled but rolled her eyes. "I know, Rose, and as much as I love you, I just wanted to do this by myself. I know that me consulting on this is because of you, but if he likes my work and offers me a job? That's because he likes what *I* can do."

Rose nodded slowly and settled back down in the soft material of the gray couch. "Yeah, okay, I get that. Really, I do. But you know if you ever need anything, you can tell me, right?"

Maia grinned and stopped bouncing, settling down next to her, dark curls springing in every direction at the sudden movement. "Yeah, I know. Thanks. I mean it."

It went silent, and Rose squealed and threw her arms around Maia. "I still can't believe you're finally back! We have so much to catch up on."

Maia grinned. "I know, we've got like, three episodes of *KUWTK* still to watch, *and* I haven't even really told you much about Thierre yet."

Rose gasped. Maia only ever told her about the guys she considered serious. For the longest time, Rose had been pretty sure there was something between Maia and Callum, Rose's cousin, but Maia'd never mentioned it, and Rose knew better than to pry. If Maia wanted Rose to know something, she'd tell her. "I want details! Is he tall? Is he gorgeous? Well, of course he is if he's dating you. I bet he's model-pretty."

Maia laughed with her head tipped back. She could easily have been a model herself what with her height and bone structure. Plus, Maia was effortlessly stylish in a way that Rose sometimes envied but mostly utilized. There was nobody else's fashion advice Rose would place higher. "Right on all counts. He's 6'5, dreamy, and he works for a Parisian design company. He flew back with me to meet up with some high-brow client of his or something."

"Cute, you sound like you're already picturing your arty babies."

"I don't know about that," Maia laughed. "How's working with Blake been so far?"

Rose let out a deep sigh and pushed her fingers through her already rumpled hair. "He's completely infuriating, entirely inappropriate, and I alternate between wanting to strangle him or myself whenever we speak for more than a few minutes at a time."

A slow grin spread across Maia's cheeks. "You like him."

Eyes wide, she glared at her best friend as heat spread across her cheeks. "Like him? *Like* him? Nine times out of ten I want to kill him, and that was before he implied to the press that we were dating. So, *no,* there's no liking here."

Maia laughed and gave her a smirk, sipping the milky coffee she'd left to cool on the coffee table in front of them. "So there's passion – I bet the sex will be great."

She gaped at Maia in disbelief. Hadn't she heard anything she had just said? Blake drove her mad. Her mind unbidden flashed back to the feeling of his mouth against her hand, his palm at the small of her back. She gulped. "There won't be any sex, Maia. He's an ass."

Maia grinned. "Hate-sex is the best kind. Besides, you know I can't stand Sam most of the time, but she does have a point. How long has it been since you last had sex?"

Rose spluttered, words getting lodged in her throat. Or was that embarrassment? She took a deep breath and let herself think back, wincing as Maia watched her face intently. "A while."

Maia snorted. "Who do you think you are? Edward

Cullen? *A while,*" she mimicked in a sulky impression of Rose.

"Well I don't remember the exact time frame," Rose huffed, and Maia patted her hand.

"If you have to think about it that hard, it's probably been too long."

"I'm perfectly content without sex," she complained and Maia raised an eyebrow, taking in Rose's bouncing leg and tight arms across her chest.

"Sure, that's why you look like you're jonesing for a fix right now. I bet Blake gives good orgasms." Maia's grin spelled trouble, and Rose narrowed her eyes as she faked a gag.

"Those are two words that don't belong in the same sentence together."

"Good orgasms?" Maia quirked, and Rose threw a pillow at her just as her phone rang again. Honestly, it was impressive her mother had waited this long to call back... or maybe it was worrying. What had she been doing in between phone calls?

With a wince, she hit the green button. "Hello, Mother."

Maia gave a quiet laugh and mouthed, "good luck," as she set up the TV for the rest of their Kardashians marathon.

"Darling! I'm *so* glad you and David are spending time together! You always did have such fun. I'm glad you can see now what an excellent idea the fundraiser was for you two."

"You know we can barely stand one another, and I have *you* to thank for having to work with him. I never would have decided to do this otherwise," Rose said slowly as a bad feeling started to swirl inside her.

"Nonsense, dear! You would be absolutely perfect together!" Her mother's voice rose shrilly in the way that only happened when she was thinking about marriage, babies, or boys.

"You mean as temporary business partners, right?"

"Well, Grace and I had hoped–"

"Mother! Are you telling me that you and Blake's mom tried to set us up? Are you *crazy*?"

Maia turned to her with wide eyes, overhearing Rose's exclamation.

"Crazy? For wanting my daughter to be happy? Taken care of? David is a lovely young man and from the news, I can see that you agree."

"There is nothing going on between me and David Blake!" Rose shrieked, frustration clawing at her insides. Damn rat bastard of a man stirring up trouble. She took two deep breaths. "Listen, I've got to go. Next time you're presented with the opportunity to meddle in my love life, please *don't*." She hung up to the sound of her mother's high-pitched protests once again and growled. Maia winced at whatever expression was currently on her face.

"That bad?" Maia asked sympathetically.

"She got together with Blake's mom to try and set us up because, and I quote, 'I need taking care of'." Her hands balled into fists and she took another short breath before releasing it and walking over to the kitchen.

"I'm sure she's just trying to look out for you, Ro," Maia said, sympathy widening her eyes.

"He's an ass! An *egotistical* ass! And a man-whore! He sleeps with everything that moves, and yet she wants me to date him?" Rose was breathing hard by the time she finished her rant. "I'm sorry, Maia, I just *hate* when my mother interferes like this." She went back to hunting down the ingredients for margaritas. "Let's just have cocktails, watch TV, have a girls' day, you know? Strictly no boy talk."

Maia smirked. "If that's what you want, sure. But if I had David Blake drooling at my feet, I would *so* take advantage. I mean, what have you got to lose? The press already thinks you're together."

"My dignity?" Maia laughed and Rose rolled her eyes, focusing on the margarita jug in her hand. "The only thing I want to do to David Blake is murder him," she said, and Maia laughed again but gave her a knowing smile as she settled into the cushions and accepted a margarita. If only Rose could forget about Blake as easily.

───

"ARE you sure this outfit is okay?" Maia, normally self-assured, confident to the point of almost cockiness, was nervous. Very nervous, if her repeatedly balled and un-balled fists, tense shoulders, and slightly damp palms were anything to go by. Rose squeezed her hand.

"You look great, you're going to kill it. You always do." She gave her best friend the most comforting smile she could and then marched through David Blake's front door. "Hello Lacy, I believe Mr. Blake is expecting us?" Lacy nodded and gestured for them to follow her.

There had been no bullshit on this visit. The gates had opened for her car and Rose had scowled. She'd worn lower heels just in case but it seemed like for now, Blake's childish games were over. That didn't help the ridiculous swarm of paparazzi waiting for them as they drove through the gates, a few cameras pressing to the tinted windows to try and get a picture of her before the gates started to close, shutting them out. Gods-damned Blake and his stupid publicity stunt. She wasn't sure how the press knew she was going to be there today, unless Blake had called in a tip which she honestly wouldn't put past him at this point. Her phone had been ringing all weekend with press trying to get her to comment about the 'engagement rumors' floating around until in the end, she'd just turned it off.

Her and Maia had enjoyed a girls' weekend of gossip, pampering, and probably a few too many margaritas in between discussing possible themes, décor, and colors for the gala. Blake's team was handling all the marketing, thankfully – Rose could do it, but it was her least favorite part of the process, maybe thanks to her less than stellar experiences with the media. Though, she was relatively popular on socials as a fashion and lifestyle influencer – whatever that meant. She just posted photos and people liked them, and occasionally she wore something for a brand. When you were already famous, it was easier to stay that way.

Maia had helped her photograph a few cute and comfy looks while Rose posed on the sofa on Sunday, so all she had to do now was edit them and she could post them to her socials later on tonight. It took a surprising amount of effort to look effortless on social media.

Despite her resentment at being forced into this gig and the still slow-simmering rage in her gut whenever she thought back to Blake's smug face as he spoke to the press, Rose could admit that she was actually... excited about this project. Maia's eye was amazing, as always, and talking shop with her made Rose strangely eager to get started.

They walked past the staircase Rose had taken the last time she had been there and she curled her fingers into her palms to stop the odd trembling that had taken over them.

She'd had a good time with Maia, but when she'd gone to bed that night her words kept floating around Rose's brain until she could no longer dismiss them. *If you have to think about it that hard, it's probably been too long.* It had probably been at least a year since Rose'd had sex. Possibly longer. She was busy, and work occupied a lot of her thoughts, and—

She could practically hear the tut Maia would give her if she knew the excuses Rose was mentally compiling. Rose sighed. The truth was that dating was *hard* and she hated it. Hated meeting new people and wondering if they liked her or just her name, or what rumors about her they'd read in the gossip column. It was part of a game she had no interest in playing. But was Maia right? Had Rose become complacent? Was she missing out?

Her thoughts had become a riot of confusion and self-doubt and, fine, *lust* as she tried to remember the last time someone other than herself had gotten her off. It was the only reason she could think of to explain the automatic smile she gave to Blake when they finally wound up in what looked like a ballroom. The cocky smirk on his mouth faded slightly and he pressed a hand to the arm of the man standing beside him as if dazed.

Her smile faded quickly, anger mixing with the desire that just wouldn't go away now that it had finally clawed itself to the surface and Blake's presence was only more confusing. Her body responded to him even as her mind wanted to shout at him until her throat was raw. It had been a year-long dry spell for her, and Rose couldn't help wondering, somewhat uncomfortably, what else she might have been repressing alongside her desire for human touch.

The ballroom was huge with dark wood floors, olive green walls with a high glass ceiling, and leafy plants scattered about. Standing in the center of the room was Blake and the unfamiliar man. They were gesturing to random things while they talked and Maia seemed to have regained her confidence by the time they made it over to them, the sway in her hips unfaltering.

Unhelpfully, Rose couldn't help but notice how perfectly Blake's suit matched his blue eyes. Damn her mother for putting unwanted thoughts in her head. Maia too, because now all she could picture was what lay under that suit as Blake pulled off his blazer, leaving him in a *very* well-fitting white shirt. Mentally shaking herself and cursing her treacherous re-awoken hormones for her reaction, she strode across the room to meet them in the middle. Her long brown leather skirt was form fitting but still professional, as was the cream turtleneck she'd paired it with, a deliberate attempt to tone down from her previous bright-red suit. Not that the press would care. For all the effort she made, they'd probably just spin the plain outfit as domestic happiness like *Infamous DuLoe So Comfortable in New Bliss, Wears Off the Rack.*

"Mr. Blake," she said when she finally stood in front of him, pretending that her earlier gut-instinct smile had only been sheer professionalism. "This is Maia Katz. She'll be working with us for the interiors at the benefit."

Blake stared at her in silence for a beat longer than was necessary as he wet his lips and cleared his throat and finally dragged his eyes from hers to greet Maia.

"It's lovely to meet you. Any friend of Rose is sure to have excellent taste." He turned to the handsome dark-haired man next to him and recognition finally lit inside her. "I'm sure you remember Christopher, Rose. He works with me over at *Horizons*. He's my second-in-command at the company and will be participating in the auction. He's just here to oversee things, maybe add a few suggestions if he feels it's necessary."

Rose gave a polite, disinterested smile to Blake and let her eyes linger on the fullness of Christopher's lips as Maia murmured her hellos and shook both their hands. Rose hadn't seen Christopher in years, and he was much less prevalent in the press than Blake, so she hadn't really seen so much as a photo. She'd always thought he was cute and the years had been kind to him. He was attractive, effortlessly embodying tall, dark, and handsome. Maybe she'd found the answer to her dry spell sooner than expected.

Rose smiled widely at Christopher as she discreetly checked his hand for a ring – not full-proof, but a good start. At the very least, he might make an excellent distraction for both her and the press from the cocky, infuriating man standing next to him, staring at her.

"Let's get started then, shall we? Is this where you're planning on holding the event? How many can this room hold? 200 people? Three?" she asked, still assessing Christopher rather than their surroundings. He was broad and had dark brown eyes that were watching her with something like amusement.

"Yes, around 300 people can fit in here. We're only looking for around 200, maybe 250 invites though. Don't want it to be overcrowded." Blake's voice interrupted her musings, and he sounded a little... put-out at her interest in Christopher. Good. She had no intention of giving into the matchmaking their mothers had schemed into motion, and Blake deserved a little payback for his stunt with the press. When she glanced at him, his blue eyes were searching her face, his mouth pulled down slightly at the corners, but most telling of all was the hand he suddenly thrust through his hair and then scrubbed over his jaw. Rose knew from personal experience that Blake only did those things when he was particularly frustrated. This was quickly becoming a very interesting visit. Maybe it was cruel, but she wanted to see just how much she could make him sweat. God knows he seemed to spend most of his time trying to irritate her whenever they were together. Or even apart, as the interview had proven, as well as the flowers.

"Maia, why don't you take Blake around the room and start telling him what you think you'd like to do with the space?" Maia smiled and nodded, bouncing over to Blake and immediately talking about how amazing the room was and raising her phone to take photos of the space. Maia was a highly visual person and Rose knew she'd need the photos to come up with a theme design that made the most of the room. Blake's low voice carried across the room as he answered Maia's questions and Rose quickly tuned them out.

"It's good to see you again, Rose."

She blinked. "Oh, so you *do* remember me." She gave him a small smirk. "It's nice to see you again, Chris."

Christopher arranged his face into a very charming grin. "How could I forget? I mean, it was you that once dumped a bowl of punch over Blake's head in the middle of your graduation party, and am I right in thinking you were also the one who pushed him into the pool once at New Year? It was both spectacular and extremely memorable."

Rose let out a startled laugh, having forgotten about that particular incident. "It *was* spectacular, wasn't it?"

Christopher stepped a fraction closer and gazed into her eyes. "So, you and Blake, huh?"

She raised a brow coolly. "I thought you'd know better than to believe the things you see on TV. There is no 'me and

Blake'. Just his attempt to irritate me, and another of my mother's plans to marry me off. Anyway, what do you think of this project? Maia is so excited to get to work with you guys at *Horizons*."

Christopher laughed a little and looked off in the direction of Blake and Maia at the other end of the giant room. From here, they could see Blake's head nodding intermittently while Maia gesticulated wildly and enthusiastically. "Well, I think it'll be great for charity, and the business. I think it could be even better for your friend, if she does a good job, and possibly good for you and Blake. If you'll let it be."

Instantly, any sort of warmth she'd been feeling disappeared. Why was the world conspiring to set her up with David damned Blake? Was she not allowed to hate someone in peace? And where did Christopher, a guy she hadn't seen since she was, what, twenty-one, get off on giving her advice?

He seemed to read her feelings straight off her face because he raised his hands in placation. "It was only a comment. What happens, happens. Just... don't take this the wrong way, Ro, but you look like you need to relax. I don't remember you being quite so... stiff when we were younger."

Stiff? *Stiff?* Crap, Maia was right. *Worse*, Samantha was right. She gave him a wry smile. "It's true, I don't make nearly as many spectacles at parties anymore. Funny how that changes once you grow up. That doesn't mean I don't have fun though... I was going to ask you out for a drink, but now I think I'll refrain."

He gave a short laugh. "It wouldn't be worth my life."

She just stared at him incredulously and then jolted as a warm hand touched her back. Maia and Blake had come around without her noticing and Blake was looking between her and Christopher with a frown on his face.

"Did you come up with some good ideas?" she asked Maia somewhat breathlessly. Her earlier lust had returned in full force with Blake's hand still on her back, rubbing little circles into the sensitive flesh there, burning so hot that for a second, she wasn't sure if his hand wasn't directly on her skin. Maia continued to tell them about the design plans they'd settled on, Christopher nodding along, but she didn't hear a word of it. She couldn't, not with Blake standing so close, not with his hands on her. *One year,* her brain taunted her. *I bet Blake gives good orgasms.* Maia's voice sent her thoughts in a spiral she couldn't accept.

"Rose," Blake said. His mouth around her name almost made her shiver. "Can I have a word, please?"

"Sure." She meant for her response to come across clipped, bored even, instead she sounded breathless. Maybe there were other ways for her voice to become hoarse that didn't involve shouting at Blake.

She didn't dare look at Christopher or Maia as Blake led her out of the ballroom and into a room just slightly farther down the corridor that turned out to be a study. He gestured her in and closed the door behind her. The room was surprisingly tasteful, just like the rest of the house, with dark wooden furnishings and lots of natural light spilling over the large desk at the back of the room.

"What, exactly, are you doing?"

She was surprised by his question, mostly because it came wholly out of the blue. "What do you mean?"

"I mean," he said, teeth gritted, "with Chris."

Her mouth dropped open. "I'm sorry – *what?*"

His eyes burned into hers as he moved closer until there

was no more room between her body and the door, his strong arms falling into place on either side of her. "He's my business partner and my best friend. If you want to get back at me for the interview, then fine. But keep him out of it."

"I don't know what you're talking about."

"Really?" Blake huffed out a laugh that she felt on her skin as he stroked a hand over his stubble. "You never were a good liar."

"And you always were an asshole," she hissed, narrowing her eyes. "You made me look like your flavor of the month."

Blake hummed and pushed his body flush against hers. "Maybe you are."

Disgusted, Rose slammed her hands into his shoulders and he immediately stepped back even as his eyes seemed to burn brighter. She was proud, then, of the steadiness in her voice, because she certainly didn't feel it. "The roses were a nice touch, I'll give you that, but I don't care how you like me best. I'm here to do a job, nothing more."

Blake's eyebrows rose as he tucked a hand into one trouser pocket. "I didn't send you any flowers."

"Now who's the liar?" she challenged, and he rolled his eyes. "Pink roses for Rose? How original."

"I don't need to send a woman flowers," Blake smirked as he lounged back against the edge of his desk, "for her to know I want her."

Rose snorted. "Good to know, and if *I* want to hook-up with Christopher, then I will. It's none of your business." The hot flush stealing through her, warming her skin, made her bold, and she tilted her chin defiantly, half-curious to see what he'd do next. If he thought he could control her, he was wrong. He may have her mother wrapped around his little finger, and the press to boot, but she couldn't be swayed so easily.

Blake stood upright and strode forward until they were eye to eye, his jaw clenched and his mouth a set, edible line. *Wait, edible?* Rose shook her head free from its daze as she paid attention to Blake's words and not his mouth. "He's off-limits."

"I don't care," she challenged, and his nostrils flared as she moved to leave the room, his hand catching her wrist and sending a bolt of electricity through her.

"What would your mother think?" Blake said, his voice smoothing as he tried a different tactic.

"She knows I loathe you, and she's so desperate to see me settle down she wouldn't care if it were with an ax murderer, let alone Christopher."

"And the press? The world thinks you're mine, Rose." Blake's eyes were like molten pools she could fall into and not realize she was drowning until her breath ran out. *Hate sex is the best kind.* The words pounded through her so forcefully that she clenched her jaw, speaking through her teeth.

"I'm not yours."

"Maybe not yet," he said, shocking her as he dragged her against him and she felt his hardness against her. Her eyes widened in shock. Did he...? Was he getting off on this? Why didn't that knowledge disgust her? In fact, why was it having the exact opposite effect? Blake's face slackened slightly as he watched this play out on her face and he stroked a finger across her bottom lip. "Why fight it?" he whispered.

"Because I don't like you," she said, but her voice sounded weak even to her own ears. "You..." Her breath stuttered as he stroked a finger down her neck towards her chest, and she gulped. "You threw me to the wolves with the press."

"Did I?" He cocked his head as he moved slowly, deliberately, walking them backwards until the door met her back again and his body pressed tightly to hers. "Or did I just give you the excuse you needed?"

The air was tight between them and she was gasping softly like there wasn't enough oxygen in the room, a strange feeling that was half-nervousness and half-desire built inside her until she felt like she was coming apart at the seams. Ready to leap, ready to let go, feeling like it was dangerous to do so and yet necessary at the same time. Like she might die if his mouth wasn't on hers, but like she might break if she gave in. She had to put an end to this now. This was *David Blake*. There were a thousand reasons she should be stopping him as he moved closer, but she couldn't bring a single one to the forefront of her mind.

Lips brushed the side of her throat and she gasped as Blake tugged on her earlobe. His breath was warm in her ear as he murmured, "Tell me. Tell me why you hate me."

The warmth from his mouth seared across her body as he pressed his lips firmly to her neck.

"You're–you–"

Blake pulled back and searched her face. A smirk formed on those plush full lips as she tried to control her ragged breathing. His mouth brushed hers in a tantalizing almost-kiss. "Cat got your tongue?"

This was madness. Utter madness. With his mouth so close to her own, close enough that they shared the same breath, she was finding it hard to think. If she could just *think*.

Seeing her hesitating, Blake murmured, "Just let go, princess. Or are you scared?"

Her eyes shot to his and narrowed as she tilted her chin stubbornly. "Well, I suppose if the press already thinks we're together you might as well make it worth my while."

He gave a low chuckle and then his lips were instantly on hers, crashing down and tasting her like he was drowning, moaning like he was happy to. They kissed like they fought, a tangle of tongues with teeth clashing and lips battling for dominance. Her fingers unwittingly slid into his hair. *Stop,* she tried to tell herself. This was *Blake,* and she knew she'd regret this, but it had been too long, and God could he kiss. She wanted more.

Maybe—maybe she could have more... it didn't need to be more than this, right? He was a bastard, and this was probably his ordinary weekday liaison. Why shouldn't she enjoy herself?

She slid her hands down the warmth of his strongly muscled back as his hips pressed her firmly into the door behind her. Slipping them under the hem of that stupidly well-fitting white shirt, she groaned at the feeling of his skin beneath her fingers. How had she forgotten how good this felt? Why had she let herself go so long without so much as a hookup? She pushed back against him and they stumbled, unwilling to let their mouths part for long as they moved deeper into the room.

Echoing her movements, he trailed a path of fire under her cream turtleneck and peaked a nipple through her white bra, and that sensation was the only plausible explanation for what she did next. Her palm slid from under Blake's shirt to stroke the rigid length of him through his trousers. He paused and pulled back a little, his eyes were wide as if he couldn't quite believe what was happening. Hell, she could hardly believe it herself. Maia was going to have a field day. Oh God, her and Christopher were waiting awkwardly somewhere outside. Yet, Blake had her burning, and she hadn't felt this way in years, maybe ever. She didn't want to let this opportunity slide. She worked damn hard and had ignored her body for too long. She *deserved* this.

Slowly, she undid the button on his trousers and pushed them part of the way down, ignoring Blake's startled intake of breath. She turned around and swept documents off the desk in front of her, smirking as she ruined his office set-up. Placing her hands on the exquisite dark wood in front of her, she let him bend her with one hand in her hair before he grasped at her waist and then her breasts as his mouth pressed to her throat. Rose reached behind to slowly unzip her leather skirt and gasped when Blake caught her wrist in one large hand.

"No," he said hoarsely, "leave it on."

She was about to protest when he managed to slide it up and over her ass and he groaned when he saw she'd gone without underwear.

"Are you trying to kill me?"

She rolled her eyes. "As if I could wear panties with a skirt that tight."

He started to move down her body from behind, pressing kisses behind her knees. She gave a surprised groan when his tongue pressed against the center of her wetness.

"Blake, not that I don't appreciate that, but our best friends are outside. Are you familiar with the concept of a quickie?"

She heard him rasp a low chuckle, and she felt a warmth press against her.

"I'm familiar – spread your hands for me," he demanded in her ear and she obliged, gripping the edges of the desk as he held her at his mercy. A soft crinkle sounded behind her and she wanted to laugh. Of course he carried condoms around. God, what was she doing?

A finger slid into her cautiously, curling inside as he rubbed the sensitive spot inside her, finding it on the first try. At her moan of approval, he withdrew and something harder, hotter pressed against her, and suddenly she was desperate for it but couldn't move with the way her skirt was bunched and his thighs stilling her. Blake sank into her until they were flush and she pushed her hips back against him as much as she could while he groaned, trying to regain control. His hand curved around her ass before smacking it, chiding her, and a long moan stole its way out of her mouth. His other hand slid from her hip to stroke the center of her and her mind went blank with pleasure for a moment until she tightened around him, rocking her hips faster and reveling in the way he cursed as he pulsed inside her. His hand fell to the desk with a thud and she let his other hand press down on her back, the roughness of it making her wetter and the wildness setting her alight. She almost wanted to laugh. Chris thought she was stiff, but look how much she could bend if she wanted to.

"Harder," she demanded, and Blake's hand slid up her back so softly she shivered and then moaned as it tugged roughly at her hair, forcing her head up and exposing her throat as he slammed into her hard enough that she knew she'd be sore tomorrow.

Jolting with the force from his thrusts she moaned, "God, you're a bastard–"

He chuckled and circled his hips tightly to hers, driving

into her faster and tighter, making her moan as she came surprisingly, perhaps embarrassingly, quickly, slumping against the desk and feeling a lick of embarrassment at the sweat beading on the wooden surface where her skin had been.

It truly had been a long time since she'd felt anything but her own fingers. How hard she'd just come likely had nothing to do with how Blake had slid in and stroked just the right spot, over and over. He gave a last pump and groaned his release before withdrawing slowly and helping her right her skirt while they panted.

"You're just as fiery when you fuck as when you're yelling at me. I can't believe you came in here and seduced me in my own office. Maybe you don't hate me as much as you thought." Blake's face was flushed, his mouth was red, and his hair had darkened at the temples with sweat and Rose was distracted again for a moment before she sat up abruptly and pushed away from his desk. She felt oddly hot, but worse was the desire still humming through her and she opted to ignore it and the slick heat starting to pulse between her legs.

"*Me* seduce *you?* I'm pretty sure you were the one begging me to 'let go'. Don't worry, Blake, I still intensely dislike you, but this was fun. Now if you'll excuse me, I have to find a bathroom before I run into Maia and Christopher."

She crossed the room and made to open the door when he caught her around her waist and spun her around. He tugged her ever so slightly closer until the warmth from his chest sank into hers and she could smell his fruity cologne. He leaned in ever so slowly and pressed his mouth to hers, searchingly tasting her.

"That's okay, princess. Run away. But next time you're lonely and fucking yourself, say my name, won't you?"

Rose glared, spinning away from him and yanking at the door, praying that she could fix her hair enough that the paparazzi wouldn't notice anything amiss. She found Maia waiting at the front door and gave Chris a nod as they swept outside, the wetness between her thighs feeling beyond uncomfortable as she climbed back into their car quickly and hoped the press didn't get a good look at her.

Maia stared long and hard at Rose the whole drive home. She pretended not to notice, focusing on the view out of the window until finally she turned and said, "What?" with a sigh of exasperation.

Maia's eyes ran from the top of Rose's rumpled hair to the wrinkle at the bottom of her top before she cleared her throat lightly. "Nothing."

"Okay," she said, relieved that Maia was apparently content to let her rumpled appearance slide for now. "I promised my mom I'd meet her and Grace for dinner at *The Hummingbird* on Wednesday, do you want to come?"

Maia grinned. "You want me to be your buffer?"

"I want you to prevent World War Three."

Maia grasped Rose's clenched fists in her hands. "Sure, I'd love to come."

Not for the first time, Rose found herself wondering what she would do without Maia. She loosened her fists and squeezed Maia's hands in silent thanks, and Maia smiled with the smallest dip of her head. In every way but blood, Maia was her sister and oh, the things we do for family.

"I'm supposed to be meeting up with Thierre for brunch tomorrow and Wednesday before he flies out again at the weekend, but I'm sure I'll be done in time for dinner." Maia smiled, and Rose nodded. "I got some great photos of the ballroom, so I'm thinking..." Maia launched into her plans for the room and Rose relaxed, the last of the weird energy she'd felt in Blake's study finally leaving her. Maia's ideas were amazing, as always, and Rose chipped in with her own thoughts here and there, making her friend's eyes light up until they pulled up in front of *The Hart* to another wave of press and Rose tensed up again. It had to be Blake telling them where she would be. She hadn't been followed around like this since the time she'd agreed to a *very* brief modeling stint for a high-profile brand she owed a favor to, and even then she'd managed to stay ahead of them most of the time. But showing up here, to what was essentially her home?

Rose smoothed her hair down again and tugged her clothes straight before stepping out of the car to a barrage of lights that nearly made her eyes water. For a second she almost lost it. Wasn't sure whether to scream or cry, just anything to make them *leave her alone*. But then Maia was there, her hand slipping into Rose's and tugging her towards the lobby, and the wave of rage faded until she could breathe and march past the cameras without so much as a glance spared in their direction.

Chapter Five

It had been a few days since Rose had proposed a shopping trip with Katie and Cara, so she reached out that morning to see if they wanted a girls' day with the hope that they might also be able to keep her mind off of the eldest Blake. One of the perks of not having to work consistently was that when you needed a mental health day, you could take one and boy did Rose need one. For some reason, the press showing up at the hotel last night had really thrown her for a loop and as hard as she tried, she couldn't think of a way they could be trailing her so accurately unless they were getting frequent tips.

So even if he had been playing nice – or what passed for it with Blake – it seemed that he still wasn't above ratting her out to the paps to annoy her. And while she *was* annoyed, she actually felt more... rattled than anything.

Shopping in privacy could be difficult, even without a trail of cameras and microphones, but Rose was hoping she could sneak out the back of the hotel and make it to the mall without being photographed. Of course, once she was there it wouldn't be long before the press turned up at the rate they were going. In fact, going there with Blake's sister would likely only fan the flames of the ridiculous engagement rumors, but she'd decided a long time ago that you couldn't control what other people said about you, only how you reacted to it. So for now, Rose was choosing denial. Nothing was wrong, she felt fine, she *hadn't* slept with Blake.

Well, one of those things wasn't quite like the others, but she was denying it to herself all the same. Temporary insanity. Or maybe the slightly more permanent kind because as she'd lain awake in her bed, their encounter was all she could think about. Several times her hand had coasted down her stomach only to pause at the waistband of her sleep shorts, unwilling to give in and knowing she wouldn't be able to look at Blake the same way – or herself – if she got off while thinking about him.

Denial wasn't as satisfying as the other D she'd spent a lot of time fantasizing about yesterday evening while Maia called her name several times from in front of the TV, sending her a curious look when Rose blinked herself out of the trance she'd fallen into, but it was by far the more sensible option.

Katie and Cara had been more than happy to join her and even travel a little way out of town to Kenwood in the hopes of losing the press and as she was about to leave, Maia opened her door dressed in a chic halter top and jeans.

"Mind if I join you guys? Thierre canceled on me, and I thought it might be a good chance to look at some fabric swatches for the gala." Her tone was calm and even, but Maia lacked her usual bounce and cheer as she tugged on a red leather jacket.

"Of course! I'm sneaking out from downstairs though. I

don't understand how the press keeps finding me. It has to be Blake, right?" Maia hummed noncommittally as they stepped into the elevator and headed down to the basement level parking lot. "So Thierre canceled brunch?"

Maia frowned as she nodded. "He said he had a meeting, but it's okay, I'll see him tomorrow anyway."

"I'm sorry, sweetie. But hey, at least you get to come shopping now, huh?" That coaxed out a small smile and Rose laughed lightly as she raised her hand in the air to her driver across the way from them as they walked over.

"Thank god for Henry," Maia sighed as they settled into their seats and Rose shot her a confused look. "Henry," Maia repeated before her mouth dropped open. "Your *driver*. Oh my god, Rose." She started to laugh as Rose tugged on the end of her hair in embarrassment. "You're such a brat."

"Good thing you love me," she said, and Maia laughed again.

Henry climbed into the car and Rose ducked down as they drove up and out of the parking lot, passing the paparazzi that were spread out in groups in the above ground parking lot to the side of the hotel. Though the crowd had thinned out a little, Rose didn't relax until they were fully on the road and she could see there weren't any news vans following them.

"So far so good," she breathed and then jumped when a horn blasted somewhere on their left. "I've been thinking," she said to Maia, who looked away from the window as Rose continued, "I think silk will be too heavy for the drapery, I don't want the room to feel too heavy. It should be light and gauzy but still feel rich. I think silk will be too oppressive."

Maia nodded slowly and Rose could practically see her mind working. They'd decided to dress Blake's ballroom in gauzy draping fabrics that would cascade from the ceiling in sweeping arches of material in various shades of green – it would look decadent but elegant.

"How about we do both?" Maia said thoughtfully. "We could have a deeper green tone as the silk and have the paler colors in the lighter material, twined around."

Rose grinned. "You're a genius. We could string the lights through the gauzy material too, maybe in a gold so that the room still feels warm."

Maia had fully perked up now as they chattered on about their plans. While Rose was happy doing some of the more boring aspects of event coordination, it was the design that really sent clients her way. She wanted guests to walk in and gasp. So long as the clients had the budget, her imagination was really her limit and she and Maia had always worked well together – it was, after all, how they'd met.

The more they spoke, the more Rose felt like she could visualize the room in her mind and that was always a good sign. When she couldn't picture what she wanted... that was usually when things started to go south.

They arrived at the mall relatively quickly. It was still early and the usual traffic had been light, Katie had texted her that she was with Cara in one of the bigger department stores already.

"You've met Katie, right?" Rose murmured to Maia as they walked into the mall and Maia bit her lip thoughtfully, not even smearing the expensive red lipstick that emphasized her full mouth.

"In passing, mostly, I think. Anyone is better than Sam though." Maia grimaced and a tinkling laugh drew both their gazes to the left where Sam stood with Cara, looking at a window display.

"Oh, you and I will get on just fine." Katie grinned and slid an arm through Maia's as Rose smiled her greeting to the two women. "Any trouble sneaking away?"

"No, I think it was fine. Thanks again for agreeing to come a little farther out."

Cara smiled and Katie waved a hand airily. "Not at all, I haven't come out here in so long. It'll make a nice change."

"If we see a fabric store, I want to go in and check out some swatches for the gala," Maia said and they nodded.

"Sounds good." Cara moved closer to Rose as they began to stroll through the mall. It was bright and airy but tried to be a little arty like most modern malls nowadays, and had odd circular lights that hung low from the ceiling in a deep blue and silver but mostly just ended up looking a little cheap. "How is the planning going?" Cara grinned. "You haven't murdered my brother yet, have you?"

"Blake lives as of yet," Rose said with a sniff but winked at the younger Blake before her mind, unbidden, flashed back to the feeling of her skin against the hardwood desk, Blake's hand in her hair keeping her bent and powerless beneath him.

"You okay?" Maia asked, and Rose jumped guiltily. "You look a little flushed."

"What? Yes, I'm fine."

They continued on, passing a jewelry store that held Katie's attention and then walking into the fabrics and crafts store a little farther down. Maia's eyes lit up, and even Rose was impressed when they walked in – how had she never been here before? The store was *huge*.

Maia strode off towards the back of the store where a hand-painted sign indicated the silks could be found and Rose trailed after her at a slightly slower pace, admiring the hardwood floors and cute kitschy design of the store. It sort of felt like stereotypical grandma vibes, homey but professional enough that you didn't want to have your hand caught in the cookie jar.

A gorgeous sage green silk caught Rose's eye as Maia held it up and examined the quality, but it was the deeper emerald behind her that would be perfect for the gala. Rose held it up for Maia to see and was rewarded with a grin that had Katie and Cara looking bemusedly back and forth between them.

"How has it been with Blake?" Katie asked, leaning against the exposed brick wall. "I didn't realize you guys had so much history until Cara filled me in after dinner at *The Hummingbird*." Her icy blue eyes narrowed on Rose and she winced, knowing Katie hated being left out of the loop.

"Yeah, sorry about that. Um, things are fine."

"Fine?" Maia snorted as she measured out a ream of fabric, being careful not to handle it too much less her fingerprints mar the silk. "You should have heard her complaining the other day. *He's such an arrogant ass, Maia.*" Her friend snickered and Katie grinned at the high falsetto Maia had used to imitate Rose.

"Well, Blake seems to be enjoying himself," Cara said, clearly trying to be peacemaker. "He was in such a good mood last night it was actually nauseating."

"Last night, huh?" Maia shot Rose a look and she could feel her cheeks growing warm again as she remembered Blake's soft moans and warm breath in her ear as he'd powered into her.

"You know, I think we can order the fabric online," Rose said brightly, gesturing blithely to the sign taped up behind the register before hurrying away.

The girls followed her out of the store a few moments later and Rose's heart was beating hard when Maia opened her mouth again, clearly not content to let this go, so Rose quickly distracted them all by ushering everyone into a boutique lingerie shop and immediately darting into the racks of lace to hide her unease.

The shop was dark with black changing curtains on silver rods and fancy leather armchairs that sat in the corner next to–

"Oh my god," Rose blurted and then clapped a hand over her mouth as she took in the display.

"Found something good?" Maia sounded amused and Rose knew then that she'd made a mistake darting into the first store she saw. There was no way Rose DuLoe would ever be caught dead inside a sex shop and Maia knew it.

Her friend walked over to the display and cooed over a bright purple dildo, complete with glitter as she held it up for Rose to see. "This one says it's flavored."

Rose choked on her own spit as Katie and Cara walked up to them and Katie waggled her eyebrows as she took the dildo from Maia. "Good for you, Rose. Maybe you should go with something a little smaller and work up to that though. That thing's monstrous and Maia was telling me it's been a while for you."

Mouth dropping open, Rose snatched the silicone cock from Katie and spun to face Maia with a gasp of outrage before thrusting her hands on her hips and turning her glare on Katie too. "Well, Blake is bigger than that and I took him just fine." Then she clamped her mouth shut again as her eyes flew wide.

"I knew it!" Maia crowed as Cara grimaced.

"Could have done without knowing that," she said, and Rose shot her an apologetic look.

"I didn't mean—I never—"

"You slept with Blake," Maia said smugly. "I knew you had sex-hair in the car yesterday."

"It just happened," she said lamely, the dildo flopping over in her hand like it too was sad and she grimaced, about to set it down when the faint *snick* of a camera reached her ears. "*No,*" she whispered, horror coiling in her chest. "How do they keep finding me?"

Rose threw the dildo down as Cara stepped closer to Katie, anxiously gripping her hand as Maia and Katie peered warily out of the store's entrance. The click came again and this time, Rose spotted them on the opposite side of the circle of shops. They were on the first floor and her body felt both hot and cold as she stomped out of the store and peered over the edge of the glass barrier to the floor beneath theirs and found another swarm of paparazzi trying to come up the escalator.

"How is he *doing* this? Did you guys tell Blake we were coming here?" Rose asked Katie and Cara, who both shook their heads. "They won't leave me alone after Blake all but told them we're dating."

"Which just to clarify..." Katie said with a raised eyebrow. "You're not?"

Rose's mouth dropped open again. "*No.* Are you crazy? No offense, Cara."

The younger woman shrugged lightly. "None taken."

"So you're just hooking up then?" Maia seemed both surprised and impressed, and Rose shook her head vehemently.

"We had sex *once* and it was a mistake. Not—" she said as

Maia looked set to interrupt her again, "another word about me and Blake."

"Well in that case, we should probably get out of here unless you want to field all of their questions," Katie nodded to the paps, who had found their way onto their floor and were determinedly striding forward. "I tell you what, we'll distract them for you." Before Rose could question that at all, Katie turned and faced Cara before sliding down onto one knee and Maia grabbed Rose's hand excitedly.

"Oh my god," she squealed, and Rose wanted to join her except shock had stolen her words. What on Earth was happening?

"I had planned on doing this later on." Katie winked as she slid out a ring and Maia practically vibrated with excitement as Cara started to cry and the paparazzi slowed down to photograph this unfolding spectacle. "But I suppose this way we'll have plenty of photos to remember this moment." Katie shot her a look. "What are you still doing here?"

Rose blinked, coming back to herself as she tugged on Maia's arm, hurrying them away as the press focused solely on the two women now crying and kissing as Cara admired a large diamond on her finger.

"Did that just happen?" she said, slightly dazed.

"Unless we just shared a fever dream," Maia grinned, "yes."

They were back in the car within minutes and still giggling like teenagers as Rose pulled out her phone and shot off a combined thank-you-congratulations text to Katie and Cara.

"You know, life with you never gets boring, Ro."

"Thank you?"

"You're welcome." Maia grinned and rested her head on Rose's shoulder as they made their way home.

"I think that's the first shopping trip I've ever done where I've not bought anything."

"Oh I don't know, you seemed pretty tempted by the purple dildo. Or has Blake ruined you for all other men now?" Maia laughed as Rose swatted at her.

"Do not even," Rose warned and continued scrolling on her phone, pleased when she didn't find any photos of her holding a dildo on the gossip sites yet. Though it was probably only a matter of time.

Chapter Six

Rose slammed her phone down onto the marble countertops with a scowl. Not only had the press grabbed several photos of her leaving Blake's on Monday and at the lingerie store yesterday, but they didn't seem to be dropping the engagement rumors that were now circling the gossip columns more frequently than ever after Katie's proposal. Rose wasn't sure what was more insulting – that the press thought she would ever marry David Blake, or that they thought she would consider sharing the limelight enough to have a double wedding with Katie and Cara.

Worse than all of that put together, Rose hadn't been able to forget the way Blake had tasted when they'd kissed or what he'd felt like inside her. It was like she was a teenager all over again. She'd thought having Maia knowing her dirty little secret would make her feel ashamed, but apparently it did the opposite. Despite what she'd told the girls yesterday, it didn't feel like a one-time thing. Not when she wanted to do it again so badly.

It was just good sex. Rose slowly untensed her jaw,

nodding to herself. It wasn't because it was Blake she'd had sex with. It was just good sex. She could have good sex with anyone, theoretically.

What she really needed was another way to keep herself occupied. Maia had gone out to see Thierre and now with nothing to distract herself from thoughts of Blake, Rose was left feeling on edge. Heaving herself up off the stool, Rose stretched and winced a little at the soreness between her thighs. Nobody had ever been that rough with her before and she'd liked it more than she'd thought she would. In the past her lovers had all been gentle, handling her with care and grace. As much as she detested Blake, she could admit that at least he listened to instructions. When she'd said harder, he hadn't hesitated.

Crap. Now she was thinking about Blake again. *No, about good sex.* Right. Distraction. Rose turned off the TV that had served as some background noise as the news reported something about some local vandalism. Usually she felt perfectly safe in the suite, but since the weird break-in she'd been feeling a little on edge. Maybe she should talk to Louis. She'd forgotten to check back in with Noah the other night, too distracted by Maia's arrival, and now was as good a time as any for an update.

Rose eyed the doors to the elevator a little warily. Logically, she knew that security was monitoring it twenty-four-seven but she couldn't help the odd skip of her heart as anxiety wormed its way inside her head. *What if someone was waiting inside behind the doors? What if she got stuck and someone appeared from within the shaft?* She shook the thoughts away and jabbed the call button angrily, striding inside confidently a few minutes later.

A dark blur moved out of the corner of her eye and Rose

screamed before she could stop herself, the doors already sliding shut and a large hand clamping down over her mouth. Rose did the only thing she could think of.

"Shit, did you just bite me?"

Rose blinked away the tears swimming in her eyes so she could see clearly and slumped forward when the hand let go, resting her arms on her knees as she fought to catch her breath. "Noah? You scared the crap out of me."

"I thought you'd see me when you marched inside." Noah brushed his hair out of his green eyes and gave her a sheepish smile. "I'm sorry, I didn't mean to startle you. We've been trying to keep at least one security personnel in the lift at all times, part of the new safety measures for the time being."

She nodded shakily. "I was just coming down to speak to you and Louis about your findings the other night, actually." She paused and then stood up straight again, ignoring the blush she could feel working its way over her face and across her chest as she said with an attempt at dignity, "I'm sorry I bit you."

Noah laughed. It boomed out of him and made her relax further as she finally reached over and pressed the button for reception. "It's alright. I know better than to accidentally sneak up on you next time. Might lose the whole arm."

Rose snorted and the silence that fell between them was comfortable. She ran her eyes down Noah's body, taking in his thick arms and flat stomach – it was just good sex, right? Noah was a guy. He could be good at sex. He was definitely attractive, she supposed, and she was obviously desperate for some action if she was still fantasizing about Blake.

Clearing her throat lightly, she tried, "Well, I mean if you really want to help keep me safe, you could come and stay in the suite with me tonight." Noah's head swung towards her instantly, surprise rounding his eyes so that they looked like they might pop out of his skull. Oh god. Had that been smooth enough? How did people flirt nowadays anyway?

"Um." Noah's cheeks pinked and Rose couldn't help her awkward chuckle. "I feel like now might be a good time to mention that I'm gay."

"Oh, okay." The wave of relief that swept through her left her both dizzy and irritated. What was wrong with Noah? Why wouldn't she want to sleep with him? Was it because she'd instinctively picked up on his preferences with some kind of internal gay-dar?

Just face the facts, a treacherous little voice inside her head whispered, *it's not just good sex. It's sex with Blake.* Rose pressed two fingers to the bridge of her nose and pinched. So maybe she was attracted to stupid fucking Blake. It didn't mean anything. She'd still rather chop her own arm off and beat herself with it than even be in the same room as him. Right?

"Er, I'm sorry, Rose–" Noah's rambling tugged her out of her own head and she blinked, having half-forgotten he was there and that she'd just awkwardly propositioned him.

"No, no, I'm sorry, Noah. I didn't mean to make you uncomfortable. It was stupid, just a weird moment. Can we just forget about it?" She winced, what had Blake done to her? She was, indirectly or not, Noah's employer.

Noah nodded and a tenser silence than before descended until they both tried to break it at the same time.

"I can arrange for some security upstairs if you're worried about–"

"You know, I'm pretty sure Louis has a crush on you–"

They paused and looked at each other before Rose

started laughing. "This is more painful than the twelve flights of stairs we did."

Noah snorted. "Do you really think Louis likes me?"

"Almost definitely." Rose grinned. "I really am sorry. I don't know what I was thinking. It's just been a weird few days."

"It's alright. If you actually do want someone up there watching out for you, I can send one of my guys up tonight."

She considered it for a moment before shaking her head, not wanting someone else in her suite and making it feel weirder in there than it already did. "No, that's okay. But thank you."

The elevator dinged cheerily as the doors opened and Noah smiled. "Sure, just let me know if you change your mind."

Rose nodded as she made her way out and towards Louis at the front desk, waving back at Noah as he settled himself in the corner of the lift again.

Louis's face was like a thundercloud as he slammed the phone down in front of him, muttering angrily when it immediately started ringing again.

"Everything okay?" she called and Louis looked up, his face easing a little at the sight of Rose standing in front of him.

"Oh it's fine, Rose, thank you. It's just the tabloids calling. They're absolutely rabid since the rumors between you and Mr. Blake surfaced." Louis paused and glanced from side to side. "So, will I get an invite?"

"To what?" Rose raised an eyebrow, not really pegging Louis for the type to be interested in charity galas like the one Blake was hosting. But what else could he be talking about?

"The wedding? Have you picked a date yet?"

A laugh crept out of her, gaining in traction until eventually she was full-on roaring, eyes watering as Louis watched her in something close to shock. "Oh my god, Louis, don't tell me you believe the crap they're touting about me and Blake? I loathe that man. I would rather set myself on fire than let him put his tongue in my mouth." Well, that wasn't strictly the truth but Rose wasn't going to let her guard down again. He was already messing with her head and that wasn't a good position to be in. She couldn't abide that she felt even a slight attraction to David Blake, but to fall in love with him? Untenable.

"Er, no." Louis laughed nervously, still watching Rose with caution as she wiped the tears of laughter out from under her eyes. "Of course not. But the reporters have been hounding the hotel and the staff, trying to bribe them into saying they've seen you here with Mr. Blake."

"Don't worry, I'll take care of it," Rose assured him. "I was actually coming down here to see if you guys found out anything more about who might have been in the elevator a few days ago?"

Louis shook his head. "Unfortunately no, all we have is the camera footage of them getting into the elevator and exiting into the shaft. We don't know how they got back out of the top floor, or out of the hotel for that matter. We've got people reviewing all our footage from that day, but in the meantime we've amped up security."

Rose sighed but nodded. "Hopefully we get some answers soon. I just don't know why they would bother going to the top floor and not even attempt to get into my suite."

"Maybe they just wanted to see if they could." Louis shrugged and Rose's stomach flipped.

"Thanks for that unsettling thought, Louis," Rose sniped, and he grinned weakly.

"Sorry."

"It's fine." She waved him off. "Oh, and while I remember, did you know Noah's gay? I accidentally hit on him in the elevator and I definitely think you've got a shot with him."

"You hit on him?" Louis laughed, and she couldn't help but join in. It *was* sort of ridiculous.

"I don't know what I was thinking," she admitted and Louis' smile turned gentle.

"Probably that he could bench press the both of us with those massive arms of his," he said lightly and Rose laughed. "Let me know if you need any help with the vultures."

She smirked. She knew exactly how to deal with the paparazzi. Give them enough that they had a story but not so much that they looked credible. She'd been letting them get away with this bullshit for too long now. It was time to remind them who they were screwing with.

"I've got it covered."

The elevator was blessedly empty when she climbed in again. Noah had likely been called away for a few minutes and that suited her just fine after her disastrous attempt at picking him up.

There were still a few hours until she and Maia had to be at *The Hummingbird* for dinner, so Rose sank down onto her sofa and flicked through the channels on the TV until she found one with a familiar headline scrolling. *DuLoe Hear Wedding Bells?* Then she propped her fluffy-slippered feet onto the coffee table and snapped a photo on her phone with just enough of the headline showing that people would feel like they'd been clever before she uploaded it online with the caption: *Quiet night in #dontbelieveevery-thingyouseeonTV*.

"DARLING! I'm so glad you're here! Oh, and Maia too! What a treat. Come, sit, sit, girls. I ordered us cocktails," Annabel DuLoe said with a wink as she waved to Cal to bring over another cocktail for Maia. Rose looked at the table suspiciously. There seemed to be way too many chairs. "Ah, here they are! I hope you don't mind, David. I didn't know what you'd like to drink, but just let Cal know, will you?"

Rose felt as if she'd been dunked in ice water. How had she forgotten that Blake would be at this dinner? Well, it wasn't like she could avoid him forever. They had to work together, after all. She turned excruciatingly slowly and winced as her eyes found Blake's. She quickly looked away and instead gave a welcoming smile to his mother, standing beside him.

"Oh Rose! It's been too long!" Grace Blake kissed both her cheeks and then Maia's before embracing Rose's mother. "I'm so glad we could finally catch-up."

"Yes," Rose said, smiling through her gritted teeth, "so lovely." It was amazing that Grace could have birthed anyone as annoying as Blake. She was unfalteringly sweet and just a little shorter than Cara, only reaching Rose's shoulders in height. Her blue eyes were a shade or two lighter than Blake's and Rose resisted pinching herself at the realization that she knew the color of Blake's eyes so precisely. They were just *blue*. Nothing special.

Somehow Maia got shuffled to one side and Rose ended up seated next to Blake and when those eyes met hers, she gulped. *Nothing special.* Heat seemed to pour off his body in waves and she found herself chugging her margarita just for something else to focus on.

"Steady, darling, there's tequila in those, you know." Annabel laughed.

"Oh, she knows," Cal said with a grin and a wink for Rose as he set Blake's drink down and then joined them at the end of the table. It was relatively quiet in the bar that evening and Cal was more manager than bartender anyway. Rose knew her mother was just grateful to have someone in the family interested in the business. "Did I ever tell you about the time I introduced Rose to my friend Nate? There was tequila involved then as well–"

"Oh I don't think they need to hear that story." She laughed tightly and shot daggers at her cousin who just laughed. A glance to her side found Blake's eyes on hers and his face oddly closed.

He seemed... off. His mouth was unusually tight at the corners as he glanced between her and Callum and Rose clamped down on a laugh. Was he jealous? She struggled not to let her eyes widen in surprise but couldn't stop the smile from forming on her lips, so she quickly busied herself with more margarita.

"You do know..." she said, leaning in after watching Blake's expression darken further the more tales Cal told of Rose's so-called 'wild' party days. The downsides to going to college with your cousin. "That the reason Cal and I are so close..."

Blake's head turned towards her the slightest amount, his hand tight around his whiskey glass, and she wanted to laugh.

"Is that he's my cousin? Practically like my brother. We went to college together, you know."

Blake jerked and Rose couldn't keep her laugh in that time. His lips rose in a smirk as he realized she'd played him for a fool. "Well, I suppose you can't still be that close, or does he know that I'm your dirty little secret?"

She rolled her eyes. "It was one measly hook-up, Blake. Sorry to deflate your ego, but I've barely thought about you since."

"I see," he murmured, but his eyes were full of amusement as if he could see straight through her lies.

Maia caught her eye across the table and gave an unabashed eyebrow wiggle and mouthed, "blushing" at her with a grin.

Rose mumbled a curse that turned into a quiet gasp as Blake's hand brushed her leg under the table. It was like electricity fired through her, tightening her body to fine points that were so pleasurable it bordered on pain as his hand languidly brushed higher. Why did it have to be *him* that had this effect on her?

"Don't you agree, darling?"

"Er–what?" she asked desperately, hand reaching down and clamping onto Blake's to prevent him from venturing any higher.

"I was saying to Grace how nice it is that you and David can work together on his project."

"Ah – yes, so nice."

Maia smirked and leaned in to whisper to Callum. Great. Now more people knew that she'd screwed Blake. Though, on the plus side, it wasn't exactly a short list of people that'd had the misfortune of Blake's company. Blake's lips curled, as if he too were remembering just how *nice* working together had been so far.

Rose kept her eyes on Maia and mouthed *traitor* to her at the first opportunity, knowing she was correct in her conclusions when Cal gave her a shit-eating grin.

Blake's hand distracted her again as it crept under the hem of her dress slowly. She was frozen. She should stop this. She should push him away. Why wasn't she pushing him away? She could have, easily. Maybe she had something to prove, maybe she just didn't want him to stop touching her just yet. She looked up and met his eyes and gave him a slow blink of disinterest, struggling to stop her mouth from twitching in laughter as he took in her challenging stare.

"I mean, I have worked with better clients, Mother, but yes, I suppose it has been *nice* catching up with Blake. Just yesterday he re-introduced me to his handsome friend, Christopher."

The heat in Blake's eyes betrayed his twinge of jealousy, but mostly he looked amused and... hungry. She gave an involuntary jerk as his fingers brushed against the outside of her panties, taunting her. The table had fallen unusually silent. Maia was looking back and forth between Rose and Blake with wide eyes while Annabel and Grace watched them with pleased pursed lips, side-eyeing each other in apparent glee.

"Well, we are glad to see you both are getting along so well. You used to be such good friends."

"Mm, yes, I have plenty of other friends now though, Mother."

Blake grinned at her words. "Well, that doesn't mean that *we* can't be friendly though, does it?" he asked as a finger slowly slid under the scrap of lace covering her.

"Quite right!" Grace chimed in and normal chatter resumed between her and Annabel. Rose lifted her eyes to Blake's. His were teasing, and a smile played around his mouth – with a small jolt she realized she wanted to kiss it. She had *promised* herself this was a one-time thing – yet here she was, David Blake's fingers perilously close to the wetness rapidly gathering between her legs. Maia would never let her live it down. But... damn, he *was* great in bed. Or, well, studies. They hadn't actually made it to a bed yet.

God, *yet*? Where had that come from? She took a steadying breath and stood up quickly. Blake muttered a curse as he quickly withdrew his hand before anyone could see but Rose thought she caught a knowing look on Maia's face and struggled to contain her blush.

"I just need the ladies'. I'll be back in a minute. Feel free to order for me."

Keeping her legs steady was the hard part as she walked down a small set of steps that led to the restrooms. Just as she reached the door, she felt a hand grasp her shoulder and gave a gasp of alarm.

"I thought you might need some help," Blake murmured into her ear as he pressed his front to her back.

"Help peeing?" she attempted to quip, but even she could hear that there was no heat to the barb.

"No. Help with... other things." Blake rocked against her, just once, but it was enough to feel the length of him against her ass. "Seeing as our last encounter was so unmemorable, well, I never like to leave a lady dissatisfied."

"Funny, that's all I ever feel around you."

"Now, now," he said directly into her ear, "I don't think that's entirely true, princess." Her hand was still pressed to the white door that led to the bathrooms and she shivered in the corridor as Blake slid a hand up the back of her thighs and slapped her ass. "That's for lying."

She whimpered with need and instantly wanted to choke the sound back. "I'm not–"

"Princess, are you lying to yourself or to me? I think there's an easy way to find out."

Rose hesitated for a moment more before pushing through the door and into the bathroom, muttering a curse as she tugged him through after her.

The countertops were dark green and black marble with splashes of gold for the sinks and taps and the chandelier light made the room seem dimly lit but the bright lights surrounding the three mirrors above the sinks showed the pink flush on Rose's cheeks clearly. Blake flipped the lock on the main door and the noise seemed too loud in the stillness of the room.

"Now, one of us is a liar, and I think it's you."

The carpet was dark and plush and Blake didn't hesitate as he sank to his knees in front of her. He was tall enough that on raised knees his head fell to just beneath her breasts and she could feel his hot breath through the material of her dress. She was grateful for the short skirt as he slid his hands up over her calves and thighs, gathering the material and shooting her a look of sheer dominance. "Hold it," he demanded and she obeyed.

"Are you ready to admit that you lied to me yet?" Blake pressed three firm kisses to the inside of one thigh and her breath left her in a ragged exhale, the material of the dress slipping a little until he grabbed her thighs and forced them to bend, so only the wall behind her supported her back as he spanked her ass. "I said hold it, princess."

He pressed three kisses to the inside of her other thigh

and she melted, still holding tightly to the skirt of her dress. Still, she wasn't ready to give in so quickly.

"I didn't lie," she repeated. "I haven't thought about you once since yesterday."

"I thought about you," he said, surprising her. "Thought about the way you moaned for me, the way you spread these pretty little thighs... just the way you are right now, princess."

A gasp left her as he pressed a kiss closer to the place she wanted him most and then placed another on the opposite side.

"Did you do as I asked?" he murmured, tongue just barely tracing over her clit through her soaked panties. "Did you call my name while you touched yourself?"

"No," she said hoarsely and couldn't control the way her hips rocked when he spanked her again, the sharp sting making her throb with want.

"Are you lying again, princess?"

"I'm not lying," she hissed out through clenched teeth. "I didn't touch myself and think of you."

"But you wanted to, didn't you?"

Rose didn't answer and his low laugh said her non-reply didn't matter. They both knew the truth. Her desire was right there for both of them to see, glistening on Blake's fingers as he pressed two inside her and curled them when she moaned for him.

"I hope you'll remember things a bit more clearly this time," he said and she opened eyes that she hadn't realized had closed and looked down at him as he smirked. "I'd hate to have to remind you again." He set a slow, aching pace as he moved his fingers in her, stretching her with a third and rewarding her with a kiss over the top of her panties when she writhed. "Say my name," he panted, blue eyes so dark they could have been black, and a lust-hazed smile draped itself across her mouth when she saw how much this was affecting him, the way his erection pressed against the tight confines of his trousers. "Say my name, princess, and I'll give you what you need." Blake pressed his tongue against her clit through her panties again for emphasis and she rocked her hips helplessly but remained silent, knowing this was teasing him more than her and laughing breathlessly when he cursed.

"What will it take to get you to beg for me, princess?" His words were husky as he pulled his fingers away, ignoring her whimpered protest, and dropped his hand to his fly. The sound of it being lowered had her eyes latching onto his movements desperately, eager for a glimpse at the naked flesh beneath even as she hated him for it. "Or maybe you just want to watch *me* beg for *you*?"

Blake's hand closed around himself as he spoke, pumping slowly beneath his tight gray pants. She reached forward before she could think too much about it, wanting to see, *needing* to see, and growling in frustration when he leaned slightly away from her. Smirking as he canted his hips so she could glimpse his head, glistening with moisture as he stroked himself, her lips parted in want.

"Tell me," Blake groaned, pants gaping wider at the front as he pulled himself free fully and she let her eyes rove his long, hard form, jutting proudly upward. "Do you like it when I'm on my knees for you, princess? Do you want me to say your name when I come?"

Rose bit her lip, conflicted. Should she give into this insanity? It felt like she already had as she stared, entranced, when Blake's hand moved faster, his dick moving in and out of the tunnel his hand made, and she wondered if it had looked so hot when it had been driving into her the other day.

"No?" he panted and Rose blinked, coming back to herself when he stood, his erection just mere breaths away from her mouth as he looked down at her. "Maybe you like it when I'm in control then, Rose."

Her name in his mouth, god, it did things to her that it shouldn't. That she *hated*. And yet, all she could think about was how it would sound spilling from his lips as he orgasmed.

Blake's hand slid into her hair, pulling her mouth closer to his dick as his eyes held hers unfalteringly. "Taste me," he demanded, pulling sharply on her hair when she didn't immediately obey. "Open your mouth, princess. I want to feel your mouth on me, all of me."

Rose eyed the long length of him in front of her doubtfully, but one more tug on her hair had her lips wrapping around his head as she looked up at him obediently, waiting for further instructions and squirming at the dampness collecting between her legs.

Blake's head tipped back as a long breath escaped him, his throat working before he looked back down at her and said tightly, "Keep going, princess. I know you can take it. I want to feel your throat working me while I fuck your mouth."

Rose moved down another inch and his hand tightened almost painfully in her hair before relaxing and stroking the small sting as if in apology. She withdrew and worked more of him in, swallowing instead of gagging when he hit the back of her throat, and Blake's hips flexed as he tried to keep himself in check. That wasn't going to work for her.

Reaching out, she wrapped her hands around his ass, pulling him closer until her lips touched his base and Blake hissed in pleasure. But when she tried to pull back he laughed, holding her head in place as she salivated around him.

"It looks like you need reminding who's in charge here," he murmured as he drew his hips away before bringing his length back against her tongue with a moan. Blake grasped her jaw gently with one hand. "I want you to watch yourself take me, princess, and when I tell you to, you're going to swallow."

Rose nodded as her tongue flicked around his dick, making him twitch in her mouth every time she did it. His pace increased until he hit the back of her throat with every thrust and her pussy clenched and unclenched repeatedly.

"Princess," he gasped as his dick sped into her, his thrusts becoming deep and ragged. "Touch yourself. Now. Slide two fingers deep and pretend they're mine while they fuck you."

Rose's eyes flew wide, she'd never touched herself in front of someone else before and the words sent an unexpected thrill through her. Her hand slid cautiously down, too slow for Blake's liking, it seemed, as he pushed into her mouth with a punishing thrust, making her eyes water.

"Now," he said in a clipped voice that told her he was close and she smirked around his dick even as he thrust in hard again. But she didn't delay any longer. Instead, she let her fingers find her clit, pushing aside her panties impatiently and moaning when the cool air hit her.

"I want to see your fingers buried inside your pussy," Blake ordered and she whimpered as she did as he told, rocking her hips as her pussy found the base of her hand. "Are you pretending they're mine, Rose? Do you wish they were?"

She could only look up at him with her mouth full of his

dick and he cursed, the hand in her hair tightening as he tipped her head back and thrust into her mouth with wild abandon.

"Swallow."

Rose did as she was told, swallowing twice as her hand brought her closer to the edge. Blake withdrew his dick, stroking her hair softly for a moment before he crouched down and nudged her thighs so wide the muscles burned.

"You're going to come for me now and I'm going to watch you. If your eyes leave mine, I'll punish you. Understand, princess?"

Her heart sped up as she nodded, anticipating the sweet sting, wanting to feel his hands on her skin even as she couldn't understand why he was having this effect on her. Rose leaned back against the bottom of the marble block countertop and let her legs fall wide, the heat from Blake's gaze making her blush as her fingers drove in and out, wringing small whimpers from her mouth as her eyes fluttered closed.

A pinch to her ass made her gasp and her eyes immediately met Blake's again as he smirked.

"Are you ready to say my name yet, Rose?"

God, she was so close but she could tell she needed more. Her eyes pleaded with Blake. Maybe later she would feel ashamed or hate herself, but right now she just needed to come. Hard. Still Blake didn't move, even as she writhed, even as her pleasure started to border on pain.

"Beg me," he said, leaning in to whisper the taunting words in her ear. "Say my name, princess, that's all you have to do." His hand skimmed over her clit and the small sensation felt ten-times more sensitive than usual.

She couldn't help it, couldn't hold it in anymore. He'd

won. Her pussy throbbed around her fingers as she cried out, "Blake, please."

The look of triumph that overtook his face nearly made her regret the decision, until his hand found her clit, bearing down hard as he worked her to a fever pitch that left her trembling as her orgasm rocketed through her.

"You see?" Blake grinned as he bent his head down to taste her with his tongue one more time before he stood and adjusted his pants. "We do work so well together, princess."

Chapter Seven

Rose found her way back to her seat on trembling legs. Excellent sex didn't make up for Blake inciting the press... but it certainly helped.

"So darling, I feel like we've barely spoken since you got home. You didn't tell me before, how was New York?" Annabel DuLoe wasted no time, peppering Rose with questions as soon as her ass hit the chair again.

"Busy."

Her mother pouted. "Now darling, I hope you're not still angry with me because of our conversation the other day."

Rose gave an un-ladylike snort as her eyes followed Blake's tight ass as he joined Maia and Cal at the bar. She turned back to the two schemers looking at her with big eyes. "Yes, I'm still annoyed with you both. Stop," she fixed her stare on her mother, "meddling around in my love life. I'm perfectly capable of finding my own dates, thank you very much."

Her mother gave a little disdainful sniff. "Oh yes? What, like poor Tom?"

"Who?"

"You see! Hopeless! Poor thing sat at the bar for over half an hour hoping you would come back the other night."

Blake sat down in the seat beside her in an elegant sprawl. "You talking about the guy she turned up with a few days ago?" He let out a short laugh and leaned in to whisper in her ear. "I'm pretty sure he wouldn't have had the balls to make you come in the bathroom."

Rose gave him a scowl and repressed the shiver his warm breath elicited as it ghosted over the sensitive spot below her ear.

"Rose?" Ally, one of the waitresses at *The Hummingbird* called, and Rose looked up, still in a slight daze, all her nerve endings alight at Blake's proximity. "This was just delivered for you."

Ally handed over a thick, cream envelope and Rose's interest was piqued. She carefully slid one long manicured nail under the flap and tugged it open, eyebrows rising at the card inside. It looked like the same material as the note Maia had left her when she'd come back from Paris, except the heart on the front was cracked in two.

"Writing me more love letters?" Rose joked and Maia frowned as she settled into her seat again.

"What?"

Rose snorted. "Okay, okay. I'll play along."

Maia was doing her best to act confused and Rose grinned again, though it faded fast when she read the inside of the card, the table's chatter fading away rapidly.

WHAT DO you call someone who fucks their enemy? Whore? Hypocrite? I thought you were better than this.

. . .

Rose looked up in shock, her heart having dropped all the way to her stomach. Someone had seen her and Blake together. But how? Her eyes roved around the restaurant, searching for someone who didn't belong – but what if it was someone close to her who had sent the message?

She looked back at Maia, trying to keep the hurt out of her voice as she closed the note and clenched it hard in her hands. "You really didn't send me this?"

Her friend looked up, dark eyes meeting Rose's. "No, what is it?"

"And you didn't leave me the other note on Thursday?" Oh god. The note that had been left *in her suite*. How had they gotten in? Who were they? What could they possibly want?

"I got back into town on Friday, remember? I didn't leave you any notes."

Rose's mouth suddenly felt dry. She'd just assumed that Maia had been in town but staying with Thierre, but if Maia hadn't got back until Friday evening and Rose had received the first note the night before... It had been waiting for her. So who had access to the suite and left it for her? The most logical answer was that it had to be a staff member. Nobody else had access. Except her mother and, by extension, Grace. Which also meant... Blake.

"Mom, did you leave me a note a couple of nights ago?" Her voice had risen in panic and she could feel a cold sweat starting up.

"No, sweetheart. Why?"

Rose pushed away from the table, breathing hard as she stared down at them. "It wasn't *any* of you?"

"Darling, what is this about?" Annabel asked as a round of shaking heads looked at Rose with pinched eyes and pursed lips. Her eyes flicked to Blake and found his face just as concerned as everyone else's, but could she trust it? Because of course *Blake* knew that they'd slept together and that she hated his guts. Most people assumed because their families got along that they did too. Only someone close to her would know that... or someone who had been watching her. None of this added up. She couldn't rule anything out yet.

She gave them all a shaky smile. "Nothing." She could get to the bottom of this herself, no need to panic anyone over a stupid note the paparazzi had probably sent. What if they were watching her now? Enjoying her meltdown? Rose wouldn't let anyone see her tremble. Blake's hand rested on her leg as he peered up at her, blue eyes warm and serious, but she looked away and slid her leg out of his reach, clenching her jaw as she forced her shoulders to appear relaxed. One thing was for sure, until she knew if he was behind this, she couldn't sleep with Blake again. Not that she would have wanted to anyway. "Nothing," Rose repeated with a laugh as she regained control of her breathing and sat back down. "Just a prank. What were you talking about?"

The attention shifted off of her and Rose pretended she couldn't feel Blake's questioning gaze burning into her face.

"We were just talking about David's gate," her mom said, sipping deeply at her mimosa.

"His gate?"

"Didn't you see it on the news, dear?" Grace chipped in, her gaze flitting between Rose and Blake before settling back on Rose. "Some hooligans spray painted it on Monday night."

Rose raised her eyebrows. "Oh, I think I did hear something about some vandals. I didn't realize it involved you though, Blake."

"Well that's the strange part," her mother said, a sly grin taking over her face and making Rose narrow her eyes. "You might have a fan, darling."

"What?" Rose's heart beat a little faster.

"They wrote *she's mine*," Blake said dryly. "Probably just some paparazzi looking for an easy story to sell."

Wasn't that what she'd literally just thought too? Just the paparazzi? Was that a coincidence? Or suspicious?

"Odd," Rose said at last and jumped when her phone buzzed with an incoming message. Her brow furrowed when she saw the name on the screen: *David Blake*. Sure enough, when she checked, she could see the glow of his phone under the table.

"Do you need to answer that, dear?" Grace asked, and there was a look in her eye that told Rose she knew exactly who the message was from.

"No, that's okay. Nothing important." Her phone buzzed again, and then again a moment later, as if to belie that fact. "Actually, I think I'm going to head out. I'm not feeling too well. It was lovely seeing you though, Grace. Blake," she said with a curt nod and then walked around the table to press a kiss to her mother's cheek. At this rate, Rose was going to get an anti-social reputation. This was the second time in almost a week that she'd left a gathering early at *The Hummingbird*. "I'll see you at home," she said to Maia, who nodded while listening intently to something Cal was saying.

Her phone buzzed again in her hand and Rose couldn't help the glare she sent Blake's way, glancing down at the message and wincing at the message on the screen:

Running scared, princess?

THE RINGING of her phone jolted Rose awake with a gasp. A light sweat made her skin feel sticky and she grimaced as she brushed strands of her hair back off her forehead. The phone on her bedside was too bright for her eyes and she squinted, groaning as she saw the time and Maia's name on the display. What was she doing calling Rose so early? Why wasn't she asleep down the hall? Rose fell back against her covers with a sigh as she answered, desperate to make that gods-damned sound stop. "Hello?" Rose croaked groggily.

"Rose? I need you to come and get me. I did something bad."

"Maia? Where are you?" Rose had left her at *The Hummingbird* just hours ago and hadn't seen her come in before Rose had gone to bed. "Are you okay?"

"I'm alright," Maia replied, and Rose relaxed fractionally. "I'm, er, at *The Hummingbird*."

"Still?" she asked, surprised. She was pretty sure it closed at one on weekdays, so what on earth could Maia be doing there? "Alright," Rose said, saving her questions for when she could properly interrogate her friend. "I'm on my way."

She dressed quickly, shoving her feet into her comfiest slippers and securing her hair more firmly in a scrunchie before grabbing a chunky knit cardigan from her closet. Her driver had likely retired for the night, or day? Rose shook her head, still half-asleep as the empty elevator carried her down to the basement parking. Maia was lucky that Rose could drive. A lot of people didn't bother when they had their own drivers, but she had always enjoyed the sense of freedom, of possibility, it gave her.

A mixture of worry and curiosity curdled in her stomach as Rose made her way to *The Hummingbird*. Her brain was drawing its own conclusions about where Maia had been and what she'd been doing, and it had her worried. Maia was a romantic at heart and while she might have sort of encouraged Rose to loosen up and enjoy some casual hate-sex with Blake, she didn't generally do casual sex herself. Then again, normally neither did Rose.

Maia's tall silhouette and head of familiar curls were easy to spot as Rose pulled up outside the entrance to the bar and her worry only increased as she took in Maia's rumpled state. Really, she was lucky that it was late-summer, otherwise Maia would have been freezing in her brightly colored A-Line skirt and sleeveless blouse.

"Thank god," Maia muttered as she climbed quickly into Rose's rental. Her normally curly, bouncy hair was wild, springing in every direction, and her eyes were smudged with the remnants of mascara. Her mouth was swollen, like she'd had the crap kissed out of her–

"You hooked up," Rose said wonderingly. "Thierre?"

Maia's laugh was short and bitter. "I left the bar not long after you and went to his hotel. He was already... occupied. Apparently," Maia gave a snort that lacked any humor, "he thought we were in an open relationship."

"Fuck," Rose breathed, keeping an eye on the road as they headed home but glancing over at Maia in the seat next to her.

"Yeah. So, I left and headed to the bar for some pity drinks–"

"Why didn't you call?" A touch of hurt colored her voice

as Rose frowned. "You know I'd have been there as soon as humanly possible."

Maia smiled and reached across to grasp one of Rose's hands. "I know, and I'm so grateful, but I needed to be alone. And I was. For a bit."

"Maia... if you didn't hook up with Thierre..." Rose had a sinking feeling she knew who Maia had fallen into bed with.

"Well, I'd had an awful lot to drink and–" Rose cursed inwardly. Maia wasn't a huge drinker, so any story of hers that included excessive amounts of alcohol always ended in disaster. "–I actually ended up staying til close with Cal. He was so sweet. He just sat and listened to me rant. We did shots. So many shots." Maia turned a little green as if just the memory was enough to make her puke.

"Okay, so you got drunk with Cal. You maybe made out a little. This doesn't sound so bad?"

Maia winced. "Well, we did kiss. But... look, I know he's your cousin, but he's hot, okay? I know that breaches the hoe-code in so many ways, but how could I not notice? Those *arms*, Ro..."

Rose blinked, startled. She had never considered that Maia might have been holding back with Cal because she thought Rose might have a problem with it. "You're an idiot," Rose said fondly and snorted. "You can date – or ogle – whoever you want, darling."

Maia's shoulders slumped with relief and there was more confidence in her voice when she continued on, pressing her fingers to her lips. "But when we started kissing, it just – I don't know, set something off inside me. I've *never* been kissed like that before, Rose. He kissed me like—like he'd been waiting to do it for years and would die if he never got to do it again."

"That's... very intense." Rose couldn't say she was surprised. It had been pretty obvious to her for a while that Cal was interested in Maia.

"Yeah," Maia said, nodding solemnly. "It just felt so good, and I like Cal. I just wanted to feel good."

"What aren't you telling me, Maia?"

"Cal and I had sex." The words seemed to tumble out of Maia's mouth in a rush and Rose gaped at her for a second. She would never judge her. It was just that it was such un-Maia like behavior. "...On the bar." Maia finished in a small voice, peeking out at Rose through her fingers.

Rose burst out laughing and Maia whipped her head up, her cheeks lightly flushed. "Oh my gosh, this is amazing! On the bar? Damn, you two are wild."

"You're not mad?"

"Mad? Why would I be mad?"

"Well, I mean, you do technically own the place, and he's your cousin, and we had sex on top of the bar–"

"–on the bar!" Rose chortled again. "You're ridiculous. As if I'd be mad. Maia, we need to celebrate! You had casual sex for the first time ever! On top of a *bar*!"

A smile began to twist Maia's mouth as she smoothed a hand over her riot of curls. "I mean, I guess it is kind of badass."

"Kind of? It's majorly badass! You one upped me – Blake and I only braved the bathroom," Rose said with a wink, and Maia finally laughed.

"Okay, okay. We'll celebrate tonight. But not til *way* later. I need to sleep, and I'm still a little drunk right now."

Rose laughed again and Maia joined in as they pulled up to the hotel. Sometimes Maia worried even more than Rose did, and that was really saying something. They'd been friends ever since they'd met on a photoshoot that Maia was styling, gone out for drinks, and the rest was history. In the five or so years that Rose had known her, Maia had never been single, and she'd never had casual sex. All her relationships went somewhere. Rose was a little more cautious. While Maia threw herself into love at every opportunity, Rose stuck to the same routine when she was dating guys. The only exception had been... Blake. Though, hate sex couldn't really be considered dating, she supposed.

"Rose, does it still count as casual sex if I might want to do it again? With Cal?" Maia's voice echoed in the underground parking as they slammed their car doors and headed to the elevator.

Unsurprised, Rose grinned. "You do whatever you want to do. Cal has had a crush on you forever. Maybe see where it goes." Rose stuck out her tongue when Maia raised a pointed brow. She knew it was basically the same thing everyone kept telling her about Blake, but it was different! Maia was carefree and trusting and looking for love. Rose could not be further from looking if she'd superglued her eyes shut.

Luckily there weren't any paparazzi around to catch her in her mismatched silky blue sleep bottoms and giant fluffy slippers, paired with her creamy thick cardigan that was actually a little too warm for the weather outside even so early in the morning. Maia had been so upset that she hadn't even noticed what Rose was wearing in the car, but was now taking the time to look Rose up and down with barely concealed laughter.

"You look like a five-year-old dressed you."

"It was like four-am! I dressed like anyone pulled from bed at the ass-crack of dawn would!"

Maia let out a snicker and soon they were both rolling up in laughter as they waltzed through the lobby of *The Hart*.

"I cannot *wait* to get into bed," Maia groaned as they got into the elevator.

"It will likely be a lot comfier than the bar at *The Hummingbird*," Rose teased, and Maia swatted at her but grinned, her even white teeth gleaming in the harsh light inside the elevator.

A strange tingle of awareness flooded through her and Rose frowned, feeling like she was forgetting something. "Hey," she said slowly as she looked around the inside of the elevator while they climbed steadily upwards. "I thought they were keeping someone stationed in here at all times since the access leak." Access leak was just a slightly less scary way of saying 'break-in' and they both knew it, but Maia let it slide.

"Guess they decided it wasn't necessary anymore." Maia shrugged as the doors *dinged* open to reveal chaos.

Rose took one step out of the elevator and Maia clung to her arm, stopping her from going too far. Glass crunched under foot and shone in the light from the open elevator as it tangled in the fluff on her slippers. The coffee table she and Maia had picked out lay in pieces on the floor, chunks of wood from the legs splintered and sticking up at odd angles, and more glass glistened on the carpet underneath. Deep gouge marks marred the fabric sofa, and feathers still drifted in the air from the cushions that had been viciously stabbed, like this had all happened only moments ago.

Her breath felt too loud, her hands trembling as her body froze up, stuck between staring at the chaos and getting the hell out of there.

The cabinet doors were all open, and the seldom-used

dinnerware inside was smashed to pieces on the floor and countertops and the TV–

"What was it that Blake was saying at dinner about his main gate?" Maia whispered, as if scared her voice would inflict more damage on the room as they stared at the words scrawled harshly in what looked like Rose's favorite red lipstick. *WHORE.* Just like the note she'd received at the restaurant.

Rose let out a long breath and spun slowly as she assessed the damage, freezing as she saw the curtains by her balcony door flutter in a breeze she hadn't conjured.

She froze, and Maia seemed to sense the change.

There was a shadow at the door.

Her body finally jolted back into action as she threw Maia forward with her outstretched hands, pushing her back into the elevator as Rose followed swiftly behind. The doors started to close as she jammed her hand down on the button for reception. Too slow, too slow...

The shadow darted forward, like it could catch the doors and prevent their escape, and Rose's mouth was too dry to even scream. All she could do was scramble back as they shut, catching a glimpse of a dark hoodie and a silver gleam of what could only have been a blade at their side.

Her heart felt like it could beat out of her chest, and she knew after seeing that carnage, after seeing the words scrawled there for her and the figure with the knife, Blake couldn't be behind this.

"What do we do?" Maia's teeth chattered as she held herself against Rose. They stayed close together as Rose hit the button for the basement before they could reach the floor for the reception.

"We just need to get out," Rose said, nodding decisively

three times, her hands shaking as she pushed her fallen hair out of her face. "Just get away, okay? We're fine, everything's going to be fine."

"What if they're waiting for us downstairs?" Maia's voice shook and Rose's breath stuttered for a moment.

"They won't be," she said with more confidence than she felt. Everything was hazy, the lights, the way the floor moved under them. Dimly, she realized this must be shock and a small giggle broke through and suddenly she couldn't stop. The doors slid open, and Rose felt like she was in a horror story, half-expecting to find her suite torn up on the other side again, but only the dark parking garage awaited them.

They stumbled back to Rose's car, hands locked between them, and Rose fumbled the keys in her hands as the car beeped to say it was unlocked, making them both jump.

A door slammed somewhere off to her left and it felt like her heartbeat was in her ears as she pulled open her door and helped Maia put on her belt. Was it the figure from upstairs? Had they raced down the stairs after them? Footsteps pounded along the concrete and Rose revved the engine, hitting the accelerator and driving them forward accidentally instead of reversing.

Maia screamed as they stopped inches away from the concrete wall and Rose swore as she instead threw the car into reverse and backed out of the lot in a harsh squeal of tires.

"Fuck, there, *there,*" Maia shouted, and Rose glanced in the direction of her shaking finger to see the same hooded figure as before watching them drive away.

"We're okay," Rose breathed, trying desperately to keep herself together, to watch the road, not even sure where she was going but knowing they needed to hurry.

Faster, faster, faster. Rose didn't realize she was saying the words out loud until Maia's hand touched her shoulder and she jumped, startled to see they'd come to a stop outside of a familiar house. God knew how they'd got there as Rose couldn't remember any of the drive. Suddenly she was desperate for air, like she'd been suffocating in the car and only just noticed, and Maia followed as Rose left her car idling and jumped out.

Maia said something to the guard at the gate and he waved them in, but Rose couldn't even take in his concern. Her mind and body felt like they were suspended underwater. Every step felt like pressing through a strong current and her mind felt like it was stuttering, drowning, only to resurface with chattering teeth. She pulled Maia closer as they stumbled up the long driveway, wrapping her arms around her like she could hold her friend together as she muttered under her breath.

At some point she'd lost her slippers without even realizing it, the sharp points of gravel dug into her feet but Rose could barely feel it, her focus strictly on the door in front of them as it grew ever closer.

It flew open before she had time to knock, the security guard having no doubt called ahead, and David Blake stared at them both with a pale face, his hair rumpled and so clearly having just rolled out of bed that Rose felt another wave of knee-shaking relief swamp her. He definitely hadn't been the one who had chased them out of the suite.

"Rose, what–"

"I didn't know where else to go." Her voice was a soft croak as she pushed Maia towards the warmth spilling out from the doorway and Blake caught her instinctively, hands flashing out to steady her as he carefully sat her down on the floor in the hall of his house.

Safe. Maia was safe and Blake, for all his perceived faults, would look after her. Her breath left her in a whoosh as her legs finally gave way and Blake let out a yell of panic that seemed distant, vibrating through her ears like they were trapped in a small tunnel.

Warm hands scooped her up, sliding under her knees, until she was pressed against warm skin.

"Fuck, princess, your feet..."

"I didn't know where else to go," she slurred again, eyes rolling in their sockets as she tried to blink his face into focus.

Arms tightened around her and Rose sighed, letting the tension slip away until her body began to shake from the spent adrenaline.

"I've got you," Blake said as the world faded into nothingness. "I've got you."

Chapter Eight

What had she been thinking? Rose sat with a heavy blanket wrapped around her shoulders, though her shock-induced shivers had long since subsided. Maia had recovered and her eyes were now bouncing back and forth between Rose and Blake like she was refereeing a tennis match as they sniped at each other.

Blake spoke to the cop at the door, shooting the occasional frown at her while they talked, giving his statement as efficiently as possible. Controlling, arrogant *ass*. She scowled at him and then at the cop as he made to step towards her again. She'd already given her statement and repeated it what felt like half a dozen times. What more could he need from her?

"Ms DuLoe, firstly, I want to commend you on your quick thinking. You did good getting out of there and to a secure location. I've spoken with Mr Blake and we're in agreement that the best place for the both of you to be to keep you safe from this guy is right here."

For a second she just stared at him, and then she started

to laugh. "Sorry, I thought you just said you agreed with Blake."

"I did." The cop frowned. "Frankly, Mr Blake's property is far easier to secure than your own, especially given that *The Hart* has now suffered two break-ins."

"Okay, so how long do I need to stay here for? A few hours?"

"As long as it takes us to catch him."

Rose's mouth gaped open. "*What?* You can't honestly expect me to stay here with him. What about Maia?"

"Ms Katz seems only to be a victim of circumstance, unlike you and Mr Blake who have been directly targeted by the perpetrator."

"I'm going to stay with Callum," Maia cut in before Rose could retort, using her most soothing voice while Rose seethed. "The police are going to escort me."

She nodded, glad that at least the cop was able to make at least one sensible decision, but leaving her here with Blake... alone... Well, her stalker wouldn't need to get to them in order for a murder to occur.

A commotion at the door signaled the arrival of her mother before the cop could try to speak again and familiar floral perfume caught in Rose's throat as her mother swept her into a hug. For a moment, her eyes filled with tears. Sometimes it didn't matter how old you were, nothing could beat the safety and comfort of your mother. Until she opened her mouth. "Gosh, darling, I'm so grateful you and Maia are okay. Thank goodness for David! I dread to think what might have happened without him."

Acid fizzed at her center as Rose stared ahead over her shoulder, caught in her mother's embrace and fuming. "Oh yes, so heroic of Blake to save us once the danger had passed.

I mean, it's not like *I* managed to get us out of there and drove us all the way here."

Her mother patted her cheek gently as she pulled away and embraced Maia too.

"Mom, you need to talk some sense into them. They want to lock me up here with Blake! I have an event to plan, a life to live! As if I'm going to let some crazy person drive me away from my home, right?" Silence followed her words as her mother glanced awkwardly between the cop and Blake. "*Right?*" Rose's voice had reached a level so high pitched that any dogs nearby would have been wincing.

"Well, darling, I don't think it's a bad idea. It's clearly not safe for you at *The Hart* right now."

"I'll be fine," she protested, dropping Blake's soft blanket to the floor as she stared at the cop and then her mother. "He's not going to go back there after such a close call, surely. I'll be *fine*," she repeated and Blake snorted, making Rose turn her glare on him.

"Fine? You were literally just chased out of there."

"Thanks for your concern," she hissed, stepping close so that her face was inches away from Blake's. "But I would literally rather gouge my own eyes out than stay here with you."

Blake rolled his eyes. "Do you always have to be so dramatic? Or do you just want me to get on my knees and beg you?" His gaze turned knowing and then triumphant when she blushed.

Her mom watched her with something close to guilt before she turned to consult the cop. "How long do you anticipate this arrangement lasting for?"

The cop shrugged. "This guy's been clumsy in the past and seems to be okay with taking risks to get close to these two... so I'd wager not long. It'll go faster if you're able to come with us to analyze the scene, Ms DuLoe."

The thought of going home sent ice spreading through her chest and she froze in remembered panic for a moment. As much as she was fighting this, some part of her didn't feel safe at *The Hart* anymore, but that didn't mean she wanted to be with Blake, even if he was one of the only people who could really understand what she was going through after being targeted by her stalker himself. She was scared, but she also had no intention of letting this guy win. Why wasn't Blake fighting this?

"Of course," she said, clearing her throat as Blake watched her with an unusually blank expression. "I'd need to get some clothes from home anyway."

"Actually, we're going to be processing most of it," the cop said apologetically. "There's just no telling what your guy might have gotten into. Can't risk bringing in anything that could affect either you or the security here."

"So you expect me to move in here without all of my stuff?" Were her hands sweatier than usual? It felt like Rose's brain was spinning as she suddenly found herself essentially homeless, without any of her creature comforts or toiletries.

"I'm sure we can make the lack of clothes work for us," Blake whispered in her ear as he brushed past her to retrieve a coat from a nearby closet that she hadn't even noticed was there, blinking when he settled it around her shoulders.

"Will she be safe back there with you?" her mom wrung her hands, and a brief flare of guilt took root. Rose might not always get on with her mom, but she never wanted to worry her either.

"Perfectly safe," the round cop said with a nod. "It'd just

be useful for us to have her there so we can see if anything is missing, stuff like that."

Her mom nodded and stepped up, pressing a kiss to her cheek. "I left your father at home, worrying, so I'm going to go and update him, unless you want me to come with you?"

"I'll go with her," Blake said before she could reply, draping an arm around her shoulders that Rose promptly shrugged off as her mom cupped Blake's face like he was some kind of savior.

"You don't need to do that," Rose tried, and Blake gave her his best smug smile.

"We should stick together, right, roomie? Why don't you take Maia to Callum's, Officer, and I'll drive with Rose to *The Hart* and wait for you there."

Dread sank like a lead weight inside her as Rose's nose wrinkled. It was going to be a long night.

Rose reluctantly followed Blake to the underground parking beneath his estate and froze at the threshold. The night's events were too recent for her to just brush off as fear burned in her throat, alleviating only when a warm hand engulfed hers.

Blake didn't say a word, just pulled her gently through the entrance and paused before an Audi that was as sleek as him but Rose grimaced when she gazed at the inside. "You covered your *Italian* leather seats with a blanket?"

Blake smirked. "I take it you've never had sex in a car." Rose just blinked at him in stunned silence. Blake leaned in close and tugged the end of her thick blonde curl teasingly. "Leather sticks."

She groaned in response. "You are so gross. You think I'm going to get in your sex-car and sit on your dirty sex-blankets? Pig."

Blake shook with silent laughter as he stood, still holding open the door. "I never said I'd had sex in *this* car. One can never be too prepared." He blinked his big blue eyes innocently at her and suddenly the inviting way he held open the door shifted in meaning. Rose's panic faded completely as she huffed but stepped inside and settled into the plush interior, slightly cool from having the car door open for so long. Blake strode around the car to the driver's seat and climbed in, settling himself behind the wheel expertly.

"You ready? All belted in?" he asked, turning to face her and his eyes rested on her chest for slightly longer than was necessary to make sure her belt was on. "Excellent. You might have to direct me when we get close. I haven't actually been to *The Hart* before."

Rose nodded absently, tension reforming and making her jaw ache as she thought about the mess waiting for her in the suite.

"I like Maia, you know," Blake said suddenly and Rose blinked, relaxing her grip on the edge of the seat. "She had some good ideas the other day."

"She's brilliant," Rose murmured absently. "She does interior design, events, and fashion too."

Blakes eyebrows rose slightly. "Impressive."

"Yes, she is."

He gave her a sly grin. "I might steal her from you."

"She only freelances for me, and I'm sure she'd find that completely agreeable."

Blake nodded thoughtfully as silence settled again. "Noted."

The drive to *The Hart* was fast and the flashing blue lights made her eyes fill unexpectedly with tears that she quickly blinked away when they arrived. Still, Blake's voice seemed softer than usual when he spoke next.

"You ready?"

"Of course," she said, throwing open her door and glaring at him over the roof of the car, "Why wouldn't I be?"

Blake opted to roll his eyes, his nice-guy threshold clearly having been maxed out as Rose swept ahead of them and through the doors to her hotel.

"I told the cop–"

"That sounds like a you-problem," she said, eyes roving the entrance hall as she searched for a familiar face with no success. She supposed it was a miracle that the press wasn't already here. "You." Rose pointed to a fresh-faced cop who stood up a little straighter as she beckoned him over. "Escort me upstairs to my room."

The cop nodded, shooting Blake a curious look as they walked over to the elevator and headed to the top floor where they found Louis, Noah, and a host of cops all pouring over every inch of the corridor and room. Dusting for fingerprints, bagging up stray items they felt were important, photographing the writing on the TV, and Rose felt like the eye at the center of a storm. Calm amidst the chaos, still even though she wanted to scream.

"Jesus," Blake swore, and she shot him a raised eyebrow.

Louis spotted them at that moment and hurried over with Noah in tow. "Oh god, Rose. I'm so glad you're okay. I tried to make them wait for you–"

"It's okay, Louis. You did the best you could, I'm sure. Who's in charge here?" Rose asked loudly and then turned her gaze to the large man with lightly graying hair as he walked over to them.

"Ms DuLoe, I presume?"

"You presume correctly. What do you need from me?"

Blake eyed her warily, clearly not having expected her to be so cooperative. She ignored him.

"I'd like for you to take a look around and see if you can spot anything out of the ordinary in this mess."

Rose rolled her eyes. "Well, I mean *whore* wasn't exactly a provocative art choice of mine."

A slow nod was his only reply as Rose moved a little farther into her rooms, trying to look past the destruction for anything missing or notable while trying to remain detached from the destruction that seemed mostly focused on the lounge and kitchen area.

"Have you noticed any unusual activity recently aside from the recent break-ins?"

This was the question she'd been dreading most, because it made her feel like an idiot. Like she'd put Maia in danger and if she'd just been a little smarter then she could have figured this out before now. "I only recently got back into town. There was a note waiting for me on the counter that I assumed was from Maia, but I realized last night that she hadn't yet arrived back into Cincy in order to leave it for me."

The cop's bushy brows rose. "Had you received any prior communication?"

"No," she hesitated before blowing out a breath. "But I also received some flowers with a note that I attributed to Mr Blake, and a message was left for me at *The Hummingbird* earlier tonight."

"I didn't send you flowers," Blake said, his face darkening in either worry or anger.

The cop nodded. "Is there a reason you waited to report this?"

Her hands clenched as she fought to keep calm. A lecture really wasn't what she needed right now. She knew she'd been blind and stupid, but why would a stalker be her first thought? Or even her second? "I didn't deem it anything of importance before tonight."

"We'll need to collect the messages as evidence." That's what she had been afraid of. If the press got their hands on the note about Blake... she sighed but murmured her agreement. The flowers were likely still in the trash.

"I expect this to be handled with discretion," she said, and he nodded.

"Is there anything else that stands out as odd to you either in the suite or otherwise?"

"Like I told Mr Greene after our first break-in – the only thing that might be different is the potted plant outside that Louis bought, but it could have been there for ages as I don't often take the stairwell."

"I didn't buy that plant," Louis said, his hands trembling finely until Noah took them in his.

For a moment they all stared at the innocuous-looking leafy plant, potted in a cheery peach planter. Then the officer seemed to leap into action as if he were coming back to himself.

"I want that plant checked for bugs and cameras *now*, mark it," he said, waving the photographer over, "dust the pot for prints too."

One officer bent over after the photographer had snapped several shots, rustling the leaves of the plant as he searched through and came back with a small, square device that had the moisture leaving Rose's mouth as she tried to swallow.

"Fuck," she said, and four sets of eyes looked at her in apparent shock. "Is that a camera? How the hell did someone bring a whole damn plant up here?"

"Looks like it," Noah said grimly when the officer in charge remained silent. "I'd wager it doubles up as a bug too. This guy obviously has access to the suite somehow."

"So he's been watching me? How many times do you think he's gained access to the suite?" Had he been in there when she had? Lurking around the corner? Watching her sleep? *No, breathe.* She was just freaking herself out needlessly. Her earlier tide of shock still floated somewhere on the outskirts of her brain but her hands were steady, her voice even as she breathed out slowly. "So we're assuming that this person is the one who got caught climbing out of the elevator, right?" She could only handle one crazed stalker at a time.

"I think it would be foolish to presume otherwise." The officer in charge scrubbed his hand over his jaw. "Given that we know for sure there was at least one bug here, I can't allow you to take anything but essential medications from the suite, Ms DuLoe. We don't know what else he may have planted."

It was the second time in as many hours that she'd had her life upended. First by a stalker mad at her for fucking Blake, and secondly by the cops dictating what tiny pieces of her life she could reclaim back. "Sorry, officer," she said, her icy calm starting to crack as a deluge of anger rolled in. Anger that this had happened in the first place, rage that she was going to have to rely on Blake whom she hated, helplessness about being uprooted, her security damaged, her safety compromised. "Remind me, who exactly *are* you?"

The man stiffened, his jaw tightening as his steely gray eyes fixed on her. "My apologies, Ms DuLoe. I'm Detective Jones. I'm leading this investigation."

Blake's hands were atop her shoulders in a flash, his fingers clamping down tightly on her skin as if to restrain her from pouncing on the man. What was her life turning into? "Get your hands off me," she said icily and Blake laughed quietly as he stepped away. "Sort out this mess, Detective Jones. Louis, when they're done, I expect the best cleaning crew you can find up here."

Both men nodded tersely and Rose didn't bother to look back as she made for the elevator, coming to an abrupt stop as Jones stepped into her path. She gave him her best haughty look, sneering down her nose until he stepped aside. Maybe she was a brat, but she'd had a *day* and it was only going to get worse.

"I assure you, Ms DuLoe, we'll catch our guy. Fast."

"Make sure that you do," she said coolly, striding forward and hitting the button for the elevator that dinged, immediately empty and waiting, and for a moment Rose's focus shifted on to how this would affect business. Though really this was all down to her parents, Rose couldn't help her concern. When her parents were worried, she worried for them.

"Where will I be able to reach you for the time being, Ms DuLoe?"

Blake's eyes had never felt heavier on her than in that moment, weighing her, assessing to see what she would say next, like it would determine their fate.

"I have the unfortunate displeasure of Mr Blake's

company for the foreseeable future." The satisfied smirk that crossed his face was there and gone so fast, Rose wasn't sure if she'd imagined it. Why would Blake be pleased at all about this arrangement?

"That's very generous." Louis looked moments away from swooning and Rose rolled her eyes. God, if this got out to the press... her and Blake holed up together...

"I really am *so* generous. Wouldn't you agree, princess?"

The heated look in Blake's eyes was impossible to miss and irritation fell swiftly onto her. She'd been kicked out of her home, chased, and was now likely to have a PR crisis once this got out, and he thought now was the time to wind her up?

"I don't know if I'd go that far," she settled on, sticking her foot onto the metal separating the elevator and the suite so the doors wouldn't close and, despite everything, wanting to grin at the frown that Blake couldn't quite hide.

"Okay," Jones said slowly. "Well, if you think of anything else or need to get in touch, you can do so on this number." He handed Blake a card and shook his hand and Rose wasn't sure whether to laugh or scream as she strode forward and plucked it from his hand.

"Don't worry, Detective, I'm certain my pretty little head won't misplace this. Blake doesn't need to hold on to it for me." Rose's smile was nothing short of sharp, and Jones' eyes flitted around the room as he cleared his throat.

"Ah, right, yes. Of course. Well..." He pointed off in the direction of a group of cops and beat a hasty retreat while she glared daggers at him.

"Take me home," she demanded of Blake, spinning to get inside the elevator again.

"Please," Blake countered and she snorted.

"You're right, I do love it when you beg for me."

Noah stepped into the elevator, maneuvering in between them as he pressed the button to go downstairs. "Thought it best that someone be here with you both to ensure we don't have another violent crime on our hands in the next few minutes."

"That would require the princess to actually get her hands dirty," Blake ground out.

"For you, Blake, I'd make an exception." She pushed her shoulders back and stared straight ahead, opting to pretend he didn't exist.

"Yes, I've noticed you're selective in your hatred for me. Is it a setting thing? Get you in a study or a bathroom—"

"Temporary losses of sanity," she hissed, her head whipping around so she could glare fully at him past Noah's profile.

Blake glared back. "How convenient."

Silence reigned thick and heavy until Noah was shifting uncomfortably between them and Rose's fingers beat out an unsteady rhythm on her arm as the elevator seemed to move too slowly between floors. Suddenly the silence was oppressive, her attention narrowing into her shallow breaths and sweaty palms.

Her vision blurred for a moment, her heart pounding too fast as she tried to focus on the numbers of the floors, but instead could only see a dark hood and the gleam of a blade. Hands were on her shoulders, fingers pressing in hard, but Rose was so numb she couldn't feel the pain. A deep voice called her name and she blinked, shocked to find Blake's face breaths away from her own. Her eyes flicked to Noah, who had moved out of the way and watched them from the back of the elevator with concern flickering in his eyes as her body trembled all over.

"We shouldn't have come back here," she could hear Blake saying, but it was like a delay between the movements of his mouth and the words reaching her ears. "Rose, Rose, focus on me..."

She couldn't, tried to wrangle her emotions back, tried to lock them down tight until she could just get out of this damned elevator, but they were like a wave dragging her under. She hadn't had a panic attack since she was eighteen and it just about killed her that Blake, of all people, was here witnessing the deterioration of her walls nearly eight years later.

A hot mouth pressed to hers, the warmth stealing her breath, the electricity igniting her bones and Rose gasped in a breath, the dark spots fading from her vision as she did so. Blake murmured nonsense against her lips, words she couldn't make out before his tongue was in her mouth and his hands were in her hair, warm body crushing hers like he could hold her together himself.

Two dings marked their descent as they grew closer to their floor and it was like the sound was an alarm, making her push back, her hand cracking across Blake's cheek so harshly that an immediate stab of regret shocked her. He stumbled away, pressing a hand to one perfectly tanned cheekbone, but there was no hurt in his eyes when he looked at her.

"Good, you're okay."

She stared at him for a moment longer before giving him a stiff nod and avoiding Noah's gaze altogether. She could feel the warmth of her skin where Blake's early morning stubble had pricked her and knew her hair was probably a disaster. All she could really hope for now was that Noah kept his mouth shut and that the press wasn't already outside ready to capture this moment.

"Make me a list," Blake said, and she focused back into reality once more.

"Of what?" The elevator dinged as they reached the first floor and Blake moved close to her side, like he wasn't sure what was out there but would protect her nonetheless. It was surprisingly... chivalrous.

"Clothes, toiletries, whatever you need. Cara is going to stay with Katie for a while so we don't compromise security with her coming and going while we're locked in. She can get you what you want and bring it back home for you. Other than that, we're not supposed to have any visitors." Rose wasn't sure when those decisions had been made and irritation reared its head again as Blake attempted to control her life.

"You don't need to do that. We're not friends."

Blake snorted. "No, right, sorry. We're just two people who occasionally fuck, is that it? God, Rose. Give me a break here. I'm trying to keep you safe."

"I never asked you to."

"Oh sorry, I guess I got mixed signals when you turned up at my house in the middle of the night and passed out in my driveway."

"I was in *shock*. I wasn't thinking clearly," she shot back, jaw clenching and unclenching as they glared at each other. "I'm not your girlfriend. I'm not *yours,* period. So I'd appreciate it if you would *stop* trying to control me."

"I'm not trying to control you!" Blake hissed out a breath and she was surprised at the soft hurt on his face when he looked down at her. "Give me the list or don't, stay with me or don't – but know that if you choose the latter, you'll be putting everyone, including yourself, in danger needlessly. You fucked up not telling people about the notes–"

"–I didn't realize–"

"Well, now you do. You know the stakes. This guy is dangerous. So just suck up your pride for once and do the right thing."

The elevator doors slid open and she was grateful because Rose wasn't sure what she would have said in response. Was she being ungrateful? Selfish? Were her negative feelings for Blake clouding her judgment?

Noah cleared his throat from behind them and she jumped, having forgotten he was there. "Stay safe, Ms DuLoe."

Rose nodded and they stepped out of the elevator and towards the exit as Noah headed back up. A camera flashed somewhere and bile burned in her stomach at the thought of the world seeing her like this – shaken and rumpled.

Blake spun to her as soon as they reached his car, a hand lifting as if to touch her face before he dropped it back to his side. "So what will it be, Rose?"

It was the most times he'd ever said her name and she should have felt relieved or vindicated that he'd dropped the *princess* moniker, but instead it made her feel... guilty.

"I'll get you a list," she said quietly and he nodded like the answer didn't matter either way to him.

"Then let's get you home."

Home wasn't a word she'd ever imagined associating with David Blake, but she supposed there was a first time for everything.

Chapter Nine

The drive to Blake's estate was quiet. The earlier tension had faded away, and the atmosphere between them was almost peaceful for maybe the first time ever. Rose was too drained to argue any more, just wanted to close her eyes and forget this night had ever happened. Weariness dogged her bones. Her hands hadn't stopped shaking since they'd left the hotel, and it was only there in the car with Blake that she finally felt the sensation of being watched – real or imagined, she didn't know – leave her.

What she wanted was a long, hot bath and to curl up in her soft bed. The bath was out of the question, thanks to the temporary wrappings on her feet. She'd sliced them up pretty badly on the driveway gravel earlier in the night without even feeling it. They throbbed steadily in time with her pulse now, and she knew that they'd likely feel worse in the morning. Her giant bed was also out of the question, having been impounded with the rest of the suite, but even if she could stay at *The Hart* tonight, she wouldn't. Everything was too fresh. The image of the man in her apartment, running towards the elevator trying to catch the doors, was all she could see in her mind's eye when she closed her eyes or drifted away. Still, she was alive. Maia was alive. It could have been worse.

It was what she'd been telling herself since she'd come around and found herself in Blake's arms and lap on the floor of his entrance hall. He'd been so warm that, for a moment, she'd moved closer instead of further away and his arms had tightened around her like he couldn't ever dream of letting her go. But the quiet moments never last, and she had eventually moved away while the paramedics checked her over. *It could have been worse.*

Maybe she should feel more guilt about the situation. Blake was only involved because of her. Had been targeted because of *her*. Rose couldn't help thinking that it wasn't worth it. She wasn't worth the trouble, not for an afternoon quickie and sex in a bathroom. That was probably Blake's average Tuesday, but he didn't usually have to give up his privacy or worry about his safety with people like Meredith, she was sure.

Then again, nobody could force David Blake to do anything he didn't want to do. He could have easily let the police place her into a safe house and rinsed his hands of the affair. His own security team were likely enough to keep himself safe. Yet, he didn't. Which begged the question, what did he want? What was he getting out of this? Was it about the press? Or was this a favor for his mother? *Maybe he's really just being nice.* She wanted to laugh at the thought because David Blake wasn't nice, and he never did anything without a reason.

They rounded the corner and drew closer to the estate's

approach, the automatic security gates coming into view, and Rose groaned. The press had finally caught wind of the situation and was ready and waiting for them. To be honest, she was shocked it had taken them this long considering they'd been so fast at tailing her recently.

They were camped out in droves, cameras flashing as they photographed Blake's car, microphones poised as they tried to make the morning news. She would need to address them eventually, but she had some time yet to figure out what to say. She was running on five hours sleep but if she went to bed now, her entire sleep schedule would be thrown off. She just needed to power through, work out what to say to the press, maybe arrange an interview exclusively so she could get her truth out there without their interference or speculation. Then she could maybe do some work for the *Horizons* gala, check in with Maia to see how she was doing at Cal's–

"Fuck," Blake said, and Rose looked up at him sharply. *What now?* "How did she get in here?"

"I thought your place was supposed to be secure. That's why I'm here, right?" Rose snorted as she looked ahead and saw what had him mad.

Blake slowed the car at the gate and the security guard peeked through the window at them before opening the gates and waving them through. "I'll take care of this. Stay here."

"Worried your girlfriend will be pissed that you're shacking up with me?"

He grimaced, his tan looking a little paler than usual in the early morning light and highlighting the shadows beneath his eyes. His thick, dark blonde hair was wild and fluffy without its normal gel and the slight tracing of stubble on his jaw was surprisingly attractive. Blake blew out a long breath as the car came to a stop facing Meredith's. "Can you do me a favor?"

It was odd enough that he was asking that Rose was immediately intrigued, plus the thought of Blake owing her... "Within reason."

"Pretend we're together."

"We literally are together right now."

He threw her a look before refocusing back on the figure waiting for them. "*Together*, together."

"What? Why?" Her nose wrinkled as Blake bit down his full lower lip.

"Because I know Meredith's type. She probably had romantic notions about how she was going to be 'the one' to change my playboy ways and get me to settle down. She's not going to leave here without a fight unless she thinks I've already moved on. That I'm serious about someone else."

"And why does that someone have to be me? She knows we hate each other."

Blake shrugged. "Make her believe it and I'll owe you a favor."

"What about the press?"

He gripped the door handle tightly and blew out another irritated breath. "I don't care about the press. Are you going to help me or not?"

Rose considered it for a moment, knowing the cameras were likely pressed as closely to the gates as they could get while they watched this unfold. "Not."

Blake muttered something under his breath but didn't say anything more to her, just pushed open the door and approached the tall and unpleasant red-headed woman who'd been at dinner with them a few nights ago.

She'd had every intention of letting Blake suffer at the

hands of Meredith, purely for Rose's own amusement, until Blake got within spitting distance and Meredith launched herself at him. Her lips found his instantly, her red hair seeming to cover his body like a shroud that gleamed in the morning sunlight as she crushed her body to Blake's and her hands found his broad shoulders. Then, suddenly, it didn't seem nearly as amusing.

She wasn't sure what she was doing, hadn't really made any conscious decision to move, was only aware of the sound of her car door opening and the crunch of her steps across the gravel until she was right next to them. Could see up close how Meredith had plastered herself to Blake, her mouth attempting to coax his into a response. Blake's eyes were open, and his hands rose to Meredith's shoulders, ready to push her away, but then he saw Rose watching and his deep blue eyes widened when she cleared her throat.

"I'd thank you to remove your tongue from my fiancé's throat, Meredith."

Meredith pulled back with a slurp that had Rose's stomach tumbling and a strange itch swept through her at the sight of Meredith's pink lipstick smeared across Blake's mouth.

"Your *what*?"

Blake smirked, and Rose felt her shoulders relax. "I hope there's no hard feelings, Mer. It was just love at first sight."

Rose bit back a laugh. "Well, not quite first sight because we have known each other for years, you see. But all that history..."

Meredith glanced back and forth between them, her green eyes wide with disbelief as she crossed her arms across her chest. "No. I don't believe it. I've seen more chemistry between potted plants than you two."

Blake raised an eyebrow and Rose wanted to curse, hating the swooping sensation in her stomach because she *knew* Blake wasn't going to let that pass. No, he wanted to convince Meredith. Unlike Rose, he didn't care who was watching as he prowled towards her, blowing past Meredith like she was nothing more than furniture and tugging Rose against his body.

"Don't slap me again," he whispered and then his mouth was on hers, slowly devouring as his hand twisted into her hair, tugging roughly, until she let out a quiet moan and bit his lip in punishment. His chuckle vibrated through his chest and her nipples hardened in response, and Rose wasn't sure what was happening anymore. Before she could work it out, Blake pulled away, panting lightly, lips slightly swollen as he glanced casually at Meredith, frozen beside them. "Is that enough to prove it to you? Or do I need to take her clothes off right here?"

Meredith made a choking sound and made for her car before pausing next to the door. "Where's the ring?"

Blake looked stumped, and Rose decided it was time she did a little more to really earn that favor. "In the car. I don't like to wear it out around the... public," she said, looking Meredith up and down in blatant dismissal. Maybe it was petty, but what kind of woman throws herself at a man who clearly isn't enjoying it? "I'm sure you understand, darling."

Meredith went pale and Blake coughed to hide a laugh, but Rose couldn't bring herself to feel badly about it. Meredith was an absolute letch, the worst kind of user and social climber trying to capitalize on Blake's money and his name, so to instead be insulted by the DuLoe heir? Well, that no doubt hit a sore spot.

She didn't say another word, just climbed into her car

while Rose and Blake looked on, his arm around her shoulders and Rose's around his waist in the picture of domestic bliss. As soon as Meredith's car was half-way up the drive the sound of camera shutters snapping finally reached her, and she held in a wince. "You owe me big, Blake."

"Luckily, I can think of lots of ways to repay you."

Crap, that hadn't been what she had in mind at all but her body seemed more than game for whatever Blake was thinking up in that sneaky little mind of his. His husky tone and the clench of his hand on her shoulder sent more than a bolt of heat to her clit, and Rose frowned at him. "Why didn't you push her away?"

Blake seemed surprised by the question as he maneuvered them so she was standing in the cage of his arms, looking up at him. "I tried. That woman is worse than a limpet." Then a grin snaked across his face that had her taking a wary step back, flustered when he followed. "Why? Jealous, princess?"

Her body relaxed at the nickname and something flickered in Blake's eyes that told her he'd noticed. "What would your fiancé have to be jealous of? I expect a big ring, by the way."

"I'd have expected nothing less, princess."

Rose snickered and then quickly smoothed her expression. What was she doing standing here cracking jokes with David Blake? Doing him favors that would only come back to bite her once those pictures the press had no doubt snapped went to print?

Blake seemed to sense her change in mood as he turned away, leading them to his front door and unlocking it with both a key and a code on a digital pad hidden in a recessed part of the wall covered by a hanging plant.

"It's Lacey's day off," he explained. "Though I suppose she and the rest of the staff will be on an extended break until we get this sorted out."

"I'm sorry," she said. "I don't mind covering their wages until this is resolved. You *are* still going to pay them, right?"

"Of course," Blake said, clearly affronted as they moved inside. "And don't be ridiculous. It's not your fault, and I'm happy to host."

"Why?"

Blake paused, picking up the cashmere blanket Rose had been using earlier from the floor and folding it. "Your sparkling personality."

"Blake–" Her protest was cut short as Cara and Katie swept down the main staircase and enfolded each of them in a hug.

"We're so glad you're alright. Cara just wanted to grab a few more things before she comes to stay with me. Have you made the list yet, darling?" Katie drew back and regarded Rose at arm's length before patting her cheek. Katie always had been a mother hen and Rose found herself smiling, glad some things never changed.

"I'll text it to you," she promised and Katie nodded, pressing a quick kiss to her cheek as Cara squeezed Blake one more time before they swept out of the room as quickly as they'd arrived.

"Those two are a force to be reckoned with," Blake said softly in the fresh quiet. "Come on." He gestured for her to follow him and led them to a kitchen-diner that was bigger than what the chefs at *The Hummingbird* had to work with. Everything was dark exposed wood and light creamy counters. It was surprisingly homey. "Coffee?"

"Thanks," she murmured. It had been a long day, and it

was only seven in the morning. If she was going to make it to the evening, then she was going to need a *lot* of caffeine – one of the biggest no-nos for anyone with anxiety – but desperate times called for desperate measures. "Does Cara like to cook?"

"Cara? No, she burns water."

Rose could relate. Cocktails and frozen food were about all she could usually manage. "So this big kitchen is going to waste then?"

"Are you writing me off because I'm a man?" Blake faced her, his back propped against the countertop as he raised a cool brow at her, and she had to admit that he did look both at home and in control in the space. It was distracting for reasons she didn't particularly want to analyze.

"Not because you're a man, no. I just figured, what with work, you wouldn't have time to cook." He handed her a mug of coffee and nodded to the large, stainless-steel fridge for milk but she shook her head. Even if she had wanted it, she wasn't about to go rifling through his stuff.

"Some of us make time for hobbies and taking care of ourselves," he said blandly and set his coffee down on the side. "This is going to be your home now too for at least the foreseeable future. If you want milk, take it. Mi casa..."

Blake had an annoying affinity of knowing exactly what she was thinking, which she hated. When he wanted to be, Blake could be unreadable.

"Thank you," she said stiffly, knowing it wasn't a hospitality she would ever be comfortable taking advantage of and he seemed to recognize that too.

"I mean it, princess. What's mine is yours, in sickness and in health, right?" The grin on his face said he was teasing, but the demanding pressure of his eyes told another story. Rose waved him off and sipped at her coffee.

"How about a tour?" she said instead.

"Now that's more like it." He winked, and she rolled her eyes.

———

THINGS HAD GONE SURPRISINGLY SMOOTHLY with the press. Rose and Blake had done a joint interview via video call with a reporter for the *Cincinnati Times,* and she'd been taken aback at how well they worked together on camera. Where Rose could occasionally be cold or closed-off about her personal life, Blake gave them just enough charm and implication that they ate it up without him really saying anything of importance so Rose still felt comfortable. Of course, it was a little harder to explain the photos of what could only be described as a 'passionate' kiss, and in all honesty, Rose thought they were being polite. It was downright pornographic. Her hands were fisted in Blake's hair and his hands had landed on her ass, and she didn't even *remember* that happening, but there it was. Immortalized in film. God, her mother was likely having a field day with this.

It was easy to forget how much she and Blake had in common, especially when it came to handling the press, but he deflected the questions surrounding their supposed engagement like a pro. Neither confirming nor denying, just in case Meredith got ideas in her head, but simply taking a page out of the red-head's book by saying, "Do you see a ring?"

It would probably drive the public rabid, but that was

okay. The majority of the interview had been about the stalker and break-in, though of course they couldn't say too much about an ongoing investigation.

By the time they'd finished in the evening, Rose was in sore need of some water and some sleep. Except, when Blake had finally shown her to the guest room she'd picked out earlier, her brain wouldn't shut off.

The bed was plush. She practically sank into the mattress, glad to be off her aching feet, and the covers were so puffy that they almost tickled her nose when they were tucked up under her chin. Everything smelt fresh and clean, like lilacs and detergent, but it was all too unfamiliar. She'd already gotten out of bed once to turn on the light for her ensuite and pull the door to, letting a faint glow illuminate the room. But every time she neared sleep, her eyes would fly open and she'd wake with a gasp, half expecting to find someone leaning over her or watching her as a dark shadow against the light from the bathroom.

It had been over an hour since she'd said goodnight to Blake and climbed into bed. He was a fairly attentive host, making sure her room was stocked with towels and giving her a spare shirt to sleep in until Cara could drop off the things Rose had asked for. But no matter how comfortable the bed was or how safe she knew she was supposed to be here, she couldn't stop picturing the carnage in the suite, the slashed pillows, the angry slant of the W swiped onto the TV in red.

Rose rolled over, stopped, and stared. There was an odd shape by the window. In her mind she saw the curtain in the suite flutter, saw the shadowy form move, and continued to stare at the curtains in her new room. They were heavy, built to keep out the light, and she knew it was her mind playing tricks on her. There was nobody there.

Moving fast, Rose rolled over and reached for the hanging chord for the lamp on her bedside table, yanking it on and then spinning back to stare at the curtains, exhaling when nothing moved.

For a moment, she just lay there panting, staring up at the ceiling with the dim light bathing the cream and seafoam room yellow. Was she just supposed to carry on like this until the cops caught this guy? Maybe it was time to refill her least favorite prescription, at the very least so she could sleep at night.

But for now...

Rose sat up slowly and swung her legs out of bed. Blake's shirt was large on her but still only came to mid-thigh because of her height, and she tugged at it self-consciously as she stared at the door to her room with her heart pounding. It was ridiculous. She felt like a kid that had gotten out of bed and was waiting for her parents to catch her.

Blake had told her *what's mine is yours* and she'd decided that actually, she did want to take advantage of that fact but perhaps not in the way that he (or even she, if she was being honest) had expected. There was no way she was going to be able to sleep in here while she felt the press of imaginary eyes on her skin, saw the devastation of her home in her mind, and imagined much worse fates than what they'd been dealt if the elevator doors hadn't closed in time.

Rose knew when to swallow her pride, when to give in, and that time was now. She needed not to think, needed to feel safe, and for whatever reason, Blake seemed to give her that.

Decision made, she slowly twisted the doorknob and padded out into the hall, wincing as each step pulled at her still-healing feet. Blake's bedroom door sat one down from hers, the door ajar, and Rose tried to breathe slowly as she approached and nudged it open further.

The lamp was on, identical to the one Rose had in her room, and the light bathed Blake's body gold. Small freckles and moles marked his back and drew her eyes until she felt dizzy just from looking at the taut muscles rippling there. David Blake was always in control and if she had to guess, that was probably why it felt so safe for her *not* to be when she was with him. Even though it terrified her.

She closed the door behind her with a thump and Blake turned to her with a jolt of surprise, eyes darkening as he saw her stood in nothing but his t-shirt.

"Princess," he said, and his voice was so low it made her toes curl. "What are you doing out of bed?"

Rose swallowed, knowing that her approaching him changed everything and nothing at the same time. "I need you."

His eyebrows furrowed and his previously sleepy gaze sharpened as he took a step towards her. "What is it?"

"I can't sleep," she whispered and then cleared her throat. "This changes nothing. Okay? I still don't like you, and you still don't like me. But tonight, I just... can't be alone." Blake's eyes hadn't left hers, like he was holding perfectly still until he knew exactly what she was offering. Rose willed her hands to remain steady as she grasped the ends of his t-shirt and pulled it up and over her head, letting it drop to the floor, and an aching satisfaction started to build inside her as she watched Blake swallow hard.

"Distraction?" he asked finally, looking his fill as she stood bare in front of him, and she half-nodded, half-shrugged.

"Pleasure," she breathed, and a smirk formed on his mouth as he moved another step closer.

"That, I definitely can do." Blake paused and dragged his eyes up from her bare legs to her face. "Who's in control here, princess? You or me?"

The thing was, as much as she detested Blake, she also trusted him. It was a weird situation to be in, wanting his touch and loathing both his company and the way he made her feel. Just this once... she wouldn't mind begging for him.

"You."

"Get on the bed," he said without missing a beat and she obeyed, walking slowly over and eyeing the smooth, cream sheets with a little trepidation. How many other women had he had here? She decided it didn't matter. She wasn't here to grill him about his exes and make love. She was here to be fucked so thoroughly she couldn't remember her name, let alone what had happened last night.

A warm hand pressed against her shoulder and bent her so her naked chest stroked against the silky sheets, her knees knocking against the edge of the bed as Blake shifted his grip to the back of her neck. "I told you to get on the bed, princess."

"I'm on the bed," she said breathlessly. As much as she'd told him, and herself, that she was relinquishing control, she was never going to be a docile damsel. She was always going to push him.

A hard smack to her ass made her gasp and her pussy throb as Blake's large hand rubbed away the sting, the cool air teasing her as she remained bare to the room and his gaze. He spanked her again, and her back arched. Blake tutted and pressed down gently on her neck. "Anyone would think you like it when you're punished for being bad, princess." He swatted her again, but lightly, and Rose wrangled her breathing back under control. "Are you going to behave now?"

She nodded into the covers and Blake stroked her ass cheeks with each hand, caressing and spreading them until the tugging sensation at her center made her hips rock slightly, and he laughed.

"Get in the middle of the bed and spread your legs for me."

The pressure on her neck let up, and Rose pushed up onto her forearms and crawled to the middle of the bed, letting him have a full view of her ass as she stretched into a downward dog position before coming up and settling down on her back with her thighs spread wide.

"Good girl," he murmured and goosebumps broke out across her skin, her nipples tightening as he continued to watch her, his eyes dipping between her legs as he licked his lips. "Spread yourself for me, I want to see you."

With only a slight hesitation, she reached down her body and followed his instructions, gasping as her fingers brushed her clit and her eyes fluttered closed. They jumped open as Blake knocked her hand away and slapped her clit, the odd pain-pleasure making her moan.

"I didn't say you could make yourself feel good," he leaned down and whispered, his fingers stroking away the pain as he rolled her clit between his thumb and forefinger. "Are you wet for me, Rose?"

A sharp pant left her mouth but no words as she stared into his blue eyes. A slight flush had begun to spread across his high cheekbones, and she was fascinated by the color.

Blake slapped her pussy again, and her hips jolted up towards him.

"Answer me."

"Yes," she gasped, and one eyebrow rose in response.

"Yes what?"

"Yes, I'm wet for you."

"Shall we check?" His mouth dipped and closed around one of her nipples and her hips shifted desperately, trying to relieve the tension as he stroked her other breast while he sucked. He released her nipple and sat back on his knees, looking down at her with a pleased expression on his face that somehow made her feel smug. "Look at that," he said as he eased first one finger and then another into her pussy. "You feel so slick on my fingers, princess. You're dripping for me. Do you want more?"

Rose writhed, wanting desperately for his hand to move while he kept torturously still. When she didn't answer, he curled his fingers, mercilessly pressing against her g-spot until she cried out.

"Yes, I want more," she managed, and he smiled as he slid in a third finger and began to rock them in and out of her, the soft, wet sounds making his eyes darken as he watched his hand between her legs. His pace increased and soon she was whimpering, rocking against him so much she could feel her own wetness against the palm of his hand from where her pussy had dripped.

He stopped before she could come and she groaned in frustration, glaring at him when he laughed quietly. Blake slid his fingers free and took his time tasting each one in his mouth before kissing her, his erection pressing solidly against her through his sleep bottoms. He nudged her over on the bed and then lay back, sliding his bottoms down and fisting his dick in his hand. She'd seen him like this before, in the bathroom, but this angle was somehow more. The slickness of his head, the tightness of his fist as he fucked himself. She'd never thought about being turned on from watching this, but she was.

Blake smirked as he watched her watching him. "Get on your knees, princess. I want you to sit on my face."

Rose hesitated. She'd never done that before and wasn't sure what exactly she was doing or what the expectations were. She moved up Blake's body and slid one leg over the other side of his head so that she had one knee on either side, and he looked up at her from below as he licked his lips.

"I said sit. Not hover."

She hesitantly lowered herself down further, and then yelped when Blake grabbed hold of her ass and pressed her wet pussy to his mouth with a groan. He lifted her again gently and she looked down at him, panting.

"Hold onto the headboard, princess. You're going to come on my tongue when I tell you."

Rose did as he said, gripping onto the headboard tightly as Blake found her clit, licking through her wetness with bold strokes that made her legs tremble as she moaned loudly for him. Her hesitation faded, her hips rocking relentlessly as he speared her with his tongue, rocketing in and out of her with single-minded focus until her arms wouldn't support her and she leaned backwards into the arm he'd brought up around her waist as he feasted.

"Rose," he mumbled around a gasp and her eyes fluttered open, glancing behind her to see his hand gripping his dick tightly as he rocked his hips quickly. Hot jets of cum started to erupt from him just as he pressed his mouth more firmly to her clit and sucked hard. "Come for me, now."

She fell apart around his mouth, shivering as the warm splashes of his cum hit her naked body while she rode his face, moaning his name as the last of the tremors swept through her.

"Thank you," she said as she moved down and slumped across his chest.

"Anytime," Blake murmured sleepily before sighing and lifting her off him. "No, don't move. I'm just going to get you a towel."

"I need to pee anyway," she said and blushed. Why she could do those things with him and then the talk of going to the bathroom made her blush, she couldn't fathom, but Blake nodded his head. His ensuite was about the same size as hers and Blake grabbed a fresh towel off of a tall white shelf, wiping her back and ass cheeks before leaving her in peace to use the toilet.

Once she was done, she crept out of the bathroom, unsure what she would find, and Blake's eyes immediately focused on her.

"Are you staying?" There was something in the casual way he asked the question that told her it was anything but, and she wondered how many women were invited to share Blake's bed as well as his body.

"If that's okay," she said and shrugged, like she would be fine either way. While her mind was definitely more relaxed now and her body was aching but in the best way, she knew she would still have trouble sleeping by herself.

Blake rolled over onto one side of the bed and opened the covers for her on the other side. Rose walked over and slid under, still naked, the sheets still warm from their body heat. He reached for the lamp to turn it off and she didn't protest, though he must have felt her tense. Wordlessly, his hand found hers and she took it even as she rolled away, keeping it pressed to her hip.

"Goodnight, Rose."

She hesitated only briefly as she squeezed his hand, looking out at the dark. "Goodnight, David."

Chapter Ten

Something wet was on her arm. Rose swiped at the moisture sleepily, and then grimaced as the wetness spread over her fingers. Last night flashed in her brain as she tried to make sense of where she was and what was happening. Was Blake *kissing* her? Last night's... activities were one thing, but morning sex had never been on the table. An odd whine made her brow furrow as she reached out her arm and found Blake's side of the bed cold and empty.

A slow drip made soft thumps as it landed on her arm and the bed, and Rose's heart thudded unevenly as she blinked open her eyes, turning her head slowly. If that wasn't Blake... Her imagination ran wild as she pictured Blake, grabbed in the night by the stalker, strung up on the ceiling and bleeding on her–

More wetness on her arm. Her head finished the turn, and a mixture of hysterical laughter and shock found its way out of her mouth as she turned to see an enormous brown labrador with its head on the pillow next to her, drool slipping out of its mouth onto her arm.

"Um, hello," she said, reaching out a hesitant hand and stroking between the dog's ears, jumping when an odd thumping started up, jiggling the bed, until she realized it was the dog's tail wagging excitedly. "What's your name?" Her strokes became a little more sure as the sleepy fog faded from her mind and she began to relax. "You're a sweetheart, that's for sure. Much too sweet to belong to Blake."

A giant pink tongue lolled out of its mouth as it yawned before sitting up, head turning to face the door as it stared out for a moment, frozen in place.

"What is it, pup?" Only then did Rose's thoughts turn to the cold sheets next to her. Did Blake regret letting her stay the night? Had he changed his mind about them staying here together after all?

The dog jumped off the bed, startling Rose as the click-clack sound of nails on the wooden flooring faded away. She slumped back against her pillow before remembering it was covered in drool and sitting bolt upright, swinging her legs to the side, and stumbling out of bed.

Other sounds began to drift to her and, curiosity piqued, Rose made her way down the main staircase and in the direction of the kitchen where she froze in the doorway. There was a veritable feast on the island in the middle of the room. Trays filled with bacon, sausages, toast (both French and normal), eggs, even small cakes, had all been laid out alongside empty plates and pitchers of juice, tea or coffee, and the brown lab stared at it all with its tongue lolling out.

Blake stood at the sink with his back to her. His blonde hair was slicked back and wet, darker than usual with moisture, like he'd just come out of the shower. It was funny how you could have fantasies and not realize it until the exact moment that you were living them. Suds ran up the corded muscles in his tanned forearms, catching the sleeve of his shirt and a few errant bubbles even floated in the air around his head, turning into rainbows in the sunlight flowing in through the window above the sink.

"I didn't think the staff were going to be here," she said in place of hello and bit back a laugh when he jumped, the water sloshing onto the wooden floor and splashing his bare toes. He had nice feet, for a guy. Why was it that seeing someone's feet peeking out of a pair of slacks seemed so much more intimate than seeing them naked at all? The dog rushed over from where it had been hovering by the bacon and started lapping up the water as Blake turned to face her.

"They aren't." He leaned back against the countertop heedless of the water, taking her measure with his eyes as the sunlight backlit his golden hair, giving him an honest-to-god halo. What was he searching her for? Regret? Desire? "I told you I can cook."

"You made all this just for us?"

"Yes."

"What if I were a vegetarian?" she challenged and a smirk tugged at his lips.

"You're not."

"You don't know everything about me, Blake."

He started walking towards her, but instead stopped as he reached the toast. "I know you like your steak rare, that you hate ice in your drinks, and that when you were twelve-years-old you ate so much chocolate cake that you projectile vomited and now can't even sniff a chocolate cake without gagging."

She blinked at him, unsure what he expected her to say or what any of that proved. They were facts. They were observable traits. Her stalker probably knew her almost as well. That wasn't the core of who she was, though. "Cute dog," she said instead, and the pup's tail started wagging again as if they knew they were being talked about.

"This is Bailey. He's three-years-old, so still pretty playful, but he's housebroken at least."

"I didn't know you had a dog."

"Why would you?"

True. She'd never been interested in knowing anything about David Blake in the past, why would that change now? Because they'd had sex? Because he'd opened his home to her? Okay, they weren't bad reasons, but it didn't change anything. She'd only been awake a scant twenty minutes or so, and already she could tell that the anxiety she'd experienced last night was reduced a lot during the day. Sometimes the sunlight could make her feel too exposed – especially when there was a gaggle of photographers watching her every move, every mistake. But other times, it had the benefit of showing you all the things that might hide in the dark.

"Cara took him for me yesterday, gave him a nice long walk before he has to resort to just the land I have here. She dropped him off this morning."

Rose nodded vaguely and silence descended again as she looked over the mountain of food.

"About last night," Blake said as he carried over a full plate to his rustic, wooden dining table and she followed suit with a cup of coffee.

"I'd rather not talk about it," she said, and his face shut down before relaxing again.

"I see."

It was quiet again for a moment as Blake chewed and Bailey drooled at his feet, whining softly for a piece of bacon and immediately leaping on a piece as soon as Blake tossed him some.

"Aren't you going to eat anything?" he asked at last and she swallowed a large mouthful of coffee before responding, wincing as it burned her throat.

"It all looks amazing. I usually drink my coffee first though."

He smiled slightly and nodded, dimples peeking out at her, and suddenly she wished she could see them on full display.

"What's on the agenda for today?" Rose tried as the silence dragged on. It wasn't uncomfortable exactly, she just felt like maybe she should be putting in more effort seeing as Blake was being such a suspiciously good host.

"What agenda?"

"Well, we still have a gala to run, right?"

Blake looked at her, blue eyes wide. "Wow, you really don't ever stop, do you?"

"What?" A frown started at her mouth and made its way across her face as he shook his head at her.

"You were literally chased out of your home less than forty-eight hours ago. Shouldn't you, I don't know, take some time to process?"

"I have things to do."

"There's more to life than working."

"Well, what am I supposed to do while I'm stuck here with you?" The words came out sharper than she really meant them to, and Blake laughed without humor.

"Oh, I don't know. You seemed to find a way to entertain yourself last night."

"I didn't see you complaining!" She stood up, her chair

screeching uncomfortably across the floor, and Blake calmly resumed eating his breakfast.

"Why don't you try relaxing? I do seem to remember you promising to call my name the next time you touched yourself. No time like the present. Or how about a bath?"

She stared at him incredulously. "I don't want a fucking bath, Blake."

He sniffed delicately. "You might want to reconsider."

Her eyes flew wide as she glared at him with her chest heaving before snapping up some of the bacon on his plate and launching it at his forehead. Bailey scrambled up excitedly, jumping onto the table and licking all over Blake's face as he attempted to retrieve the scrap of food. The sight of the pup's butt wriggling in the air as it dove down over Blake, trampling his plate of food under his paws was so comical that Rose couldn't help it, she burst out laughing and both the dog and Blake stopped what they were doing to stare at her as she wheezed breathlessly.

They were still staring as she spun around to leave the room and Blake called after her.

"Where are you going?"

"To run a bath." She glanced back and snickered as he wiped puppy spit off his face with one sleeve.

"You haven't had any breakfast yet."

"What are you, my mother?" she sniped, but scooped a piece of toast up as she left, waving it in the air for him to see. "Happy now?"

"Not particularly."

"Ass."

"Brat."

Claws tapped the floor as Bailey followed her back up the stairs and towards the guest room. Despite her annoyance, she couldn't help but admire the interiors in Blake's house and knew that Maia would be drooling over it if she were here. Everything was painted in fresh white, with dark wood accents and random pops of color in the form of art on the walls or the curtains hanging over the bay windows set in the hall. It was relaxing, and Rose had to wonder whether Blake was right – when *was* the last time she'd had a break?

It was no secret that Rose loved her work but, more than that, she needed a busy mind, though it was clear to her now that she'd been neglecting her body. Yoga and work trips weren't enough to feed a libido and now she was reaping the consequences, being driven temporarily insane by lust. That was the only explanation for the way she'd sought out Blake last night. Well, that and the fact she needed not to be alone and he was literally the only person available as they were on a police-mandated lockdown.

So maybe the gala prep could wait a day. It wasn't healthy for her to go through... trauma, like she had last night, and simply bounce back like it'd never happened. Because it had, and it was clearly triggering her more than she cared to admit if she was voluntarily seeking out Blake for refuge.

Rose sighed as she walked into the guest room and plucked her phone off of the bedside where it had been charging, huffing slightly as Bailey ran in after her and made himself comfortable in the cloud of covers on her bed. She shot off a quick text to Maia, wanting to make sure she was alright, before hesitantly pressing the button to call someone she'd hoped not to have to call ever again. It had been unrealistic. Anxiety didn't ever just go away. But she'd been doing so well with her lists and her routines, she'd thought it was under control. Now she wondered if that had ever been good or healthy for her at all, whether she'd been naive to think so in the first place. Routines were good until they couldn't be maintained and then you either had to learn to bend or you broke.

"Good morning, this is Doctor Makers' office. How can I help?"

"Hi," she said and cleared her throat lightly before continuing, "this is Rose DuLoe. I'm calling to get a refill of a prescription."

"Hold on just a moment, Ms DuLoe, and I'll get the doctor on the line."

"Okay," she murmured, "thanks."

Maybe this wasn't a step back at all, maybe it was a step forward. There was nothing wrong with asking for help, hell, even her subconscious knew that if it had picked Blake's house to turn up to yesterday.

"Rose," a pleasantly deep voice came over the line and, instinctively, she relaxed. "I've been expecting your call."

"You have?"

"You're the talk of the city with what happened at *The Hart*. I would have been concerned if I didn't hear from you." That made her breathe a little easier, knowing she was making the right decision. She'd seen Doctor Makers a lot when she'd been in her late teens and early twenties, mostly for exam pressure at college, and her mother believed everyone could benefit from therapy.

"I was thinking about renewing my anxiety meds."

"We can do that, certainly, but I'd also like to schedule some time in with you – say once a week? I heard they've got you on house arrest, so you shouldn't be too pressed for time," he teased, and she let out a small laugh.

"Sure, that would be great."

"Excellent, I'll have my team set up the appointment with you, and I'll get someone to courier over the prescription, seeing as you can't come and collect them."

"I appreciate that, thank you."

"No problem, Rose. Take care of yourself."

It was funny. He always ended their conversations with that same phrase – *take care of yourself*, and she wondered whether she had ever actually paid attention to it before. Resolved, she stood and placed the phone back down next to the bed and made her way to the ensuite. The bath wasn't quite as big as her one in the suite at *The Hart*, but it was deep and made of a gorgeous copper that reflected the flowers on the small window ledge and the walk-in shower. For an ensuite, it was a generous size.

She flicked on the taps, running her fingertips under the water idly to test the temperature before setting it running. When she turned, she found Bailey in the doorway, eyes fixed on the running water. Rose had never had a dog before, but she wasn't stupid enough to miss the warning signs of a puppy looking to hijack her bath.

"Right, Bailey, *out*."

He gave her big brown puppy eyes but scooted backwards when she walked towards him, closing the door behind her. She settled down on the floor with her back against the door, and Bailey stood between her legs, panting softly as she mussed his ears and stroked the soft line down his nose. Maybe there was something to those therapy animals because Rose definitely felt her mind settle as she focused on the pup, laughing when he licked her fingers as she scratched under his chin.

"He likes you."

She looked up, startled to find Blake standing in the

doorway watching them. Pressing a small kiss to Bailey's head, she patted his side and stood up. "When did you get him?"

"I got him as a puppy. Chris had a friend whose dog had a litter and he thought it would be good for me."

"And was it?"

Blake grinned, a twist of his lips that was somehow both boyish and reluctant. "Yes. But don't tell Chris I said so." It was quiet for a moment as they looked at each other and then away. "He was so tiny when I got him, hard to believe given he's practically a giant now."

"Do you have pictures?" She found herself asking, and Blake looked surprised.

"Yeah, I, um, actually had an album made. I can show you, if you like."

A blush coated his cheeks, making the dark freckle next to his nose stand out and a dimple on the left side of his face repeatedly pop into existence like he was biting his cheek.

"Sure," she said with a shrug. "I'm waiting on the bath, so as long as you can endure the stench–" she threw him a withering look "–then I'd love to see."

"I'll manage," he replied as he led them out of her room and into the hall where he walked to the end of the corridor and turned left, stopping at a small, chest-height bookshelf next to a window. Framed photos decorated the top of Blake and Cara together with Grace. Rose knew their father had passed when she was young but could recognize him easily in the photo to her right. A young man who was a dark-haired version of Blake sat with what looked like a four or five-year-old golden-haired child on his lap and a baby in the crook of his arms that had to be Cara. There were clearly more recent additions too, like Katie and Cara kissing on a beach and Blake and Grace at her fiftieth birthday party a few years back. Then there was–

"Oh my god, where did you get this photo?" Her face felt hot, and she wanted to blink out of existence at that moment.

Blake chuckled when he saw where she was looking and she wanted to shriek at him to look away. Why did he even have it?

Her blonde hair was sporting straight choppy bangs and loose curls were falling out of her waist-length hair. She was tanned from the summer and her eyes were bright, but if you looked close enough you could see the slight puffiness where she'd cried for an hour straight after her date stood her up. Of course, she'd later found out that Blake had paid her date not to come. Bastard. Thankfully, it was only her junior prom, Blake's senior, so she'd had a Blake-free go of it a couple years after, but still. Her dress was a hideous shade of peach that was trendy for the mid-two-thousands but clashed awfully with her tan and blonde hair. Blake looked effortlessly handsome even then, and she still wanted to smack that smug smile off his face years later.

Her mom stood on one side with her arm wrapped around Rose's shoulders and her dad stood on the other, a large smile taking over his whole face. Blake stood on her dad's other side with Grace leaning on his arm in an old-school Hollywood pose that somehow worked for her. Rose could remember the photo being taken – maybe by Christopher? – but had never actually seen it in print.

"I can't believe you have this," she said softly as she ran her eyes over her parents. She'd never thought of them as getting older until she saw how young they were in this photo and thought of the new lines in their faces, the gray hairs creeping in as much as her mother tried to cover them up.

Blake held out a cream-colored photo album for her to take, and she couldn't help her smile at the pawprint emblazoned on the cover in brown. It was hard to imagine Blake commissioning anything so... cute.

"That's actually his paw print from when he was a puppy." Blake grinned, and she watched him closely from the corner of her eye as she turned pages. No wonder he'd given in and taken the puppy. Bailey was adorable, all floppy ears and giant paws and eyes too big for his little face.

She turned the page and paused at the next photo, a warmth flashing through her chest that she promptly ignored, and feeling Blake's eyes on her face, she quickly hurried past. A slow grin formed on his face and she snapped the book shut as she handed it back to him without meeting his eyes. "I'd better go and check on my bath."

"Of course," he said mockingly, and she wanted to growl. Men as ripped as David Blake should not be allowed to hold tiny, cute puppies to their naked chest. They also shouldn't be allowed to be so ridiculously photogenic. It should be illegal. *Especially* when they were egotistical, cocky asshats.

The bath was full and steaming when she got back to her room and Bailey skidded on the hardwood floors as he tried to sneak into the bathroom.

"No," she told him sternly and nearly melted at the puppy eyes he sent her. "Fine, but you're *not* getting in."

Bailey wagged his tail where he sat as she brushed her teeth, his eyes darting to the bath and then back to her as if to check if she was watching him. Blake was an ass, but damn did he have a cute dog.

"Bailey," she said warningly as he scooted a little closer to the copper tub, his paws grazing the fluffy cream bath mat. He whined, and she wanted to laugh but knew he might take that for permission. "If you're staying in here, you cannot get into the bath. It's mine." He turned his head away as if sulking and she snorted. "You're almost as spoiled as me, sweetheart."

She shucked Blake's tee and unwrapped the bandages on her feet before stepping into the scorching hot water with a sigh of relief and a slight wince. Her feet were better than they were, but the water still stung like a bitch. She'd added in some bubble bath from a tiny bottle in a basket on the countertops that ran the length of the back wall and now everything smelled like mangoes. Bailey trotted over and placed his paws on the rim of the bath and she lifted a hand out of the water and stroked his ears. "Down you get, pup."

She sat in the bath until she acclimated to the heat and then started to wash away the crazy day – or was it a night? – that she'd had yesterday, rinsing away Blake's touch and scent as well as the sheer terror. Her breathing quickened as she remembered the knife, the slamming of the stairwell door as the figure had run after her and Maia.

Bailey whined, his head propping under the fingers she'd left hanging over the bath, licking at them when she said nothing, just continued to rasp in harsh breaths that left her dizzy. Was this what dying felt like? This slow climb of terror until your heart gave out? The feeling of suffocating even when you can still breathe?

A splash knocked her from her thoughts and the breath back into her as Bailey dove in the bath, his paws landing half on top of her and she ducked under the water, the last of the suds in her hair streaming out.

"You're so naughty," she said as she resurfaced and looked at the drenched puppy sitting opposite her, licking the streams of water on his face. But she gave him a shaky smile, knowing that if he hadn't jumped in, she might have hyperventilated her way to the bottom of the tub. "Thank you, pup."

A knock came at the door and Blake's voice filtered through. "Everything okay? I heard a splash."

"Bailey jumped in. I'm going to need some extra towels." Her eyes found the water sloshed across the floor, running slowly to the back of the room. "Um, make that a mop too."

It was quiet for a minute, and then Rose heard his footsteps leave. Bailey whined, and she smoothed a hand along his wet face as the tread of Blake's feet sounded outside the door again. "Can I come in?"

Rose stood and wiped her hands down her arms and body, not that dripping all over the floor mattered too much now anyway. She reached for the fluffy towel she'd hung up on one of the little black wall hooks and called for Bailey to get out of the bath, grimacing when he shook himself off and sprayed her with tiny droplets. Stepping carefully out of the bath so she didn't slip, Rose called out for Blake to come in. The bath mat was soaked under her toes, but the water hadn't yet cooled, thank god for small mercies.

The door swung open and Blake took in the soaked chaos with a quirked brow. "He jumped in?"

"Yeah, but it was my fault, so don't punish him."

He gave her a quizzical look but waved her off. "Go and get dressed, I'll clear this up. Bailey, *no*." The dog paused in the doorway with one paw in the air, clearly intending to head back out into the warm and drip everywhere while he was at it. "Come here," Blake said, kneeling in the water heedless of his pants as he opened a big towel in his arms, laughing when Bailey ran to him, barking, and Blake began to towel him down.

Rose smiled slightly as she left the room, using the side of her towel to squeeze the water from the ends of her hair before a mild panic hit her as she remembered she had no clothes to wear, moisturizer to use, not even a hairbrush.

"Blake–" she called, realizing she was going to have to borrow something of his, or maybe Cara's, but he answered before she could even speak.

"Cara dropped off some stuff for you, it's on the island in the kitchen."

A relieved breath flew out of her. "Thank you." She wrapped her towel more firmly around herself and headed down the stairs to the kitchen, spotting the plethora of bags from the doorway and relaxing. She was still stuck here, but at least she had her stuff now. An envelope sat on the table too, shoved off to the side like the bags had swept it away, and her hand paused as she reached for a bag when she saw it was her name written on the envelope in a careful cursive. *Rose.*

Curious, she put down the bag she'd been about to rummage through and instead picked it up, smiling at the ceiling as she heard Bailey finally break free from the bathroom and Blake cursing up a storm. The seal was broken already, the flap sticking up and slightly creased, and Rose frowned. Had Blake opened her mail? Or had it been the security guard? It would make sense that they were checking everything that came into the house. She wondered how long it must have taken for them to painstakingly search all of Cara's bags and stifled a snicker.

It wasn't funny really, but what would they possibly be looking for inside a bag of face creams and perfumes?

Rose slid the contents of the envelope out and dropped it like it burned at the first glimpse. It was a photo. Her and

Blake outside *The Hart* on Thursday morning. She was stood next to his car and his hand was hovering next to her face in the instant before he'd dropped it and opted not to touch her. The way their heads were tilted towards each other made this moment look more intimate than it really had been, hell, it made *them* look more intimate than they were. Sure, they'd had sex, and maybe that familiarity could translate for the camera, but the reality was that they rubbed each other the wrong way. Always had. There was nothing between them but history and maybe some awkward and unwanted attraction.

Who had taken this? And why? She could only think of one person and her hands grew clammy at the thought of them there, watching her when she'd thought she was safe. But then she remembered that prickly feeling she'd had in the car and shivered. He'd been watching her even then.

She flipped the photo over and her breath caught in her chest. *I'm coming.* That was it. Just two words. Two words that held more threat and promise than a whole slew of words. He knew where she was – well, she supposed everyone did. Her arrival to Blake's had been recorded by dozens of cameras. But that didn't mean he could get in.

Did Blake know about this and not tell her? God, when would he stop trying to control her life? He was as bad as her mother, scheming and lying and only giving her half the information in a bid to control her better.

"Princess, where did you–" Blake stopped in the doorway, face going blank as he saw what she held in her hand.

"It had my name on it," she said quietly, and he took a single step forward. "Were you going to tell me?"

He looked away. "Yes."

"When?"

A hand pushed through his hair, leaving it damp as he met her eyes again. "Once you'd had a chance to settle in. You barely ate breakfast this morning and you never stop, Rose. I just wanted to give you a day without worry."

"That's not a decision for you to make for me." She grit her teeth as she slammed the photo and envelope back down onto the counter. "This is *my* life. What I eat, what I do with my time, who I fuck, that's for *me* to decide. Not you. Don't ever keep things from me again, Blake. Or–"

"Or what?" he interrupted silkily. "You'll cuss me out? Leave? The funny thing is, Rose, even if you do that, we both know you'll end up right back here in my bed anyway."

She recoiled. "That's–"

"Not the truth? That you don't like it when I fuck you? If you want to lie to yourself, fine. But don't lie to me."

She stared at him, towel clutched tightly to her chest as her hair continued to slowly drip down her back, droplets forming on the floor beneath her. He wanted to poke and prod at the tender parts of her, then fine. As long as he knew she would poke back.

"Christopher would never speak to me the way you just did."

"And yet, you turned up on *my* doorstep. Not his."

Her hands flew up as she took a frustrated step forward before her towel slipped and she quickly slapped them down, tugging the material back into place and exhaling roughly as she turned away.

"Get this to Jones," she said as she brushed past him, ignoring the warmth from his skin and the tic of his jaw as his eyes followed her out.

"That's it?"

"That's it."

"That's seriously all you have to say to me." His voice was flat and Rose turned at the bottom of the staircase to look back at him.

"I have a delivery coming later today. Don't let your security guards leak the contents to the press."

"Fine."

"Fine."

Chapter Eleven

They had spent the remainder of Friday afternoon and evening avoiding each other. The good thing about a house as large as Blake's was that it was easy to do. The bad thing was that she was bored. Relaxing was hard. When she wasn't playing with Bailey, she alternated between texting Maia and making aesthetic boards for imaginary events she might one day run.

Rose had never really been the type to fantasize about her wedding, except for the decor. She liked to think about what theme she might have, what sort of center pieces might pop, but she'd never stopped to think about who the man at the end of the aisle might be. In all honesty, she'd never had a relationship serious enough to even put a temporary face onto the imaginary groom in her mind.

Blake had put together another oversized meal for the two of them at dinner time on Saturday with endless amounts of potatoes, vegetables, and some kind of flavored rice that she had to begrudgingly admit was amazing. He'd cooked her steak to perfection and Bailey had drooled by her chair the whole time she'd been eating until she'd tossed him a tiny bit of the fat rind, and he'd given her a happy tongue loll after gobbling it down. The conversation had been sparse, nothing beyond *could you pass me the salt* or confirming that Blake had, in fact, passed the photo on to Jones.

It had been hot and humid all day, the skies remaining a baleful gray, but Rose had at least hoped for a breeze and was left disappointed. Bailey was an active pup and needed walking a few times a day, but luckily Blake's estate sat on a long run of land, the borders of which he had secured with motion detector cameras, barbed wire, and he'd even added a few extra security guards to patrol the area to ensure nobody snuck onto the land. It made her wonder why Blake took his security so seriously, even before all of this had happened. Or maybe she hadn't been taking hers seriously enough.

It was true that she'd received plenty of both hate and fan mail, but she'd always opted not to have a personal security detail. She had her driver who pretty much took her everywhere, so she was unlikely to be accosted on the streets, but it just seemed so unnecessary – until it wasn't.

Saturday's gray clouds had given way to a rainy deluge overnight and left the green forested area Blake had outside both muddy and delectable. The scent of fresh earth drifted in through the open window and soothed her. It was odd being on the outside of the city. You could get to the heart of Cincinnati in about twenty minutes in the car, but what a difference it made in terms of privacy and the quiet. She could hear herself think, but she hadn't yet determined whether or not that was a good thing. She'd tried to go out on a walk with Bailey yesterday, but the outdoors still left her feeling too exposed at the moment, so she'd simply waved them off and headed back upstairs, sitting in the cushioned nook of one of the bay windows as the rain slowly began to come down again.

The rain had stopped today, but the mud persisted and muddy paw prints were scattered along the wooden floor downstairs, ranging from the kitchen to the entrance hall, and she could hear Blake cursing as he chased the dog down to clean his feet. So far, Blake had managed fine without the staff members he usually had on hand to maintain the house and gardens, but Rose did wonder what would happen once they ran out of clean towels. A smile cracked across her face, there and gone in an instant. Her mood had been gently swinging up and down since her prescription had arrived Friday afternoon. She'd taken a pill before bed and knew she would need to wait until her body adjusted for them to start doing much good. Though fortunately, they'd made her drowsy when she'd first taken them years ago, and that seemed much the same this time around too, so at least she'd had a couple of decent night's sleep without making her way to Blake's room again.

Her body just needed to find a new rhythm, but if it would help stop the panic attacks that had begun creeping up on her more and more often, then it was worth it.

One thing she definitely didn't remember from last time was the change in her libido. Most people were worried about it being stifled but, frankly, she could have done with that while she was living with Blake and thoughts of his taut, gold chest cradling a tiny Bailey drifted into her brain. Unfortunately, the opposite seemed to be true. It was like her skin was crawling with desire, almost like hot flashes of lust that had her gripping the edges of her seat. A few times Blake had asked if she was okay and she'd wanted to shout at him to *shut up* because even the sound of his smooth, deep voice had shivers skating over her skin and her core heating.

It would probably fade. She just needed to wait it out. The problem was, the hotter she got, the more she couldn't stop thinking about things she really had no business to be fantasizing about, which then turned her on more. It was a vicious cycle of being horny, remembering Blake's tongue in her, feeling it even more strongly until she was pacing up and down trying to resist the urge to hunt him down in the house. That was another pro to the large estate. Even if she succumbed to temptation, actually finding Blake was near impossible unless he was cooking or clattering about in his office.

She was so overly sensitized she wasn't sure she could take it anymore. If she'd been in the privacy of her own home, with her vibrator, this wouldn't have been a problem. She'd have just touched herself and come until her body stopped torturing her. She sat down heavily on her bed in the guest room as a tingling swept through her stomach at the thought, the temptation. But no, she couldn't. She was in Blake's house. He slept right down the hall. It would be... weird. A breeze swept through the window and lifted the escaping tendrils of her hair off her neck, sending another tingle through her skin. Her breasts began to feel heavier with anticipation, the nipples tightening even as she still mentally battled over whether or not to do this.

Rose let out a long breath and she shook her head in an attempt to clear it before making her way to the hallway outside. Maia had thoughtfully re-directed the dresses Rose had ordered for the gala to Blake's house. They still had over a month to go until the event, but she wanted to make sure that her dress would off-set the room's design perfectly. Plus, she would likely need a bit of time to get everything tailored.

Decision made, Rose headed for the small room opposite Blake's that he'd left the bags of dresses in for her. Apparently, it was Cara's dressing room and had at least three different floor length mirrors so she could properly assess each dress as she tried them on. Sometimes brands sent her dresses to wear and, if Rose liked them, she would snap a few photos of her in it for her socials. Other times, she would reach out to designers or fashion houses personally with a commission request.

Three dresses had been couriered over by a private firm, and she had tipped extra considering it was a Sunday rush delivery, but the problem was that she liked them all. Two of the dresses were wispy and gauzy, almost insubstantial even as they covered everything. They clung to her modest curves in just the right way and made her waist look even smaller than it was. They were pretty. Beautiful, even. But the third... it was striking.

Rose winced as she twisted her arm around to catch the zipper and let out a growl of frustration when it refused to budge all the way to the top.

"Let me," a deep voice said and she jumped, catching Blake's eyes in the mirror in front of her. A shiver skated across her skin as his warm hands balanced lightly on her back, and she cleared her throat, trying to push the sensations down. She'd tried to distract herself by coming in here to try on the dresses and now here was Blake, the reason she'd needed the distraction, busting in the room and putting his hands on her.

"Thanks," she said, and silence descended, the sound of the zipper moving raising the hairs on her arms.

Blake stepped back and she let out a breath even as the tingling tightening of her breasts didn't let up as their eyes collided once more. Rose bit her lip. The dress. She was supposed to be looking at the dress.

It was silver silk but was surprisingly heavy and when she moved, glimpses of red flared out from carefully concealed slits in the dress, almost giving her a train that made the air ripple when she walked.

It was stunning. It would also clash with the decor horrifically.

"What's wrong?" Blake had moved closer to her while she'd been examining the dress and she took a hasty half-step away as the fresh smell of the outside drifted to her, mixing pleasantly with his cologne.

"Nothing, this just isn't the dress."

"What are you talking about?" he protested, laying his hands on her shoulders as he steered her back in front of the central mirror, and Rose couldn't help but admire the way the fabric flared out again at the small movement. "You look beautiful."

She gulped and looked away again. "I think one of the other dresses will look better. I can always save this for another time."

Blake raised an eyebrow. "Trust me, this is the dress."

"How do you know? You didn't even see the other two."

"I saw them," he said, voice a little husky, and Rose licked her lips, ignoring her body's desire to step closer to him.

"You were watching me?" She wanted to sound outraged. Instead she sounded... curious.

"Don't worry," he smirked, "I looked away when you got naked."

God, she wished she hadn't just heard Blake say the word *naked,* now she was never going to get her thoughts back on track. This had been pointless.

"I should hope so," she said weakly, and his eyes ran over her face searchingly. "Unzip me," she demanded, and he blinked. She needed to get out of here, away from Blake before she came out of her skin and did something she regretted. "Now."

He obeyed, sliding the zipper down to the bottom of her spine before walking slowly out of the room, leaving the door open. Rose quickly stepped out of the dress, trying to ignore her quickening breaths, the ache of her pussy as pressure built inside her again, and she slipped her clothes back on. The corridor was empty, and Rose nearly shook with relief as she practically ran back into her room and flopped down onto the bed, wincing as the air tickled her sensitive skin.

She'd tried distraction and it hadn't worked.

The bedroom door was slightly ajar, but she didn't move, scared if she did she might break the spell that was coming over her. Knowing that she couldn't keep on like this and surely it was better to fuck herself than to let Blake do it? Slowly, she laid back against her pillows and tentatively squeezed her breast, her breath leaving her in a short gasp as the tension inside her wound tighter. Her fingers plucked her nipple and her breath eased in and out of her as she did the same to the other breast. Glancing quickly at the door to make sure there was no sign of Blake, she reached her right hand down and traced the outline of her aching flesh through her thin shorts, panting at the light touch as she clenched almost to the point of pain.

Her eyes found the empty doorway once again and then her hands slid under the waistband, hooking her fingers over the edge as she pushed the shorts down to her ankles. The cool breeze stroked across her skin and she lifted her hips to meet her hand, teasing the outer edges of her pussy as she felt her own wetness against the pads of her fingers. Why did this feel so forbidden? She flicked her eyes to the door, found the hall empty, and let her fingers part her folds to press down on her clit until her eyes closed and a gasp tore itself from her throat. She rocked against her hand slowly as her fingers found a circular motion that squeezed her clit and more wetness gathered between her legs, starting to leak down the backs of her thighs.

It wasn't enough. She needed to be filled, stretched. Fuck, she was still tempted to find Blake. *No.* No. She didn't need him. Had never needed a man to get her off before. Though that was before she'd realized what she was missing. Unbidden, her thoughts turned to the way Blake's mouth had felt pressed against her pussy as his tongue dove in and out of her, licking and sucking at her juices like a man starved and served his favorite buffet. One finger slid inside her pussy as her left hand squeezed her boob, her hips rocking as she remembered the way his cum had felt on her skin, hot and wet as he ate her through her orgasm.

A second finger filled her, and she moaned. Blake's dick, hard and long, pumping in his hand as he looked his fill of her, bare and glistening before him. The finger he'd teased her with, achingly slow. Rose pressed a third finger inside her pussy, plunging them in and out in a rocking motion that made her whimper his name, her thoughts filled with his tongue, his hands, the way his dick had felt buried inside her.

Her pussy sloshed with wetness as she worked herself higher, pushing her fingers in harder, desperate to reach the edge, tears slipping free as she realized it wasn't enough. Her hand stilled momentarily before resuming a much slower pace. It felt good. She could feel herself dripping down her fingers, but she needed more.

"Well don't stop on my account. I know you didn't come yet." Blake's voice had a strange mixture of panic and desperation seizing through her as she looked up and found the door open wide, his broad shoulders taking up the space in the frame and a large bulge in his pants contradicting the calm tone of his voice.

"What are you doing in here?" Her voice was hoarse, and belatedly she wondered how loud she'd been moaning.

"I heard my name." He smirked. "I thought you needed me again. I guess I was right." He took a step into her room and dropped his hands to his belt, watching her eyes follow his hands eagerly, and when she looked back to his face, there was no more amusement there, just hunger. "Do you need my dick, princess?"

Slowly, her fingers began to move inside her again and she whimpered. Blake's eyes dropped as he watched her, his gaze hooded as he licked his lips. "I could watch that forever."

He reached for his belt and undid the buckle, freeing his fly, and she watched, entranced, as his dick sprung out. He was hard as a rock and moisture smeared across his stomach, leaking more as he watched her pace increase.

Her pussy clenched around her fingers, throbbing, and he chuckled. "Do you like it when I watch you, princess?" His hand curled around his shaft as he began to stroke softly, moving closer to her with each thrust of her fingers. "What do you want me to do with this?" he asked, pumping his dick harder for emphasis and moaning for her as he kicked off his pants and knelt on the bed between her legs. "Tell me."

"I want," she choked out as her thighs moved impossibly wider, "you to fuck me with it."

Blake smiled, letting go of his dick as he grabbed her legs, pressing her knees down until they burned and her pussy shone up at him, so soaked she was sure there would be a wet patch on the bed when she was done. He moved closer, pressing his dick to her folds and stroking her clit with his head, watching the way it pulsed for him like he was hypnotized. Pre-cum leaked out and mixed with her wetness as he slid his dick through her folds, rocking against her and creating a friction against her clit that had her hips writhing helplessly until his head pressed into her entrance and made her gasp.

He was big. She couldn't remember him stretching her so much that time they'd had sex in his study, but maybe he was just harder now. Blake didn't let up, thrusting into her so hard she saw stars as his hand came under her hips and he lifted her against him, grinding against her so that his balls hit her ass and her pussy dripped around his base.

"How's that, princess? Is that filling you more than your fingers?"

Rose couldn't do anything but moan as Blake fucked her harder, thrusting into her with such savagery that she knew it was part punishment for the other day and for not coming to him the past couple of nights.

She could feel his dick twitching inside her and knew she wasn't far from the edge. His eyes met hers as he shifted his angle, moving into her with long, languid strokes that made her head fall back as she gasped. Blake's head lowered to her breast as he sank all the way back in, grinding deep as he licked and bit her breasts until she was riding him desperately from beneath and he panted her name into her mouth.

Blake's fingers found her clit, slapping it and pressing down hard as he thrust into her desperately enough that her body jolted backwards as she finally came, and he followed three thrusts later.

Their bodies were sweat slicked, Blake's shirt sticking to his back and turning see-through across his chest and tight stomach as he rolled off her, arms flexing.

"That better, princess?"

"Um, yeah. Yeah, thanks."

Blake rolled over and looked at her, taking in her no-doubt red cheeks and moving his gaze down over her body, cataloging her still-hard nipples and the wriggling of her hips as she tried to get comfortable.

"Rose?" His eyes were uncharacteristically serious as they met hers. "Did you come?"

"Yes," she said honestly and he nodded, a small frown tugging at his mouth.

"Princess," Blake's voice had dropped and the lower tone made her stomach swoop, "do you need more?"

"It's fine," she said, still feeling like her skin was burning, like her itch was on the verge of being scratched.

"That's not what I asked," he said, sitting up, placing his warm hands on her waist and dragging her back into the middle of the bed. "I said, do you need more?"

Crouched between her legs like some kind of stubborn god of sex, Rose couldn't lie. He'd loosened a few of his shirt buttons so the broad expanse of this chest and upper abdomen were visible, and his forearms flexed beneath his rolled-up cuffs.

"Yes," she whispered, and a grin flitted across his face.

"Well, then," he purred, "I'd better get to work." He lowered his mouth to her clit and pressed a long lick to the center of her, repeating it over and over until her legs trembled as he watched for her reaction, blue eyes mischievous as he worked her. Sucking it into his mouth, Blake didn't let up, and her head eventually fell back against the sheets, unable to hold it up any longer as he pushed a finger into her pussy while he ate her out. Talented tongue dancing across her flesh as he wrung whimpers from her.

She was close, so close to an orgasm bigger than the one she'd just had, and she knew instinctively it was this her body had been craving. Blake was giving her exactly what she needed, one lick at a time. Her hand sank into his thick, blonde hair, pulling and yanking as her muscles trembled in her legs until her pussy couldn't take it anymore, orgasming so hard she was breathless as Blake left her with two long licks and then looked up at her with a satisfied smirk on his face.

"Better?"

She nodded, too out of breath and exhausted to talk, and he chuckled as he sat up. The tension of the past few days had dissolved, and he gave her one of his genuine smiles, the ones that made both his dimples dig in deep to his cheeks.

"I don't know why we aren't doing this all the time."

"Because I don't like you," she sighed contentedly, sitting up and stretching before heading to the ensuite to pee and clean up. "Have you got spare sheets? Those ones are kind of messy now."

Blake didn't respond, and when she turned, he was staring at her intently. "But *why* don't you like me?"

She huffed, pissed that he was ruining her post-orgasm high. "Well, why don't *you* like me?"

"I never said I didn't." He winked, and she rolled her eyes. Some things didn't need to be said. Blake had always been an ass to her, from brushing her off as too young to play with the big boys, to the stupid pranks he'd play on only her – she could swear he'd teased her more than he had Cara. Though to be fair, his sister hadn't always been around very much. But paying off her prom date... junior or no, that was a dick move. You didn't do that to someone you liked. Plus, every interaction since then had been overly antagonistic. He did his best to piss her off, did it *deliberately,* and then had the cheek to say he didn't hate her? This was all just part of one of his mind games, winding her up by pretending he liked her.

"Actions speak louder than words," she sniffed and he laughed loudly, startling her.

"So when I invited you into my home, cooked you breakfast, kept you safe...?"

"You honestly expect me to believe you did those things for me?" she scoffed.

"Who else would I do them for?" He stood and seemed at a loss, hands held loosely at his sides as the easy air between them became foggy once more.

"I don't know, Blake! Your mom, as a favor to mine?" She hurriedly washed her hands, glaring at him in the mirror, watching as he sighed.

"Nobody asked me to do this," he said finally, breathing out a long breath and looking at her deeply before glancing away into the hall. "It was my idea."

She moved a step closer, her head cocked. "But why?"

"To keep you safe."

Head shaking, she backed away again. "No. I don't believe that."

"Why?" he asked, and if Rose didn't know better she would have said he was begging. "Why won't you trust me?"

"Because you've given me no reason to – at every opportunity you lie to me. You're arrogant and controlling and you don't have any faith in me!" She hadn't expected to say, or even feel, that last part and for a second, she just blinked at him as he regarded her.

"I think you're wildly competent, and I respect the hell out of you. Wanting to protect you doesn't negate that." He moved close to her as he looked into her eyes before shaking his head and heading for the door. Blake paused in the frame. "Do you remember how you asked me last week about the guy I paid off to ditch you at prom?"

"Yes," she said curtly.

"I paid him off because I overheard him bragging to his small-dick friends about how he was going to 'bag the precious DuLoe pussy' on prom night, which he apparently found hilarious because he'd also been sleeping with your friend – Chelsie, I think her name was?" Blake didn't wait for her to reply, just walked out of her bedroom and whistled for Bailey. She listened to his footsteps go all the way down the stairs and jumped at the bang of the back door as he took Bailey outside, leaving her to stew in her thoughts.

Blake had paid off her prom date to protect her? Rose wasn't sure how to feel about that. Sure, she had been sixteen and not nearly as capable or confident as she was now, but it didn't give him the right to swoop in like some kind of white knight and make decisions for her. But why had he even bothered in the first place? He'd never liked her, even as kids, so why would he care if she was dating some douchebag? The questions swirled around her brain until she wanted to scream. Had he just told her that to manipulate her?

Confuse her? This was Blake's problem all over – when push came to shove, he didn't know how to share control.

What about in the bedroom? Okay, so maybe he was willing to give up a little control sometimes, but great sex could be found anywhere. Alright, maybe not *anywhere,* but it was nothing worth giving up your freedom to an overbearing prick for.

Who's in control here, princess? Blake's voice whispered to her. *You or me?*

Rose flopped back onto her bed with a groan, not sure where the direction of her thoughts left her in regards to David Blake.

Chapter Twelve

Blake had been short-tempered all day and Rose was ninety-percent sure it was her fault. She'd been sat downstairs, in what she'd dubbed the TV room, with Bailey most of the afternoon. There was a large sliding glass door to their right that overlooked the woodland greenery and though it was raining again, the gray weather just made the plush room feel cozier.

Blake had a large L-shaped couch in soft brown leather and she'd laid out a blanket on it for Bailey to sit and then grabbed her own from a big wicker basket by the door. The couch faced a TV so large it took up most of the back wall, with big speakers hooked up to it on each side and smaller ones installed behind where they were sitting for surround sound. The room was quiet though. She felt awkward trying to work out how the TV worked and so hadn't attempted it. It had four remotes. *Four*. It just seemed like an obscene amount. The TV at the suite had one remote – on, off. Except now she wished she hadn't compared them because now all she could see was the word *WHORE* scrawled in bright red lipstick across its surface.

Rose shook the thought away and pulled Blake's laptop closer. He'd let her borrow one of his to continue working on the gala, seeing as hers had been impounded with everything else in the suite, and Maia had sent over her latest mock-up of the ballroom. It was stunning in shades of green and gauze, and Rose could imagine how the golden glow of the string lights would catch on the bubbles in the champagne... they'd decided to go for old-school elegance, almost royal, and who knew? It might turn out to be her favorite project yet. All she needed to do now was show Blake the plans and have him approve them, which was easier said than done when he left the room every time she walked in.

She stroked one finger over the smooth top of the laptop as she thought. Even though she'd been working here and there on the gala, she had actually tried to bear in mind what Blake had said to her before, something she could recognize was true – *you never stop*. It had only taken a break-in and confrontation with an angry stalker to trigger the anxiety she'd mostly kept at bay before and to realize that perhaps her coping mechanisms hadn't been as healthy as she'd wanted to believe. Her panic attacks had been less frequent since starting up her anxiety meds again, but it would take a little while for her to tell if they were still working for her after all this time. What she really needed was for this guy to be caught so she could stop worrying about going outside or feeling uncomfortable in the dark, like she could be being watched. She hadn't slept with the lights on since she was a kid, but it was what she had resorted to doing to keep herself out of Blake's bed and firmly in her own.

Blake had asked her yesterday at dinner who she thought

it might have been in her apartment that night. Generally, she'd been avoiding remembering. The way the light from the elevator had caught on the metal of the knife still had her heart beating too fast, and at the time she'd just shrugged. But now it was a question she couldn't get out of her mind. Why was this person targeting her? Was it just some crazed fan? Or, the question she'd been worried to look at too closely, was it someone she knew?

She ran a hand between Bailey's ears, frown morphing into a grin when his eyes twitched but his snoring never stopped. It seemed like Blake had worn him out on their walk earlier, but while Bailey was snoozy and content, Blake seemed fouler than usual. She could only assume he'd been out stewing on the things they'd said yesterday. In truth, she'd been stewing too. Maybe she had been unfair to Blake. Maybe. But she still wasn't going to just take everything he said on blind faith. He was still a controlling ass even if his intentions were good.

Blake strolled into the room at that exact moment and Bailey opened a sleepy eye to look at him. Were they talking? Should she say something? From the way he'd been slamming about in the kitchen earlier it definitely seemed like he had something he wanted to say to her.

"He's not supposed to be on the couch," Blake said at the same time that she asked, "Are you pissed at me?"

He blinked. "No." He grabbed the blanket that was pooled on her lap and tugged half of it onto him as he sat down, and she glared as she tugged it back.

"You definitely *seem* pissed at me," she needled and relented when he reached for her blanket again, tucking it around his legs as he reached for a skinny black remote.

"Not everything is about you," he replied tersely, and yeah, ouch. What stick had got up his ass?

"I never said it was. So it's just coincidence that we had an uncomfortable chat yesterday and today you're moody?"

Blake sighed, running a hand over his face as he looked at her. "I didn't find our chat uncomfortable," he said pointedly, and she grimaced.

"Well, then what is it? Spit it out," she said, opting to ignore his retort. Maybe she could have been gentler, but somehow it seemed like the time for tough love.

"It's my mother."

"What? Is she okay?" Maybe tough love hadn't been the right approach after all.

"She's fine." Blake sighed. "Or at least she is right now, but she's getting older. She won't be here forever, and when you lose one parent you become incredibly aware of that fact."

Rose was silent, unsure what she could really say to help. She was lucky enough to have both parents happy and healthy and alive. Blake wasn't.

"So you're worried about her?" she asked a little more gently, and he half-shrugged.

"I don't want to miss out on time with her."

"That makes sense," she said slowly. "But I don't get why that means you're moody right now."

"I'm not moody," Blake pouted, and her lip twitched. "On a Sunday, Mom, Cara, and I normally do family dinner. We do movies and snacks, and yesterday was the first one I've missed in a long time and, well, I didn't even really notice because I was focused on you."

"Cara and Grace did it without you?" She was a little envious. Her mom and dad were great, but they'd never had that sort of family relationship where they had traditions. Sure, they met up for food or drinks but a lot of the time... Rose looked away from Blake to the woods outside, guilt churning. *A lot of the time she simply didn't have time*, was what she had been going to say, but the truth was... she could make time. Blake clearly did. And he was right, her parents weren't going to be around forever, if not now, then when?

"You look deep in thought," Blake said. "Did you hear anything I just said?"

"Um, sorry. No," she admitted, and he snorted.

"You are one of the most self-absorbed people I've ever met." She would have been offended, but he almost made it sound like a compliment. Besides, she knew it was true. She was used to being the only child, used to getting her way and being the center of attention. She was a self-confessed brat. "Vain too," he added, and Rose swatted his arm as he laughed, face seeming lighter than before he sat down. "I told them it was okay to do it without me."

"Well," she said, plucking the remote from his hand and wafting it around uselessly, "we can do our own frenemies day today instead. Just me, you, and Bailey."

"I've been upgraded." Blake grinned as he grabbed the remote back and selected the category *Movies* on the screen. "No longer the man you loathe, huh? *Frenemies,*" he mocked, and she glowered.

"It's probationary," she hissed, and he winked at her.

"So, what do you want to watch while I cook?" Blake scrolled through, and her eyes flew wide at the amount of choice. The guy was clearly a movie buff.

"Don't Grace and Cara usually help you in the kitchen?"

Blake snorted. "No. If Cara is even in the vicinity of an

oven, things burn. Katie joins us on a Sunday now too, and she can at least chop and peel. My mom is usually in charge of the wine." Rose laughed, and he blinked at her for a moment before turning back to the TV. "Are you still into those murder mystery movies? The old black and white ones?"

Shocked, her head snapped around to look at him. "You *remember* that?"

"Ugh, yes, how could I forget? It was when you got into French cinema that it was the worst, you had a beret in every color and refused to speak in anything but French, despite the fact that you didn't actually know a lick of it."

"I was eleven," she protested, and he laughed.

"So what do you like now?" Blake's eyes were intent on hers as he waited for her answer.

She shrugged. "I don't really watch movies anymore. I don't..."

"Have the time?" he said knowingly. "Well, we're going to change that right now, princess."

"I want to help you cook though."

"Sure," he said with an easy grin, dimples flashing. "Normally I would do fresh veggies and cook from scratch, but until Cara does a grocery run for us we're stuck with the frozen stuff."

Rose shrugged. "Fine by me, I can use a microwave. It's not often I have any semblance of a home cooked meal anyway."

Blake looked horrified as he mouthed the word 'microwave'. "We'll put the frozen veg in boiling water. I'm not going to just nuke them."

"Why not?" Her face scrunched up and then smoothed out as she laughed at the disgust on Blake's.

"I'm going to pretend you didn't ask me that. Sit, watch, I'll be back once the chicken is in the oven."

She nodded absently, closing her eyes while he picked out a film and opening them in a daze at the quick press of lips to her forehead. "Blake?"

"Yeah?"

She hesitated for a second before swallowing and letting it drop. "Maia sent over her mock-up of the room for the gala. I love it, but we need your final approval to go ahead."

A smile quirked his lips and caught her attention for a second before she pulled her eyes back up to meet his. "If you love it then that's good enough for me, princess. I trust you."

MONDAY'S FRENEMY dinner had been nice, homey, and despite its moniker, she was pretty sure none of the food had been poisoned by Blake. It was probably the longest she and Blake had gone without arguing maybe ever. Plus, it was essentially her fault that he'd had to miss his first Sunday family dinner the night before, so letting him cook for her and watching movies together had been the least she could do. A temporary ceasefire. He'd picked an action movie for her to watch, which had been okay, and then a romantic comedy that she thought she might have already seen on TV with Maia, and then he'd settled down next to her and turned on what she knew was his favorite genre: fantasy.

All in all, she couldn't remember ever having an evening more relaxing. With Bailey sprawled across her lap and a belly full of immaculately cooked chicken, it almost felt like home.

Reality was now intruding though, making up for the ease of yesterday with a phone call with Detective Jones this morning. Rose had sunk right back into her normal schedule, up at six-thirty, ready in an hour, sipping coffee by eight. Blake blinked at the sight of her sitting at the dining table when he walked into the kitchen with only a half-hour until the video call with Jones. For a moment, she was too distracted by all the abs on show to complain that he was going to make them late.

Blake's towel was slung low on his hips, the white complimenting his tan in a way that made her envious of never getting outside. When was the last time she'd taken a holiday? Rose swallowed hard, trying to drag her eyes off of the bead of water slowly rolling down, down, down...

"Rose?"

"Hm?" Her eyes flashed upwards and caught a cocky smile playing across Blake's face that he tried to hide, unsuccessfully.

"Just checking on you. Think you had a bit of drool escaping."

Her spine straightened as she glared at him. "I was *not* drooling. What are you doing walking around half naked anyway? We're supposed to be on a call with Jones in less than thirty minutes." Rose knew she was a stress head. Especially about appointments. It was even worse when she traveled. But she couldn't help it. She wasn't sure what Jones was going to tell them or what questions he might ask, and the uncertainty of it all wasn't helping her already-shot nerves.

Blake grabbed a cup of coffee and reclined against the counter, not even bothering to hold his towel as it slipped dangerously low. "Relax, princess. It only takes me ten minutes to get ready. I've got plenty of time."

She sniffed disbelievingly, opting to stare out at the garden through the backdoor than at him while he stood half-naked. "Do you want me to take Bailey out while you get dressed?" It was a big concession for her, voluntarily offering to go outside with all this still going on, and so she was more than a little bit relieved when he shook his head. Still, Doctor Makers would be pleased with her for challenging herself when she spoke to him later in the week.

"No, that's alright. I took him out earlier."

She nodded absently, still staring outside, glad that rain had cleared up and that it was proving to be a bright and blue day. A tree shook to the right of the woodland trail and her eyes shot to it, breathing out when a bird hopped out from the brush and pecked at something on the floor.

"You okay?"

Rose looked up, surprised to find Blake still watching her. "Yeah. I'm fine."

He nodded and drained his coffee, placing the mug into the large sink before heading past the island again to go and get ready upstairs. She might have been watching him leave, and she *might* have gasped when he dropped the towel, showing off his toned, tan ass. She heard him chuckle and knew she was busted but looked away quickly, not daring to lift her eyes until she heard his bedroom door close.

He emerged about twenty minutes later and found her in almost the same position as before, drinking her second cup of coffee. Caffeine had been the hardest thing for her to give up when she'd been taking her meds before, and she was still working on it now. To only be on her second cup was actually pretty good for her, and she now switched to tea after lunchtime.

Blake had a laptop under his arm as he looked in through the kitchen doorway and gestured for her to follow him. It was strange how different a place could look once you got used to it. This place now felt very different from where she'd had her first meeting with Blake, and then subsequently had sex with him, but as he led them into the study, the images started to marry up. Papers were in an orderly pile on the desk, and he'd set up a table in front of the long couch against the back wall for them to sit on while they spoke to Jones.

Rose avoided looking at the desk but thought she saw a smirk on Blake's face a few times as he set up wires and logged into the computer before moving away and lounging back against the desk he'd had her bent on just over a week ago. Jones' face soon took up the screen and Rose could feel her tension ratcheting up several degrees at the tight expression on his face as Blake strode over and settled next to her on the leather couch that faced the rest of the room. Blake smiled, but Rose could only nod as the Detective greeted them.

"There's not much news yet, I'm afraid. We've been working on tracing the photograph they sent you, maybe work out where it was printed, but right now it's like looking for a needle in a haystack. I did want to follow up with you though, Mr Blake about the security breach you believe you experienced yesterday evening. Do you have any updates on that yet?" Blake's eyes flickered to her and back again, and if possible, her stony expression became flatter. *Bastard.* Chicken-cooking, movie-watching, controlling, lying *bastard.*

I trust you, he'd said, and she wanted to laugh for being such an idiot.

Blake must have noticed her expression darkening on the screen in front of them, but he didn't so much as look at her. "We don't know yet if the security device flagged a human trying to break in or a rabbit too close to the sensor. My team is looking into it, but in the meantime, I've got the security team doing extra patrols. The cameras didn't capture anything, so the likelihood is that it was an animal." Jones replied, but Rose didn't even hear it as Blake whispered to her, "That's why I didn't mention it. It was so unlikely that it was them I didn't want to worry you needlessly."

She didn't bother to respond, just kept her jaw clenched and her mouth shut. She was an idiot to relax at all around him. This wasn't her home, he wasn't her friend, and they needed to catch this guy so that she could get the hell out of here.

"Thank you for the update, Detective. Did the cameras at *The Hart* yield anything useful in seeing who snapped the photo of us in the parking lot?"

Jones shook his head. "The angle was wrong, I'm afraid. Plus, whoever took that photo could have been using a long-range lens."

She nodded absently as Jones rambled on about the importance of staying put and reporting any changes immediately before he hung up.

"Rose–" Blake tried as soon as the call ended.

She stood up and brushed down the blouse she was wearing before looking down at him. "If anything like that ever happens again, I want you to tell me."

He opened his mouth like he was going to argue before sighing. "I'm sorry. I thought it was the right decision."

"Yes, well, you were wrong." How many times did she have to tell him? She wasn't fragile. She wasn't going to break. In fact, she was the one who got her and Maia out of there. Why did he insist on not worrying her unless– "You looked inside my package, didn't you?"

"What? No."

"I'm not ashamed," she hissed, "and I'm not weak either. I can handle things. Having anxiety doesn't change that. Needing medication doesn't change that."

His blue eyes were wide and he stood in a rush of motion, grabbing one of her wildly gesticulating hands in his. "I had no idea. I didn't look in the package. You've already been through so much. I just thought I could take care of this for you."

She tugged her hand free, warmth curling low in her stomach. "I don't *need* you to take care of me. I'm not a child, Blake."

"I know," he said in a low voice that made her heart flipflop in her chest as he moved closer, her chest heaving with deep breaths against his. "Would I do this if I thought you were?" His mouth crashed down onto hers, teeth tugging at her lip, hands spanning her waist as he dragged her impossibly closer. Her senses were full of Blake, his taste, his smell, until he broke away and she was left gasping. "Would I have fucked you if I thought you were some dumb kid? You're two years younger than me, Rose. That's nothing."

"I didn't think you were picky," she whispered, knowing it was a low blow and needing him to hurt.

He snorted, moving back from her with a look of disappointment pinching his mouth. "I thought you'd know better than to pay attention to the rumor mill, princess. Sure, I fuck around, but I have standards just like anyone else. Just because I don't date doesn't make me a fuckboy. It just means I already know what I want."

His eyes were heavy on hers with some meaning she didn't understand before he turned and walked away, leaving her standing in the study with frustration a beating drum in her chest. What else was he hiding from her? How was she ever supposed to trust Blake if he steamrolled over her at every opportunity? Her eyes drifted to the desk, that *infernal* desk that had the blood rising in her cheeks as she looked at it. She inched closer and rested her hands on the edge before glancing back at the doorway and finding it empty.

The first drawer slid open easily, full of knickknacks and junk like highlighter pens, a stapler, and a squishy red ball that at first she'd thought was a stress ball, but when she squeezed it let out a loud *squeak* that made her freeze. When the tell-tale sound of Bailey's paws didn't come, she let out a long breath and slipped the ball back where she'd found it before moving onto the next drawer.

Inside was a myriad of files for *Horizons* all labeled in a way that was surprisingly organized – she might have thought someone else had done it if not for the fact that she recognized the curling lilt to Blake's handwriting. Two other drawers were the same, but the top drawer on the right-hand-side gave her pause.

There were photographs inside, one of Blake and Grace, and another of him and his Dad with a very young Cara, and the other was... her. It was just the one photo, hardly a shrine, but it was *just* her. Not her with her mom or her dad, just Rose and the sunset, her hair whipping out in the beach wind and glinting off of a lens flare while she laughed. It was... beautiful, and she'd absolutely never seen it before. She looked about eighteen in the photo, and thinking back, she could remember going to see her parents at a beach house they'd hired for a month in the summer all the way in Malibu. She'd been mid-way through her first year at college and had flown out on the weekend for a cookout on the beach. In all honesty, she'd forgotten Blake had been there because she'd spent the majority of the time avoiding him and Christopher – the memory clicked into place all of a sudden, and it was like she could almost smell the salty air and hear the gulls. Chris had been going through a photographer phase and had been snapping candids all weekend, but Rose had never seen any of them. It seemed Blake, on the other hand, had. But why this photo? Why her?

It just means I already know what I want. As she stood there with the sunset photo in her hand, Rose had to wonder, for the first time in a long time, what exactly she meant to David Blake.

Chapter Thirteen

A knock on her door woke her the next morning and Blake's voice was strained, instantly sending worry spearing through her. "Rose, you're going to want to come and see this."

She was up and out of bed a moment later, the floorboards cold against her toes. Bailey was whining as he bounced in front of Blake, desperate for his attention, but Blake was focused absolutely on her as he nodded down the stairs. She followed the sound of voices to the TV room where her mouth dropped open.

"Son of a bitch," she breathed and felt, rather than saw, Blake stop and stand next to her. The large screen threw the reporter's face into relief, every hair magnified as she spoke to the camera while standing outside the large gates of Blake's house.

"Whether the break-in resulted in any loss of life we cannot yet say for sure, but sources have confirmed that the walls of the Blake estate were in fact breached on Monday night. Our thoughts are with the DuLoe family at this difficult time." The reporter's clear gaze was appropriately solemn, but Rose couldn't believe what she was hearing.

"Is... is she saying that I'm *dead*?" she shrieked, frantically patting down her hair and checking her reflection in her phone before seeing all the notifications continuing to blow it up. "Oh my god. I need to call my mom. Or, wait, are they still outside?"

"Rose, you can't go out there."

She blew out a long breath. "I can't fucking believe this! Who let that information out about the potential security breach? And who told them I *died*?"

Blake's hands fell to her shoulders, halting her pacing as he looked down at her. "I don't know, but we'll find out and deal with it, okay? Right now you need to call your mom."

Rose nodded, breathing out shakily. "I will in just a second."

"What are you—"

Rose held her phone at arm's length and beamed into the camera now live recording to her, approximately, four-hundred-thousand followers. "I know I've been a little quieter on here than usual lately, but if you've been keeping up with the news, then you know I'm in police-mandated seclusion with David Blake at his estate. However, this morning I woke up to the news that I'm apparently dead. I have a whole bunch of notifications that I honestly don't know if I'll ever get through, but I want to say thank you to those of you who have reached out or tagged me in posts. However, I'd like to assure everyone that I'm alive and well and that the *Cincinnati Times* better get themselves a damn good lawyer." She ended the live, her hands trembling and a headache starting to pound beneath her left eye. "My life has become a media circus.

And *don't think* for one second that I've forgotten about your role in it all, you ass."

Blake raised his hands innocently but couldn't help a small grin that said he had no regrets about driving the press rabid with supposed dating rumors. Her phone rang in her hand before she could call her mom, and she breathed a sigh of relief as she answered.

"Mom, I was just about to call. I have no idea why they said that–" It was then that she noticed that her mom wasn't speaking over her. Alarm bells began to ring in her head and Blake stepped closer, face pinching with concern at whatever expression she was wearing. She turned away. "Mom? Are you there? Is everything okay?"

"I–" Every muscle in Rose's body stiffened up. Her mom was never lost for words.

"Mom. Tell me what's going on." She used her calmest, most authoritative voice, and at last her mother choked out some words.

"I-it's your dad. He just stopped moving. Rose, why isn't he moving?"

Rose swallowed harshly, fear like she'd never felt before freezing her insides as she turned to Blake and said, "Call an ambulance. Tell them my dad collapsed and my mom is in shock." Blake blinked at her dumbly for a second, mouth hanging open until she said, "*Now*," voice breaking.

"Can you tell me what happened, Mom? It's alright, someone is on their way."

"We were watching the news. We were just watching and then he just made this sound, like he was choking, and then I just couldn't get him to wake up."

"Okay, it's alright. He's going to be okay. Mom?" The sound

of voices came through the line, and she sagged back against Blake as he came up behind her and then the line cut-off. "I think the ambulance arrived. She said they were watching the news. I bet it was that damned reporter. Oh god, Blake, what if he's dead? What if he died thinking I was dead? I need to get to the hospital. I need to see him. He needs to know I'm okay. What if he–"

Blake pressed his lips to hers quickly, hands on either side of her face, cutting off the words and forcing her to breathe even as the panic continued swirling inside her. "You're not going anywhere."

"But I–"

"No," he said gently, but firmly, stopping her as she tried to walk towards the front door. "That's what this guy has been waiting for, to get you alone, vulnerable. I will go and see your dad. I'll take one of my security guys with me, okay? I'll check things out and update you. If I think you need to come then... well, we'll cross that bridge if we come to it. Alright? You stay here with Bailey where it's safe."

"I can't just *sit* here! Not while he's off in some hospital, while he could be... he could be..."

"He's going to be fine. And you're not going to just sit here, okay? You're going to call Jones and ream him the fuck out. Then you're going to sit and watch the drama unfold on the TV until I call you with an update. Okay?"

"No," she said sharply. "*Not* okay. How can you, of all people, not understand that I need to be there with my dad right now? My mom could barely talk to me through shock on the phone, Blake. I need to be there and I'm going."

"It's not safe–" he said, eyebrows pulled together and eyes pinched in concern when she threw her hands up in the air.

"*I don't care.* So what if this guy finds me or chases me? If he wanted to kill me, he could have done it in the suite–"

"Maybe he would have and you didn't give him the chance," Blake said firmly, and she shook her head.

"You really think I'm going to just sit here nice and safe on the off chance this guy tries something while my dad could be d-dead or dying?" Her words stuttered out and the harsh lines of Blake's face softened as he scrubbed a hand through his hair. "I'm not asking for your permission. I'm going to the hospital to see my dad and the longer we argue about this, the less time..." She couldn't finish the words aloud, but Blake seemed to understand them anyway. *The less time my dad might have left.*

"Fine," he said and reached for his jacket, "but I'm coming with you."

"You don't need to–"

"I do," he said firmly, and she didn't waste any more time arguing as she grabbed a pair of boots Cara and Katie had picked out for her and slipped them on roughly. If it weren't for the reporters... Hell, if it weren't for the damned stalker, this never would have happened.

A cold feeling started in her fingertips and stopped only when Blake grabbed a hold of her hands and crouched down to peer into her eyes. "This isn't your fault, and we don't have time for you to panic. Be mad now and then you can freak out later if you need to, okay? Stevie and one of my other guys are going to escort us to the hospital, and I've called Jones too. He's going to set a perimeter at the hospital in case this guy tries to get to you there."

She nodded woodenly and allowed him to pull her up from the floor and towards the door. A sea of reporters and cameras waited beyond the gate and they immediately started hurling questions at them as soon as they were in sight.

Rose ignored them for now. But later there was going to be one hell of a reckoning.

Stevie climbed into their car with them and gave her a polite but sympathetic smile in the rearview mirror that she tried her best to return as Blake murmured that they also had another of his guys who was going to be tailing them for security purposes. It all felt overkill. Maybe this guy had lost interest, maybe he hadn't seen the news. She hadn't ever had armed security following her about before and it felt ridiculous, but Blake was clearly used to it.

The gates opened for them and Rose fought the wave of rage inside her when she spotted the reporter from the TV still stood outside. The urge to roll down the window and rip the woman to shreds was strong but she refrained. After all, that woman wasn't in charge. What they really needed to know was where the news station had got that tip from.

It would probably only take them twenty-five minutes to get to the hospital, maybe more if the traffic was bad, and every second felt like it was slipping through her fingers too fast as she tried to hold on.

"He's going to be fine," Blake said. At some point he'd taken hold of her hand in his again and she hadn't even noticed as she numbly watched out of her tinted window.

"You don't know that." Her lips felt numb, and she swallowed painfully as the car seemed to move like it was going through toffee.

"I do know that," Blake said fiercely enough that her eyes found his and held for a moment. "He's strong, just like you, and healthy. Whatever this is, they'll help him. It's not too late."

Was this one of the stages of grief? Denial? She supposed that Graham DuLoe had been something of a father-figure to Blake after his own dad had passed. It felt like she'd skipped right over denial, sped through anger, and had now settled somewhere colder than acceptance, somewhere that speared ice through her bones until her teeth wanted to chatter, but instead, she bit her lip until she almost drew blood.

Rose turned back to the window as they took the turn that would lead them to *The Christ* hospital, one of the best in the US. *He's going to be fine,* she tried to tell herself. *Everything is going to be fine.*

That was when she noticed the car. Silver, bulky, like it could take on a trucker and maybe win. It was relatively inconspicuous except for the fact that it was barreling towards them with no sign of brake lights.

"Blake!"

He turned his head and Rose watched his eyes widen, heard Stevie's yell of fear, and then glass flew as the car hit, rattling her teeth in her skull. The initial jolt made her gasp and the screech of metal made her ears vibrate painfully until all she could hear was tires scrambling for traction as Stevie braked, and the thump as their car flipped and all her blood rushed to her face.

For a second everything fell silent, and then her eyes fluttered and the sounds of shouts and horns beeping came back to her. Glass crunched by her ear and a pair of thick black boots, professionally knotted and tucked into black cargo pants, walked away from her as she tried to make her voice work.

There was glass in her hair. She could feel it pinching when she tried to look around for Blake, for someone to help, but she froze when moving her neck made her head pound, and nausea kicked up so badly she thought she might throw up then and there. The glass made a pretty tinkle as it hit the roof of the car when it fell out of her hair and clothes, and her face stung with what had to be a dozen cuts from the spray of glass when the windows had shattered, and all she could think about was that they weren't supposed to do that. It was safety glass, meant to crack but not shatter, so the fact that it had... How fast had that driver been going?

Hands finally reached in and she nearly cried with relief. She couldn't feel her seatbelt button with her fingertips and didn't know if that meant something was very wrong or if she simply couldn't find it. Hands pulled her free from the wreckage easily, and the kind face of a paramedic met her as he shone a light in her eyes.

"How do you feel?"

"Where's Blake?"

"They're getting him out now, okay? I need you to tell me what hurts."

"Everything," she slurred, and he cursed when her eyes rolled in their sockets.

"Okay, stay awake now for me. What's your name?"

She pried her heavy lids up and her heart seemed to beat quicker and slower at the same time when she finally caught a glimpse of Blake's body being pulled from the car. A tear blurred her vision, unable to fall because of how she lay on her back, and all she could do was grip the paramedic's arm for a moment until his colleague sent a thumbs up. Alive.

"Your friends are okay," he said and relief made her head loll. "What's your name?"

"Princess," she murmured, confusion making her brain swim and her hands shake as she tried to lift them again. "David."

"Concussion," she thought she heard him say, and then the last of her adrenaline slipped away as the world faded.

———

HER THROAT WAS sore from shouting, and the rest of her body ached to match. She'd come around about an hour ago and the nurse had practically pinned her to the bed when Rose had made a move to get up and find her father. Of course, she wouldn't have gotten far with her head spinning and nausea swirling whenever she was upright. Mild concussion, they'd said. She was lucky. The car had been aiming for the driver's side, and if not for the flip, she probably would have been up and about faster. Rose had tried to ask about Blake and Stevie, but the nurse couldn't tell her much beyond that they were both alive. For now, she'd been forced into bedrest until she could stand without needing to puke.

Thankfully, she didn't need to be able to stand in order to yell down the phone at Jones for about twenty minutes. She could admit that she'd been an idiot and hadn't really taken the threat seriously enough. Sure, it was possible the car that had hit them had been a coincidence and sheer bad luck, except for the flowers that had arrived just before she'd woken up. Twelve solid pink roses with an apology note and a photograph. It was her, unconscious in the car with blood on her face. The nurse had gone pale when she'd seen it, but Rose had just clenched her jaw before turning it around to find a drawn-on sad face and apology message. After that, she hadn't been able to stop thinking about those boots. Had that been the person who'd taken the picture? If so, then why not kill her then and there? Did they think it would attract too much attention? But then how did they get close enough to take the photo of her without anyone seeing? The only thing she could think of was that the man in the boots had to have been the currently-missing driver of the other car. Jones had fucked up not once with the car crash, but twice in allowing his perimeter to somehow be breached enough for the flowers to get through. But it did make her wonder just how this guy was slipping into all these places unseen or unquestioned.

She'd also contacted her lawyer who had assured her that they would sort out the mess with the reporter from the *Cincinnati Times,* and Jones had promised to liaise with them about the tip-off that they were assuming had been used in an effort to lure Rose and David out of the house. And it had worked, thanks to her. But after one CT scan and three more hours of resting, Rose couldn't regret the decision to leave, not when she was finally able to stand and make her way to her dad's room.

The beeping in there was louder than in her room, and several wires peeked out from under the hospital garb they had him in, washing out his usually tanned features. Seeing him there, eyes closed and face relaxed, made her notice the details she'd been overlooking for years – the new lines, the gray hair at his temples, and the circles beneath his eyes. Much like Rose, her parents didn't *need* to work, and it was beyond clear to her now that it was taking a toll on them more than ever. She was going to have to have a conversation with them about slowing down. It wasn't just herself that she'd been neglecting, she now realized. It was her job to make sure they were okay, to look out for them. Maybe it was time to have a chat with her cousin about how they could be doing more for the business.

"I can feel you worrying from here," her dad said without opening his eyes, but a small smile twitched his lips until, finally, eyes the same shade of brown as hers opened and twinkled at her. "Your mother went on a coffee run."

"I saw her earlier," she said, moving closer and sitting down in the empty seat by his bed, wincing at the soreness in her back and side as she did so.

"How are you doing?" His hand was soft as it covered her own and she squeezed it lightly.

"I think I'm supposed to be the one asking you that."

He laughed but stopped quickly as a pinch of pain showed on his face. "I'm the parent here, darling. Now, don't worry your old dad, hm? How's Blake?"

Mom had clearly filled him in on what had been going on and she blew out a long breath at not having to re-hash it all again so soon. "I don't know yet. They haven't told me anything."

"And what about you?"

"They've said I can likely be discharged by this evening as long as my scans come back clear."

"That's great!"

"Yeah..."

"You don't sound pleased," he said with a raised eyebrow and Rose grimaced.

"I don't want to leave without him," she said and kept her eyes on the ceiling, ignoring her dad's quiet chuckle that somehow managed to sound smug. "Well, it is his house," she went on, ignoring her blush, "it feels weird to be there without him."

"I see," he said carefully, and thankfully she was spared from responding as her mom swept back into the room with a coffee in each hand. Her dad eyed the cups hopefully, making his wife glower.

"No, Graham. You know the doctors said no caffeine!"

"Ever?" she asked, horrified, and squeezed her dad's hand tighter when he nodded.

"They're putting a stent into his heart," her mom told Rose for the third time, but she didn't mind, knowing her mom was saying it more for herself than for Rose. "So he's going on a strict diet until the surgery."

"What about after?"

A stern look was leveled at both her and her dad. "We'll see."

Her mom fussed about with her dad's covers and Rose looked up at the white, chunky clock that looked like it'd been glued to the gray wall. "They told me they'd have more news about Blake and Stevie around seven, so I'm going to go and pester the nurse again." She wrapped her mom in a hug and pressed a quick kiss to her cheek before doing the same for her dad. "I'm so glad you're okay."

"Me too, darling."

The corridors were quiet, and Rose walked as quickly as her bruised body would let her, the sound of her footsteps echoing and raising the hairs on her arms until the nurse's station was in sight and she paused at the tall figure standing there. He paced back and forth anxiously, like he'd been waiting for a while, and her mouth went dry as she watched from a safe distance before slowly walking forward again.

The nurse behind the desk looked up with a smile and nodded to her left. "He's almost as persistent as you."

Rose laughed but it sounded breathless and finally he looked up and saw her, face breaking out in the relief that was mirrored inside her too as Blake swept forward and pulled her against him.

"Thank god." He pressed the words into the top of her head and the warmth of his breath made her shiver as his hands ghosted over her sides, stroking upwards until they found her face. "Are you alright?"

There was a deep gash on his forehead and one of his lips had a split that she touched lightly as she nodded and Blake relaxed, like he'd been waiting for her to confirm it before he'd believe it.

"And your dad?"

"He's okay." She smiled, but it faded quickly when she noticed the bandage around his arm. "I'm sorry–"

"You don't need to apologize." Blake smiled slightly at the slight look of irritation she couldn't hold back. "You didn't do this, that bastard did. I knew the risks. So did Stevie."

"Is he going to be okay? Jones said the car was aiming for the driver's side."

"I know." A muscle in Blake's jaw popped before he relaxed it again. "They think *he* thought that I would be driving."

"Bastard," she whispered as the anger she'd been suppressing started to kindle again and Blake nodded, stepping even closer as one hand came up to cup her cheek as he peered anxiously into her face before letting her go again. "When are they clearing you?"

"I can go whenever you're ready," he said and she nodded, content to just enjoy his warmth for a quiet moment before clearing her throat and stepping back. Now that she knew everyone was okay, she just felt tired. The nurse called her name and they walked back over to her desk as she confirmed Rose's scans were all normal. They were free to go.

"Jones is escorting us out of here personally," Blake said, somehow knowing again what she'd been thinking about. "I don't think he's going to try again."

The truth was, she didn't either. Otherwise, why would he have apologized? "He sent me flowers and an apology note."

Blake frowned, his hand tightening around hers as he tugged her to a stop so they could collect their meager belongings and sign their insurance paperwork, before they moved towards the exit. "We're going to find him and we're going to stop him. I promise I won't let anything happen to you."

Rose gave him a thin smile as she pushed through the doors to the parking lot outside. "It's not me I'm worried about."

Chapter Fourteen

J ones had dropped Rose off at Blake's estate before continuing on to the station with Blake in tow. Now that this guy had escalated things so drastically, Jones needed someone to give an official recorded statement – by the book, he'd said. The potential charges had jumped from destruction of property to assault and attempted murder and Rose wanted to scream that the cops were only now paying attention after they'd almost been killed. Wasn't it their job to *stop* those things from happening in the first place?

The sun had started to set, and Rose couldn't stop her anxious pacing as she waited for Blake to call and tell her they were back on the road. Somewhere along the way she'd lost track of whether today was Wednesday or Thursday, but it was the evening, and the darker it got outside the more anxious she became. Bailey watched her from his place on the couch, his eyes going back and forth with her movements. He was surprisingly calm considering he'd only been out for one walk earlier that morning. She'd let him out of the house as soon as she'd got in but couldn't bear to be so exposed outside and had called him back in twenty-minutes later.

Finally, her phone rang and relief struck through her.

"Blake?"

"Sorry, Rose. Doctor Makers here. I heard about what happened on the news and thought it might be better to check in with you now instead of Friday."

"Oh, right. Thanks for calling."

"How are the new meds working for you?" he said, and that was one thing she'd always appreciated about him – his ability to cut to the chase.

"They're okay so far. Things are starting to settle down now, I think. Hard to tell with everything going on. I was a bit up and down for a few days, and I also noticed an, um, increased libido."

The Doctor hummed over the phone, and she imagined him scribbling notes down in his little black notebook that he'd always carried for their sessions before. "That's good. Nothing to worry about there. Do you have any concerns?"

"Well, I was worried about the libido increase, actually. It's a little better than it was for the first few days, but still higher than I'm used to."

"You don't need to be concerned there, Rose. The likelihood is that your own anxiety was reducing your sex drive, so now that it's being regulated, your sex drive is returning. You'll get back into the swing of things soon I'm sure. Any word on your father yet?"

"He's going to be alright. They're giving him a stent. I'm actually just waiting on Blake to get home with an update from the cops after the crash." She bit the inside of her cheek with a sigh, and Makers made a sympathetic noise. She'd already torn the skin there to shreds on the inside from anxiously chewing but couldn't stop herself even with the pinch of pain and metallic taste in her mouth.

"Did the hospital give you any medication?"

"No," she said, relieved. "So I'm all good to keep taking my meds?"

"Yes, I don't foresee any issues there, but I would like to keep up with our check-ins."

"Of course. Listen, Blake is supposed to be calling me any minute to let me know when they're on the road, would it be okay to pick this up another time?"

"Of course," he said carefully. "I'll get off the line so you can keep an ear out. Any questions about your prescription please get in touch, and I'll give you a call on Friday anyway to see how things are progressing, seeing as this was only a short chat instead of our usual session."

"That'd be great. Thanks so much. Take care," she murmured and then sank onto the couch, resting a hand on Bailey's back and just feeling him breathe, timing her breaths to coincide with his until her head stopped spinning so much.

God, she was absolutely parched. Other than being knocked out, it felt like she hadn't stopped since everything had happened. There had always been someone else to think about or a new thing to worry about. She was just relieved to finally sit and reflect in silence.

Until her leg started to bounce and her brain started to conjure scenarios up from thin air about what might happen to Blake on the way home. Why hadn't he called yet? Rose shivered, brushing off the imaginary feeling of glass shards tickling her skin, and then pushed up from the couch and went to get a drink, walking back into the TV room as footage from the car wreck rolled across the screen. From this angle it looked even worse. The left side of the car was crumpled and dented, the paint scraped off and a smear of silver ripping across the black exterior. The windows had shattered when the car flipped, and footage from a bystander caught a glimpse of Rose's blonde hair as the car settled back down onto the ground with a bounce and groan of metal. It was horrifying, so naturally, the news station replayed it in slow motion.

Rose sat on the floor for a little while longer, just watching the news through sightless eyes with Bailey curled in her lap, until a key rattled in the door and he took off running with a bark. She wanted to follow him, but when she stood her legs shook, and when she blinked her eyes felt full of grit. For the first time in a long time, all Rose really wanted to do was get in bed and cry.

Instead, she made her way to the front door and pushed Bailey down and off of Blake before he could knock him over. Then she looked at him, and her eyes flooded with tears that she quickly blinked away. She'd seen him in the hospital, but in the hours they'd been apart his bruises had deepened, and the effect it had on her was almost as bad as when she'd seen him for the first time in the hospital, so many hours after she'd woken up and demanded to know if he was okay.

His face was bruised at the left temple, a raw purple splotch that told her exactly how he'd ended up unconscious before. Blake's perfect bottom lip was split down the middle with two stitches holding it together that she hadn't noticed before, and he winced when he tried to smile or talk. One faltering step towards her had him swaying, and she quickly brought an arm up and around his waist as she led him back to the couch one small step at a time. He'd been sitting on the side that had taken the brunt of the impact before they'd flipped and while her concussion was already healing, it would take him a little longer to recover.

"Why didn't you call?" Blake opened his mouth, but she pressed a finger gently across his lips before he could speak. "Never mind. The nurse told you to take it easy. I should have gone with Jones."

Blake shot her a defiant look that was mostly just tired and Bailey whined as he followed them into the room, but she ignored him in favor of tucking a cushion under Blake's head and draping him in the blankets from the basket. The TV was on mute but the bright lights played out across his face as his eyes fluttered closed and she stroked a hand across his brow. Who knew she would actually care if something happened to David Blake? She wasn't even sure if she really trusted him. But it was becoming very clear to her that she did care, and if she'd lost him today she never would have forgiven herself.

"David," she whispered, and he lifted his eyes ever so slightly to show he was listening. "Nod or shake. Did you really only ask me to stay here with you just to keep me safe?"

She held her breath, not sure what exactly the answer would mean to her but knowing it was important that she ask and actually listen this time, and if her heart got hurt in the process... well, it turned out she could take a little pain.

One nod.

Yes.

Chapter Fifteen

Blake slept through Thursday night and most of Friday, and she could tell he was in more pain now than when he'd arrived home initially. She knew that to be the case firsthand too, had experienced it the night after hurting her feet in Blake's driveway, and now her entire body ached as well. Luckily, she wasn't exactly going anywhere that required either heels or a lot of walking at the moment, but she'd known that they would feel worse the day-after the crash than the day-of. The truth was, they'd been lucky. The cops had put out alerts at the local hospitals in case the driver had been injured, but Rose couldn't get the memory of those boots walking away from her out of her head and she knew that this guy had to be a pro of some kind. He'd driven a car into them and hadn't been injured. He was either even luckier than them or he knew what he was doing. But how? Cop? Firefighter?

Blake couldn't make it up the stairs to his bedroom yet, so she took care of him in the TV room, bringing him drinks and soup, helping him walk to the bathroom and then stumble back to the couch. Somehow, being the one in charge while she took care of him made her feel more comfortable than she had been before in the house. She decided it was probably time to wash her towels and bedding and went hunting for the washer and detergent, and she came to a shocked stop when she finally located them in a room just off of the kitchen.

Mounds of towels, bedding, and clothes sat in neatly organized piles next to the machine, and Rose peeked inside to check there wasn't a load going around or forgotten about – nothing. A giggle snuck out as Rose stared at the piles of laundry. Then another. So. Blake wasn't doing amazingly at everything since he'd had to let the staff go. He could cook for sure, but clean?

Rose wound up laughing, clutching her stomach as she shook silently. David Blake didn't know how to do washing. Once her laughter had mostly got itself under control again, she got to work on the piles. Thankfully, Blake had one of those crazy big industrial sized washers that could fit in a *lot* of laundry, so it probably wouldn't take too long to sort. It occurred to her in that moment that since she'd been here, she'd been feeling so anxious and tense that she hadn't even really snooped about, barring the study, which was so unlike her it actually made her stop in her tracks to consider that for just a second.

She checked in on Blake and found him asleep, blonde lashes fanned out across his cheek and breaths deep and even. His bruise had come up fully and covered his left temple, brushing all the way down to the peak of his cheekbone. She'd iced it for him last night, and thankfully most of the swelling had gone down, but she was still hit with a strong amount of both guilt and gratitude when she saw his injuries. He hadn't needed to go with her, but he had anyway. What she still didn't really understand was why. They weren't friends, hadn't ever been friends. Having sex definitely didn't change that. Her mind flashed back to the photo of her he kept in his desk and settled there uncomfortably. She hadn't mentioned the photo to him – both because she'd have to admit to snooping and because she wasn't sure she wanted to hear what he would say.

She pulled her eyes away from his bruise, only for them to fall to his mouth, and she cursed a little as she spun around to leave the room. Luckily his lip wasn't totally busted all the way through, just a deep cut with dissolvable stitches that should heal up by next week if he was lucky – not that she'd been doing much research while she lay upstairs in bed awake each night. A quiet whine drew her attention, and she followed the sound to see Bailey through the doorway waiting patiently by the backdoor, one paw up on the wood and big eyes looking to her for help. She'd known it was going to have to happen some time. Bailey was too young to be allowed out by himself, too curious. She had to go outside with him.

Thoughts of further snooping abandoned, Rose walked reluctantly into the kitchen and rubbed Bailey's ears. "You're lucky you're cute, pup."

Breathing in through her nose and out through her mouth, Rose reached down and tugged on a pair of boots that were left by the door and grabbed a whistle hanging on a hook. She probably wouldn't need it, but better safe than sorry. She didn't want to have to tell Blake she'd lost his dog in his own garden.

She opened the door and Bailey was off like a shot,

sniffing around bushes that were clearly his favorites as she worked to stop the prickly feeling sweeping over her from freezing her movements. Instead, she kept her head up and her eyes alert, the cool air helping with the sweats that had suddenly come on, scanning the landscape for anything that looked amiss or anything Bailey could potentially get into that he shouldn't.

He was still sniffing at the bushes near the door, but he quickly ran over when she called him and they made quick progress across the trail. It was actually... nice to be back in the outside world. Especially away from the paparazzi. One of Blake's private security guards stood alert up ahead, and Rose offered him a smile as she passed by. She was safe here. The bastard that had been watching her couldn't get in without half a dozen people knowing. Couldn't hurt her or Blake again as long as they stayed here, and the rest of her family all had either private security or police escorts keeping an eye on them now that they knew just how real the danger was. If they had been willing to run them off the road, what else were they capable of?

Something else had caught Bailey's attention on the side of the trail as he sniffed eagerly, ignoring her spoken commands when she called him. Rose moved closer and froze at the sight of blood, dark red and splattered thickly in the grass.

"Help!" she called, and the security guard looked up and over at her before breaking into a fast jog. "There's something in the grass there. Bailey, here. Come." The pup finally trotted over to her side, and her eyes fixed on the dot of blood on the fur of his front paw. "What is it?" she asked as the security personnel pulled on rubber gloves.

"Rabbit," he said gruffly and offered nothing more as his dark eyes examined the grass.

"Do you think Bailey killed it?" The dog looked up at his name, panting before looking out at the tree line.

"No, not enough blood on him or in the brush." It certainly looked like a lot of blood on the grass to her, but then again, she'd never killed an animal so she didn't have a good reference to compare it to. "I'd say it was killed elsewhere and then dropped here."

"Are you sure?"

The guard stood up with the small rabbit clasped in his hands by its ears, and her lunch threatened to make a reappearance. "If the dog was going to kill it, I doubt it would have used a blade."

Fear had her blood running cold as she looked around the woods surrounding them, gray spots hovering at the edges of her vision. "Put it back down on the ground and take a photo," her teeth started to chatter, and she knew she needed to get inside and call Jones before she passed out. "I need you to send it to me. Do you have a radio?" The guard nodded, and she let out a relieved breath. "Great, get someone up here to make sure nobody else messes with the scene, and then you're going to walk me back to the house, okay?" Another nod, and then he did exactly as instructed, which she appreciated.

Another guard made it over to them in a couple of minutes and turned pale at the sight of the blood on the floor and the fleshy jelly of the rabbit's neck. "Stay here, don't look at it if you think it'll make you puke. This is a crime scene. Don't let anyone else approach unless they show you a badge. Okay?"

The younger guard nodded, and then she set off back for

the house with the quieter guard trailing her. Bailey trotted ahead, oblivious to the panic she felt that increased the longer it took to get back to the house. How far had they gone? Shouldn't they be back by now? Just as her breaths started to veer into dangerous territory, the backdoor came into view and she asked the guard to stand and wait to escort the officers she would be calling back to the site in question and thanking him for walking her back.

Blake was awake and propped up against the island as they walked in, and she growled. "What are you doing up?"

"I'm fine," he said, waving her off. "I'm just a little sore. What's Scott doing outside?"

"We found something," she said and took his hand without thinking too much about it when he looked alarmed. "Would Bailey kill a rabbit?"

"A rabbit? I mean, there's always a chance, but it's not happened in all the time I've had him."

"Okay," she said, rubbing two fingers over the bridge of her nose. "Scott thinks the throat was slit anyway, but I had to check. We've got one of the other guards looking after the crime scene. I'm going to call Jones, and then your guys can escort them through the grounds to the scene."

Blake nodded, blue eyes watching her with something close to worry as she hit call on her phone and explained the situation to Jones. In all honesty, she was tired of being one step behind all the time, tired of having to do the detective's job for him while his department couldn't even prevent information being leaked to the press.

"Are you okay?" Blake asked when she was done, and Rose looked at him frankly, letting him see the tiredness, the frustration in her eyes.

"No. I'm tired and I'm angry and I hate feeling like I'm dealing with this alone."

"You're not alone." Blake took a wincing step forward and brushed his hair out of his eyes. She liked seeing it like this, a little fluffy and a lot messy, free from the gel he usually controlled it with. "You have me. We're a team."

Was that what they were now? A team? "Teammates don't lie to each other."

"I'm sorry." His face was soft, vulnerable, like he was showing her his underbelly knowing full well she could slice if she wanted to. "It won't happen again. I promise."

"You've said that to me twice now. Third time's the charm?" She crossed her arms over her chest and then dropped them when his eyes lowered.

"I was wrong to keep it from you before. If you like, as soon as I can actually bend my knees, I'll grovel on them for you."

Rose coughed lightly, her cheeks turning slightly pink as she tried not to picture a very naked Blake doing just that. "I'll hold you to that," she said, and surprise and delight seemed to fight for dominance on his face until he gave in and smirked. "But this is your last warning, David." He blinked at the use of his first name, and she kept her face cold and blank. "If you lie to me one more time, I won't ever trust you again."

Blake's blue eyes held hers, and when he licked his lips she didn't look away. "I promise."

"Okay." She breathed out and closed her eyes, finding him still watching her when she opened them again. "Now what? Do we like, get tees made or something?"

He snorted and she grinned, though it faded quickly as she spotted tell-tale blue lights flashing through the foggy glass next to the front door. "Looks like they're here," Blake said, and she nodded.

"Can I get you anything?" She wanted to be busy. As tired as she was, it was the bone-deep kind that couldn't be cured with sleep. The kind that let you know that something had to give otherwise you would break. This had to be over soon. It just had to. "Soup?"

Blake groaned. "I've had enough soup to last me a lifetime."

"It's literally been two days, yet they call me dramatic."

"Two days of your cooking feels like–" He gave her wide eyes and coughed. "Um, heaven."

"Yeah, that's where I thought you were going with that," she said while he nodded earnestly and she tried not to laugh.

"I think there should be leftovers in the freezer," Blake murmured, limping over and rummaging through a drawer.

"Oh, now he tells me," she complained to Bailey, and he sneezed in agreement. "I found your hoard, by the way."

Blake froze with his head in the freezer. "My what?"

"Tell me, Blake..."

He looked up, eyes darting from side to side as he cleared his throat, and his nervousness made her curious about what, exactly, he thought she'd found. "Yes?"

"Do you know how to use the washer?"

A hint of a blush slowly crawled over his cheeks, and she bit back a grin. "Of course I do."

"Oh? So you were just, what, saving all those piles for later?"

"Yeah," he said, tugging at the unbuttoned collar of his shirt. "I, um–"

Rose couldn't hold it in any longer, bursting out laughing

at the uncomfortable look on his face, cackling louder when he blushed even more. "I know your secret now," she said breathlessly, and he scowled.

"You don't know nearly as much as you think, princess." There was a silky note in his voice that had her heart pounding, and she shot him a glare.

"Keep it in your pants, Blake."

"With sincere regret, DuLoe."

Grinning at each other over the kitchen island, for a second everything felt lighter, like their lives hadn't gone to absolute shit recently. Then her phone vibrated in her hand, and she sighed. "What is it, Jones?"

"A letter just arrived for you at the front gate. One of Mr Blake's guys is bringing it to you now. Call me back once you've opened it. I'm still out in the field."

"Why am I the one opening it?" Rose protested, but the beep of the call ending was all that answered her. "These guys are absolute jokes," she muttered. Had they not heard of the chain of evidence? Wouldn't it mess up any prints on the letter if she were to open it without them dusting it first? It was like they weren't even trying to catch this guy. What if she opened the letter and it had poison in it? Rose winced. She wouldn't be able to sue them from beyond the grave.

Blake raised an eyebrow as she walked through the hall and opened the front door, leaving it open as the security guard handed her the envelope. It was heavy, expensive paper just like the others, and the fear she felt was so strong it almost seemed ridiculous that it was because of the innocuous looking square in her hand.

"Do you want me to open it?"

Rose looked up at Blake's voice, knowing from the tight set of his mouth that he didn't like this any more than she did. "No, it's okay. I can do it, though I don't know why they're making me."

"You can do anything," he said, and she smiled, believing he meant every word. "Do you want to know something funny?" Blake's voice was closer now as he walked slowly over to her as her thumb opened the edge of the envelope.

"Sure," she said. He was trying to distract her, and she appreciated it, but there wasn't much that would be able to mute the horror of what was happening to them both.

"When I was at the hospital trying to find out what happened to you, they didn't want to tell me anything because I wasn't family."

Rose looked at him, the envelope now almost forgotten as she listened to his voice. She'd had the same thing when she was there too. The nurses had been tight-lipped about other patients but had put her in touch with her mom after confirming Rose's identity. She'd actually messaged her mom a few times since she'd left the hospital, and she'd said her dad was resting but recovering well, which had filled her with enough relief that she'd felt faint.

"So I leaned across the counter and into the nurse," Blake smiled slightly, and Rose wrinkled her nose, unsure she wanted to know where this was going, "and I asked *can you keep a secret?* And of course, everyone wants to know the gossip. Plus, I'm not dumb. I'm recognizable. A secret from David Blake? Irresistible." Blake smirked, and for a moment she was too caught up in his story to even think about looking at the envelope. "She said yes, of course. So I told her that it was under wraps right now because of the press, but that I very much considered my fiancée to be family. Her eyes got all wide and gooey – everybody loves to be in on a secret, you know, especially one about secret love

– and she had just called your floor when you found me first."

She was staring at him, she knew. Also knew that Jones was likely impatiently waiting on an update right now, but all she could do was carry on looking at Blake, like if she looked away he might become a mirage.

"So I suppose being my wife has some benefits after all, huh?" He grinned, and she let out a dry laugh and coughed. *My wife*. Crazy, ridiculous talk. She would sooner dissolve into goo than become Blake's anything, tentative friendship or no.

She turned back to the envelope and carefully peeled it open, feeling like her head was somehow clearer after talking to Blake. It was all undone when she saw the photograph. The blood on his face, the dirt and gravel and glass that stuck into him and the unnatural cant to his neck. The hand holding the photo shook, and her other hand pressed itself to her mouth as if to hold back her gasp of horror.

She'd never understood what people meant before when they spoke about trainwrecks, how they were awful but you couldn't look away. That was how she felt right then, like she would give anything to just close her eyes but knew the instant that she did so the image would be forever imprinted on her brain anyway so she just. kept. staring. For the first time since the crash, Rose was grateful she hadn't been able to turn and check he was okay because of her neck pain because seeing this... would have undone her.

Blake limped his way over to her and swore once he saw what she held in her hand. "Rose, it's okay. I'm fine. See?" His words didn't reach her, all she could see when she looked at him was the stillness of his face in the photo superimposed over the here and now. "Rose?"

She reached a shaking hand out and cupped his jaw, trying just to breathe, to remember how to cry so that maybe she could wash that image out of her eyes.

"Princess?" he said, and she didn't think she'd ever heard him say the nickname tenderly before, but he was now and she didn't know what to make of that, didn't know what to do with the way he was making her feel as he stood next to her but lay in complete devastation in the photograph gripped in her still shaking hand.

"Bastard," she managed to say through lips she realized were trembling, hadn't noticed the wetness running down her face until it trickled over her lips and she tasted salt. "H-he took our photo like a sick fucking souvenir. Who does that, Blake? Why would they do that to us?"

Blake grabbed her arms, pulling them into her chest before he wrapped his own around her and tucked her in close. "Oh, don't act like you've never thought about running me over for pleasure, princess."

It was like she'd opened a floodgate though, and now that the tears had started they weren't going to stop, and fuck Jones, fuck the bastard who was doing this to them. She was going to take this moment for her. For Blake. For her dad. And she sobbed into his shirt with the force of an elastic band snapping, like she'd been stretched too thin and this was her unleashing.

His hand found her hair, stroking it softly as he murmured words to her that she couldn't make out until her sobs started to ease and she realized he was singing a lullaby she'd once heard Grace murmur for Cara.

"David?"

"Yes?"

"I'm sorry I ruined your shirt."

His laugh rumbled through his chest and tickled her cheek. "It's okay, Rose."

She pulled away and wiped her long sleeve across her face, though it would do nothing for the puffiness that was probably starting to set in around her eyes. Her throat felt raw as she called Jones back and he answered with a sharp, "Well?"

"It's a photo of Blake, bleeding in the road after he was hit by the car."

"Okay," Jones said after a beat of silence. "Is there anything written on the back this time?"

She turned it over and bit her lip, feeling sick all over again. "It says, *Gotcha*."

"That's it?"

"Isn't that enough?" she snapped, and he fell silent. "I'm handing it back to the same guard as before. He'll meet you at the gate. And Jones? If you don't catch this guy soon, it's your head." She hung up and for a moment just clenched her phone in her hands, her head hanging forwards until she breathed out and looked up. "Are you ready for a real bed tonight?" Blake raised his eyebrows in interest, and she snorted. "As flattered as I am that you'd have me in this state, I mean to sleep. *Just* to sleep," she clarified when he looked set to interrupt her.

He sighed. "If you insist."

"I do," she said primly and linked one arm in his to help him up the stairs to his room. A few painful moments later, he was sliding under the covers, and she gave him a small smile as she made to leave, pausing as his hand caught hers.

"Do you want to stay? Just to sleep, I swear. Sometimes it's just nice to have someone there." Blake's voice was so quiet that if she hadn't strained her ears, she might have missed it, but she did, and so she squeezed his hand back.

"Just to sleep." Rose climbed into the bed on his other side, and for a moment it was quiet, the covers warm and the air cool. "Goodnight Blake."

"Sweet dreams, princess."

Chapter Sixteen

The thing they never show you on TV is how slow the cops work in real life. The time it takes them to get all their experts to analyze a scene, check out their databases for hits, identify random fibers that could be clues. Jones got in touch with them the day after she'd received the photo of Blake, predictably with nothing new to tell them, but she'd woken up in Blake's bed that morning surprisingly satisfied considering the lack of sex that had occurred.

They'd found nothing at the site of the rabbit killing. Their theory was it had been dropped into Blake's land from above via drone, but Rose was pretty sure they had no idea what was going on. The only thing they did seem sure of was that her 'admirer' was currently fixated on taking Blake out, at least that's why the cops thought he'd sent the photo of Blake injured to them separately from the one with her apology flowers. Like it was a warning of things to come.

The other thing they don't show you on TV is the red tape, the bureaucracy cops got caught in. They thought the escalation of violence meant their guy might attack tonight and were preparing to set-up a sting. Why they thought this would be successful, she had no idea. It wasn't like a swarm of cops outside Blake's house was exactly subtle.

"They're like a bunch of chickens, running around with their heads cut off but somehow still managing to squawk," Rose complained to Maia while Blake dealt with Jones.

"Damn," Maia sighed. "If they're treating the white folk like this, I shudder to think what the rest of us are dealing with."

Rose couldn't help but agree. "It's a fucking mess."

"How is it at Blake's though?" Maia's voice was sly, and Rose knew that what her friend really wanted to know was whether she'd had sex with Blake again.

"Blake's is fine," she said evasively. "Are you still staying with Cal?"

"Yes," Maia giggled, and Rose snickered.

"You have it bad."

"So do you," Maia retorted, and Rose pouted.

"Do not."

"That's funny because I'm pretty sure I saw in the paper that you're engaged–"

"Yeah well, they also said I was dead," Rose snorted. "Can't believe anything you read, darling."

They chatted for a few more minutes, and Rose closed her eyes. With Maia's voice in her ear, she could almost pretend that things were normal. A gentle tap on her bedroom door startled Rose awake, and she blinked around blearily.

The sun had gone down, and at some point Maia must have hung up. Blake stuck his head around the door, his hair sticking up at the back like he'd also just woken up from a nap.

He grinned at her. "Sleeping on the job, princess?"

The job? Her eyes flew wide. "Oh crap, have they started already?"

Blake nodded. He looked tired. Dark circles were smudged under his eyes, and his usual cocky smile had a sharp edge that she understood all too well. Rose groaned as she stood up and grabbed his hand, walking them both carefully down the stairs while Blake followed bemusedly.

"This is pointless," she said, breathing out deeply as they reached the kitchen and she snagged sodas for them both. "So what the guy sent me a photo of you? It doesn't mean he's coming after you any more than he was before. Maybe he was just trying to upset me."

Blake raised an eyebrow. "Upset you?"

"Well, yeah, you're my–" She glanced up as she spoke and saw the intrigued look in his eyes as he smirked.

"Your...?"

"Host," she blurted, and Blake bit his lip.

"Right." He winked. "Well, I think they're more worried about the escalation. He trashed your apartment before, but physically harming someone is on another level."

"Yeah, because he seemed so friendly when he was scrawling 'whore' all over my walls." Rose rolled her eyes, expecting Blake to laugh, and instead staring at him when he frowned. "Come on, let's go and sit down. This is a waste of time. I don't see how they expect this to be a success. A truckload of cops in your driveway isn't my idea of inconspicuous."

Blake shrugged. "I'm sure they know what they're doing."

"I'm not," she muttered and plopped down onto the sofa, careful not to slosh her drink. "So where are we at with the Gala? Are people still accepting invites?"

"Yep, some want in because they want the inside scoop on our situation, and the rest are just wanting to rub elbows with everyone else as usual." Blake eased himself down into the corner seat, smiling wryly, and she swallowed as his casual tee rode up. It was probably the most relaxed she'd seen him since she'd been here. Normally, he spent a portion of the day working and was in his usual shirt and slacks, but today...

Dark gray joggers that looked soft and well-worn made him seem more vulnerable than usual, and as she watched his long, tanned fingers tap an uneven beat on the sofa she realized she was staring.

"No such thing as bad press," she said eventually, and he chuckled. "Have your must-haves RSVPed yet?"

"Yep." Blake's leg jiggled as he turned on the TV, and she wondered what had him so keyed up. "Honestly, the only thing left to do is run the thing. Maia's been sending me vendor updates." She had?

"Oh," Rose said, and Blake shot her a look before glancing back to the TV.

"She didn't mention it?"

"We mostly spoke about Cal."

"Your cousin," Blake's smile became devious, and she knew without a doubt that he was remembering their encounter in the restroom at *The Hummingbird*. A torch shone past the window, and the muscles in his arm tensed. He was nervous, she realized. She had been so focused on her own belief that this 'sting' was a waste of time that she hadn't even noticed he was worried the cops might be right.

It made sense. The bastard had run them off the road, but in all the time she'd known him, she didn't think she'd ever seen David Blake *unsure.*

Rose stood and walked to the door, looking out past the blinds at the cops as they found their places inside bushes and the maintenance shed before she pulled on the lever to flip the slats over.

"What are you doing?"

The truth was that she wasn't sure, but it didn't seem right that this guy had taken away Blake's confidence. Her anxiety had already been through the roof. It was just presenting in a different way than before, so really, her stalker had done her a favor by showing her just how bad things had gotten without her even realizing it. But Blake? He'd always been cocky. Always been ready to meet her toe-to-toe with an insult or retort.

"Rose?" She turned to face him, and he leaned forward, resting his forearms on his knees. "I think we need to stay alert—"

"I think you need to relax," she said smoothly, and his mouth snapped shut as she walked over to him. When she sank onto her knees, he released a breath that shook. "Do you want this?" She rested a hand lightly on his knee, and his eyes burned with heat as he watched her.

"Yes."

"Then take what you want from me, Blake."

He was quiet for a moment, assessing her, maybe considering how much he could really do while his body still healed itself but, eventually, he reached down to the bulge that had been growing bigger since she'd knelt down. "Open your mouth for me, princess."

She did as he said and tried not to squirm impatiently

when he pulled his dick out and began stroking it languidly before raising his hips up closer to her lips. One hand reached out and sank into her hair, massaging her scalp as he guided her face down to meet him.

He was warm on her tongue, salty and smoky, and she let out a hum of appreciation as her tongue curled around his tip and he hissed out a breath.

Rose looked up at Blake as her mouth took more of him in, and he swore, watching her like he couldn't look away even if the house burned down around them. "That's it, baby. More."

Moving farther down, she gagged a little, and he tugged at her hair lightly until she slowed her pace, working her mouth up and down his shaft as he let out a groan.

The hand in her hair tightened and she knew what he wanted, giving him a nod as she suctioned so hard her cheeks hollowed and he gave a shout, hips bucking upwards.

"Do you like the feel of me on your tongue?" Blake panted, and she licked him in response. "Do you want me to fuck your mouth now, princess?" Rose moaned around him, and he smirked. "That's what I thought."

His hand slid around to the back of her head as he held her head in place, slamming his hips upwards so that he could drive between her lips, ragged breaths leaving him as he got closer to the edge, and her eyes watered but she didn't move away. "Good girl. You can take it, baby."

She pressed her legs together to alleviate some of the tension she could feel building inside herself too, and his eyes darkened when he noticed.

"Are you wet, baby? Do you want me inside you?"

She moaned around his head as he slid out of her mouth

almost all the way before sliding back in, his hips moving faster and faster.

"I'm going to come in your mouth, princess. You're going to swallow, aren't you?"

Rose flicked her tongue around his head as he pushed in and he moaned her name when he came, shooting down her throat and panting in satisfaction when he watched her swallow.

"Lie back on the sofa, Rose."

She stood on shaky legs and sat backwards, shivering at the feel of his warm hands on her legs as he pulled down her yoga pants. He smiled slightly when he saw the wet patch forming through her panties and stroked a finger lightly over it.

"It's your turn to come now, princess."

She nodded eagerly and sighed with relief when he hooked her panties with two fingers and dragged them down over her hips. He wasted no time, watching intently as his finger parted her folds and stroked over her clit before lifting it away and tasting her on his skin.

"Next time," he promised, a gleam in his eye that said he planned on keeping his word. "Is this what you want, baby?" One finger slid into her pussy, curling upwards and making her gasp as she bore down on it. "Or maybe two?" Another finger joined the first as his thumb circled her clit. "You make the most delicious sounds, princess."

As if for emphasis, she couldn't hold back the long moan that escaped her mouth as Blake began to slowly finger-fuck her.

"You took three before, right? I think you can take even more than that, princess, but we'll see." A third finger filled her too, and she felt deliciously tight as they rubbed her from the inside. She squirmed for him, wanting his hand to *move,* and he chuckled. "Faster?" he asked, and she nodded. Blake sped up minimally, and she moaned in frustration. "Say my name, baby, and I'll make you come."

"Blake," she panted, and he rewarded her, speeding up and pressing down on her g-spot until her legs fell open wide, needing everything he would give her. Then he slowed again, and she growled.

"Say my name," he repeated, and she scowled while he laughed.

"Bla—"

"That's not my name."

She blinked at him as he plunged into her deeply, and her breath stuttered out of her.

"I want you to moan it for me, and then I'll make you come, princess."

She moved her hips restlessly, trying to fuck herself on his fingers, but he just tutted and pulled them slightly farther away while she swore.

Two fingers rolled over her clit, and then suddenly he was in her again, pumping hard, and she was almost there, so close to orgasming her eyes were slipping closed when he spoke.

"Say it for me, Rose." He curled his fingers at exactly the right spot, and she exploded.

"David!" His eyes were so blue as they locked onto hers, watching her as she came on his fingers.

"I guess we just have to hope that they didn't hear that outside." He grinned, and she blushed but the truth was that she wasn't sure anymore if she cared whether they'd been heard. They settled back against the couch as Blake put on some cooking show that immediately made her zone out while she replayed what had just happened in her mind. She'd called Blake's name. He'd called her *baby*. Rose got the feeling that they were entering dangerous waters if they continued playing with fire like this.

A knock on the patio door made them look up and Blake headed over, nodding at Jones through the glass when he indicated his phone.

They picked up a moment later when it rang. "No sign of anything so far. We'll stay the night, but nothing is looking likely at this point. We'll wake you if there are any developments."

Blake nodded, murmuring his thanks while she stared pointedly away from the phone. If this went on much longer, she was going to have to see about hiring someone privately who actually knew what they were doing, because at this point, she didn't feel like that was really the Cincinnati PD.

Chapter Seventeen

Bailey was barking – that in and of itself was odd, as he was generally very quiet and well-behaved. Stranger still, it didn't seem to be at any one thing. He was just zooming all over the house growling.

"Maybe the officers yesterday night spooked him?" She suggested when Blake tried in vain again to quieten him down.

Blake ran his hands through his hair. "I've got no idea what's wrong with him. He's never been like this before. Maybe all the tension finally got to him? Do you think I should call the vets?"

Rose paused, surprised that he'd asked for her opinion. "Animals are supposed to be more sensitive than humans, right? But if it'll give you peace of mind, you could call them for some advice." Rose shrugged, mostly just wishing Bailey would shut up soon. She loved the pup but damn did his bark echo.

"Bailey, *enough*," Blake groaned, and then they both

sighed in relief when Bailey finally stopped, sinking down on his bed in the kitchen with a whine.

They'd been sitting at the kitchen island for the last two hours and Rose's ass was now numb. She missed the plush stools that Maia had picked for their breakfast bar in the suite – she'd been able to sit and drink margaritas for hours in those.

Another photo had arrived earlier that day and now sat innocuously on the counter like it wasn't the most worrying of them all. On the surface it wasn't that bad. It was a photo of a house. Nowhere near so bad as Blake's beat-up face, looking like he was dead.

The problem was that it was Blake's house, and it looked like the photo had been taken from inside the gates, but it was far enough away that it was hard to tell. The cops had, of course, taken it as another sign that things were escalating and were staking the house out again. It was no wonder Bailey was on edge. They all were.

"What are you going to do when you get your freedom back?" She grinned at Blake and was surprised when he didn't smile back.

"I haven't thought much about it."

"Really?" God, it felt like it was all she was thinking about lately. Unbidden, she remembered the way she'd called his name last night, the way he'd slipped from *princess* to *baby*. That was... intimate, right? It had definitely felt intimate.

Blake shrugged. "It's been nice having the more permanent type of company."

She blinked, not expecting any variation of that sentiment to ever come out of Blake's mouth. What was it he'd said to her before? *Just because I don't date doesn't make me a fuckboy. It just means I already know what I want.* So if Blake wasn't looking forward to resuming normal practice with his rotating door of women, what *did* he want?

Rose drank the last of her soda and stood up, intending to head for bed, and was surprised when Blake did so too. She raised an eyebrow at him, but he just shrugged nonchalantly as they made their way up the stairs.

Bailey had settled down, now only softly growling as they made their way upstairs, and as she turned away to go into her room, Blake's hand slid around her waist.

She'd expected a cocky smile, or even a dirty remark, and instead found a thoughtful look on his face as he pulled her a little closer.

"Sleep with me again tonight."

"*Just* sleep?"

He frowned like he was thinking about it again, before he nodded and then came the cocky smile she'd been expecting before. "If you want."

She could only assume she was so taken aback that she'd found herself in a temporary state of madness because she hesitated only for a second before saying, "Okay."

It had felt natural the other night. They'd been through something crazy together, and sometimes you just needed to not be alone. But this... sure, things were still crazy, but it just felt less about that and more about... them.

Blake's eyebrows flew up like he'd expected her to say no but, instead of replying, he just gripped her waist tighter as they made their way to his room, releasing her only when they got inside so he could take off his shirt and she looked hastily away from his chest.

She did her teeth in his bathroom and took her evening dose of medication without feeling self-conscious and when they settled down into bed, she was shocked at how *right* it felt, falling asleep in the dark almost immediately.

BLAKE WAS GONE when she woke up, his side of the bed still warm and smelling faintly of his cologne. He was an even earlier riser than Rose, and she suspected that was when he usually worked out because she hadn't seen him do so much as a press up since she'd been here, but there was no way he looked like *that* if he wasn't doing some serious upkeep.

Rose sniffed delicately and then propped herself up in confusion at the lack of bacon-smell that usually wafted up the stairs. The only times Blake hadn't cooked her breakfast was when he'd been recovering and was too sore to leave the couch. But he'd cooked for her yesterday and had no trouble. Maybe he was simply busy and she had been spoiled, getting used to the smell of cooking food waking her up instead of her alarm clock.

She swung her feet out of bed and something crinkled under her heel. God, if that was a condom wrapper...

It was a photograph. There was nothing written on the back and face down it could have just been Blake's, but dread started in her stomach and began to clog up her airways as she slowly reached down to pluck it from the floor.

It was the TV room. Blake was reclined on the sofa, his arm stretched out and tangled in a familiar blonde head of hair. Her hand flew over her mouth as she realized that this was from the other night and in the photo she had Blake's dick in her mouth. From the angle it looked like someone had grabbed a quick shot in between a gap in the slats covering the glass door. Someone had been there, watching them, that whole time.

Rose was grateful for her empty stomach then as it rolled and she gagged. Had Blake found this when he woke up and gone to speak to Jones? No, surely he wouldn't have left without telling her or just left the photo carelessly on the ground.

She stood up, the room swaying violently in front of her as she fought to calibrate her senses. Where was Bailey? Maybe he'd taken the dog out for a walk. Rose checked the time on her phone and bit her lip. It was later than she'd expected. The tension from the last few days had clearly worn her down, but if he had taken Bailey out they would have been back by now usually. She tried whistling for him and waited with her breath held to hear the clatter of claws on wood. Her heart beat faster when the house remained silent.

Something was wrong. But how could it be when the cops had been outside the house all night? Should still be out there right now? Nobody could have gotten in or out without them knowing... Unless the stalker was one of them. Those damned boots rose up in her mind again, and Rose felt her heart beating in her throat.

If she couldn't trust the cops, it made sense that she couldn't trust the security team either. Who knew where this guy had infiltrated? It was the only thing that made sense – how else would he be able to get in and out of anywhere, send her these messages, and know where she was constantly unless he'd been getting that information on the inside? So who could she trust?

She took two deep breaths and decided to text a quick 911 to Noah and hoped he was awake to see it. If he'd been on the night shift... The message showed as read and she breathed a sigh of relief. Maybe it was overzealous, but her gut told her something wasn't right here and that photo... It was next to the bed. Noah was a good guy. She knew she could trust him. But even if he did get here to help, it would take him at least twenty minutes in the car without traffic interfering.

Rose made her way to the bedroom door and opened it slowly, her heart beating so wildly she wondered if it could be heard outside her chest. Her palms were slick on the metal knob, half-expecting there to be a face waiting for her on the other side like in a horror movie.

The hall was empty. Rose let out a shallow breath that got stuck in her throat as she spotted another photo on the floor just a few steps outside the bedroom door. It was the fridge in the kitchen. The room was dark, but she could make out the glow of Bailey's eyes in the flash, the baring of his teeth as he growled. She dropped the photo to the floor and turned her head to check both ends of the corridor. One of the cons to a house this size, it was hard to know whether you were the hunter or the hunted. Another glimmer of white on the floor had her stepping towards the main staircase, adrenaline coursing through her and making her legs tingle as she bent, looking at the photos from random parts of the house that were scattered down the steps. Her eyes caught on a picture that made her freeze with one foot in the air, about to descend. It was her face, asleep. Her lashes were curled peacefully across her cheeks, Blake was just a large form to her right, the camera was clearly focused on her.

How had the flash not woken her up? What should she do now? This guy was clearly inside the house, had been for a while judging by the photos – Bailey's odd behavior last night suddenly added up and she groaned. They had been so stupid.

She didn't know where Blake or Bailey were, didn't know where the intruder was either. What was she supposed to do now? Should she alert the cops on the off chance this guy wasn't one of their own?

Decision made, Rose followed the trail of photos downstairs, looking at them only to avoid slipping as she made her way down and to the front door and came to a shocked stop as she saw the chains folded around the double handle. She could try and get to the back door in the kitchen, but she could see the trail of photos led her that way and she doubted very much that the intruder was leading her to an escape. Or, she could get this over with and let them know she was awake and done playing.

Hoping Blake wouldn't mind too much about the damage, Rose reached for the ceramic bowl where Blake kept his keys and strode for the skinny window next to the front door, slinging her arm back and punching out with it as hard as she could. Her arm felt like it was on fire as the bowl shattered and the glass cracked, a small hole forming as the sound split the quiet.

Her breathing was harsh as she looked at the small break. The cops were trained to notice that stuff, right? She could try and widen the hole and escape but... Blake. She couldn't leave him here with this psycho. *If he was even alive.* The thought made her breath hitch. No. Of course he was alive. He had to be.

Nothing seemed to move, like the house was holding its breath as she moved out of the foyer and towards the kitchen, trying to look ahead and see if anyone was in there. Nothing. It looked empty. There was a pile of more photos sitting on the counter, right on top was one of Blake, his blue eyes defiant as blood dripped into his eye and stuck to his hair. Tape covered his mouth and Rose gripped the edge of the picture tightly, forcing herself to focus on the other elements in the photo like the color of the wall behind him (beige), the reflection of a window in his pupils (bright). She was so focused on trying to work out where Blake was being held that she didn't hear the first footstep as the door to the laundry room swung open.

A hand gripped her elbow tightly and she didn't waste another breath, just screamed as loudly as she could, straight from her belly. If the cops didn't notice the smashed glass, surely they would hear *that*. They couldn't all be in on it.

Her face whipped to the side as she was backhanded, landing in a sprawl on the floor. She flipped her hair out of her face, glad that most of it was still tied up, but not thrilled about facing this guy in her PJs. She scrambled up, touching her still-bleeding hand to her mouth and cursing at the sting. That was definitely going to swell.

"So glad you could make it," she said sarcastically. "We wondered if you were ever going to show. I don't like to be kept waiting."

"I'm sorry, Rose. Busy schedule and all." His hood obscured his face, but the voice was vaguely familiar.

"Leaving your hood up in-doors? How gauche." The man laughed as she put the island between them and the sound made her skin crawl because he genuinely sounded *happy,* like they were friends meeting up for drinks.

"I figured we knew each other well enough by now to do away with the rules for company," the man said pleasantly and Rose shifted uneasily, trying to ignore the blood slowly dripping onto the floor by her bare feet. "Oh dear, look what you've done to yourself," he tutted. "Stupid bitch."

"Well that took a turn," she said mildly, willing her voice not to shake even as her head ached from the force of adrenaline no doubt tunneling through her. "It definitely seems like you think you know a lot about me, darling. But I can assure you that I don't know anything about you."

"Liar," he laughed, and she wasn't sure what to say. Did he really think they had some sort of relationship? Like he was leaving her sweet gifts this whole time? "It's sad, really," he continued on, "you think that *he* knows you? You think he'll whisper sweet nothings in your ear while you whore yourself out for him on the bathroom floor?"

"Is he alive?"

"Sure." She wasn't sure she believed the casual way he said as much and she thought she could see a shadow of a grin beneath his hood. "But only because I want to take my time with him after."

"After what?"

"After we talk, Rose. After I make you see how right we are for each other."

Rose rolled her eyes even as her mouth dried out, who the hell was this guy?

He didn't like that, slamming his fist down onto the counter. "He's no good for you, Rose. He doesn't know you like I know you." There was a kind of hysteria to his words, a desperation for her to, what? Agree?

"How cliché. You know, the kitchen is where the knives are kept," she said, reaching for the longest one and drawing it out with a hand that shook. "Did you not think this through before leading me here? Or are you just stupid?"

A small twist of lips was visible as the man lifted his head and reached into his hoodie pocket, pulling out a gun and laying it down on the counter like it was more of an offering than a threat, and it felt like her blood turned to ice in her veins.

"Where's Blake and Bailey?" she repeated, hating the way her voice shook.

"The mutt? He tried to bite me and then ran off before I could wring its skinny neck."

Relief made her hand shake so violently that she wasn't sure if holding the knife was still a good idea.

"And Blake?" she tried again.

"Didn't you look at my photos? I already told you. He's busy." A pale hand reached up and slid his hood back, a smile ready and waiting on his face as he took in her shock. "So now there's nothing stopping us from being together, Rose."

She could only stare. When the cops had initially asked her if she had any enemies or anyone that would attempt to harm her, *he* hadn't even made the list, but that was the drawback of the internet – hell, even the papers. You saw enough about someone that after a while you felt like you knew them. "Tim?"

His smile dropped and he picked up the gun. "My name is *Tom*."

"Right, right, of course," she said, keeping one eye on the gun his hand had tightened on. "Silly me." How long had she been down here? She glanced quickly at the fancy-ass clock Blake had installed above his sink and wanted to groan. How had it been only five minutes since she'd got out of bed? Noah would barely be on his way. She needed to stall Tom if she wanted to walk away from this.

A scowl darkened his face, and her stomach clenched so

hard she thought she might throw up at any second. "This is the problem with girls like you, more air in your head than brains. So entitled. So *blind* to what's right in front of you!"

"And what's right in front of me would be... you?" Tom's eyes were flat and dark and she shivered as his stare seemed to spread a coldness within her that felt penetrating, like she'd never shake it. "Is Blake okay?"

Tom laughed harshly, and she flinched. "Blake this, Blake that, *why do you care?* Is his dick really that good?"

Her temper flared, and she snapped before thinking. "He's my – friend."

"Oh yeah, you looked so friendly on the sofa the other night."

Nausea churned through her again at the thought of him watching them and she dropped any sort of pleasantness her face might have held up until that moment. They always teach you to stay calm if you're ever held at gunpoint, to just keep quiet, keep your head down. It was easier said than done. This guy had wrecked her life, and for what? "That's the problem with guys like *you,* Tim. You're a fucking pervert who thinks they're entitled to a woman's attention just because she smiled at you one time. For the record, I *hate* red wine and you were an inconceivable ass on that *one* date we had. Get over yourself."

The safety clicked off as he pointed the gun at her, face white with rage. "You don't know what you're talking about."

"No? You think you know me, Tim?"

"*Tom.*"

"Right, that's what I said." She smiled at him even though her tongue felt heavy and dark spots danced at the edges of her vision. She just had to hold on a little longer. Noah would come. He had to. "You don't know anything about me, Tim. Blake, though? He knows *everything* – what expression I make when I come, what my pussy tastes like after he's fucked me, does that make me a slut to you?" She laughed. "What, did you follow me on socials? Read about me in your magazines and jack off? Pathetic." His finger twitched on the trigger and she knew she needed to de-escalate the situation, shouldn't have let her temper run away with her as much as she had but, god, it felt good to finally let loose. "What about Samantha?" she said, trying to distract him and letting out a slow breath when it worked and Tom's eyebrows furrowed.

"What about her?" His finger relaxed on the trigger, and she tried not to signal her relief.

"How did you get her to set me up on the date with you?"

He shrugged lightly. "She's my cousin." Of course she fucking was. God, she'd always known Samantha was a psychopath – clearly it ran in the family. "We're meant to be together, Rose. You know it, too."

"But what was the point in all this? The flowers, the photos, the *threats,* did you think it would make me love you?"

"I wanted to make you see." Tom waved a hand airily, and she kept her eyes trained on the gun. "I wanted to win you back."

"By running me off the road?"

"I apologized for that," he said, jaw tight. "I never meant to hurt you."

"Just Blake, right?"

Tom shrugged. "All's fair in love and war."

God, how deluded could a person be? Rose looked at the clock out of the corner of her eye. Fifteen minutes. She just needed to stall a little longer. "How did you even get in here? The cops are outside, looking for you."

He smirked and leaned forward against the counter casually. "If you weren't so self-absorbed, maybe you'd remember me telling you I work in private security."

Gee, for someone who claimed to love her, he sure had a lot of shitty things to say. "You have a badge."

"It does help, yes, but more than anything I *blend in*."

God, she'd been right not to trust the cops. They were the ones who'd put them at risk in the first place! Tom had probably waltzed in with them yesterday and then never left. "That's why you left the rabbit, to get inside." He nodded with a smug smile and she wanted to scream because that was on her, she'd fallen for his trick along with the rest of them. Rose took a calming breath and said as pleasantly as she could manage, "And the paparazzi tailing me? The press leaks? Those were all you?"

His footsteps were heavy as he rounded the counter, laughing cruelly as she scrambled back in the other direction and then reversed when he moved back to his original position. "The leaks, yes. The paps I can't claim all the credit for, but I did give them the occasional nudge knowing you would blame *him*. Annoying little bastards."

It disturbed her that she agreed. "If not the paps, then how did you always know how to find me?"

"You haven't exactly been inconspicuous." Tom grinned and she shivered, sensing an end to his patience soon. "I might have had to sneak around at first to get that camera in – did you know it came with audio? – but once I realized how far I could get with my uniform on, I didn't have to hide or sneak around to get a keycard for the suite. You should probably fix that."

"I'll get right on it," she said dryly and then swore when the knife shook and she almost nicked herself. "What are you going to do with me, Tom?" It had been over twenty minutes since she'd first texted Noah. Unless the traffic was horrific – which was possible but unlikely at this time on a Sunday – he wasn't coming.

He tilted his head to the side, a piece of milky blonde hair falling onto his forehead. "Whatever I want." She swallowed thickly, and he smiled. "That alarms you, I see. But it's okay, Rose. I know that you want me. Deep down you know I would be better to you than Blake ever would." His face twisted as he said Blake's name, and she knew that she'd stalled as long as she could. It was now or never.

There was no way all of the cops outside could miss a gunshot. At the very least, they would be able to find and help Blake, and if she played her cards right he might even shoot her somewhere that she could survive.

"I would rather die," she said honestly and smiled gently as she remembered what she'd said to Blake when he'd proposed her moving in – *I would rather gouge out my own eyes*. Maybe she did have a flair for the dramatic after all, but if she was going to die she wasn't going to do it being nice to this bastard.

"Bitch," he said, swinging the gun up again and aiming at her head as his face closed off to her, and Rose swayed on her feet.

"Original," she rasped and flinched as he cocked the gun.

"You are nothing." Tom sneered at her, spit flying through the air as he gestured, and each wave of the gun made her shrink back farther. "You weren't worth it. You bitches never are."

A scuff in the doorway made her look up hopefully – *Noah?*

Instead, a familiar blue gaze locked onto hers as Blake snarled. "She's worth everything."

The world became a blur as he charged Tom, knocking him to the ground and hitting him with a punch that clearly dazed him – or maybe he just couldn't decide who to aim for: her or Blake. They tangled together on the floor and then the gun fired with a boom of sound that made her ears vibrate, unable to even hear her own scream as Blake rolled off of Tom and onto the wooden flooring. Her hearing came back fuzzy as the sound of the front door breaking floated to her but all she could see was Blake on the floor.

She ran and slipped on her own blood as she sank down beside him and pressed her hands to his lower shoulder where the blood seemed to be gushing from, trying to ignore how warm his blood was on her toes. Tears obscured her vision and she blinked them away, trying to focus on Blake. Was he breathing?

A hand grasped her chin as Tom staggered upright and then let go as he fell again. Voices called out to her, but she was frozen. Her skin felt like ice, and Tom's touch still burned on her face despite him letting go. He aimed the barrel at her between her eyes as he stumbled upright once more and she could see where it still faintly smoked from the bullet that had taken down Blake.

Something hard dug into her hand and it was only then that she noticed the deep, throbbing ache in her leg. The knife. She yanked it out from where it had sunk into her thigh when she fell just as Tom smirked at her, saying words she couldn't hear past the pounding of her pulse in her ears.

Rose thrust the knife forward, screaming unintelligibly, or maybe she was crying, she couldn't be sure anymore.

The knife sliced into his arm holding the gun, and she knew she would never forget the way it tugged at his flesh. Tom's mouth dropped open in shock even as his finger tightened on the trigger. She closed her eyes, leaving her hand pressed against Blake's shoulder to try and stem the bleeding. Not wanting to see when her end came for her.

A bang exploded and she instinctively ducked down, her head pressed into Blake's neck, but it had come from the wrong direction. She tried to look up, but Blake's hand tightened in her hair, forcing her eyes to his as he breathed shallowly.

"Fuck, that hurt more than I expected it to," he said, and she didn't know whether to laugh or cry or scream. "Why the tears, princess? I thought you'd be glad to get rid of me."

She sobbed harder as she cradled his face, ignoring the bloody handprint she left behind. "How could you do this to me? How could you do this?"

Blake's face was pale but he smiled as he closed his eyes. "Save your life, you mean? Oh, I don't know. Had nothing in the calendar, I guess. Plus, I suppose when you've been in love with someone for most of your life, it's hard to just watch them die."

She hissed in a shaking breath. "You're delirious. This is *not* okay." His breathing stuttered and she moaned with fear. "Blake, I–" she choked, and he coughed out a laugh.

"Wow, I'm bleeding out and you still can't admit it."

Dizziness swept in, and she slurred words without knowing what she was saying as her hand became weightless. Hands grasped her shoulders and the yelling resumed.

"Princess? Princess, where are you hurt?"

"Was she shot?"

"I don't think so."

A hand tugged Blake's arm off her lap. "Fuck."

Then she couldn't remember anything except a gentle pull on her hair and Blake's voice. "I can't believe you outdid me taking a bullet for you. Not everything's a competition, princess." His voice wobbled and she sighed against him, awash in a sea of warmth as the darkness finally consumed her.

Chapter Eighteen

"You know you're going to have to talk to him at some point, right?" Maia fluffed her hair in the mirror hanging on the wall in the foyer as Rose finished lacing up her strappy silver heels.

"Why's that?" she asked, and Maia frowned disapprovingly until Rose sighed. "I'm grateful for what he did–"

"The man took a bullet for you!"

"Keep your voice *down*," Rose gritted out, glancing around to make sure her mother hadn't heard. It was bad enough listening to her crow about Blake's heroic feats constantly, but to have Maia doing it too? Rose's mother needed no encouragement. "So, what? I owe him now?"

"That's not what I'm saying and you know it." Maia pouted as she slicked on a pretty pink gloss that popped against her dark skin.

"Whatever, I'm going to his stupid gala because I organized it. I can't really mix booze with my anxiety meds, so the free bar isn't worth staying for."

Maia sighed but wisely shut up when Rose's mom swanned into the room on a cloud of blue organza. "Going to snag yourself a hot date, Mom?"

"Well, I will be if Graham doesn't get his sweet behind down those stairs pronto," she called overly loudly, and Rose couldn't help but smile as her dad called down from upstairs.

"Gross," she said affectionately, pressing a kiss to her mom's cheek. "We'll see you there."

"You are not leaving this house until I get a photo of you both!"

They left the house twenty minutes later, cheeks aching from holding their smiles in place for so long while her mom darted around grabbing photos from various angles.

"Got to give her props," Maia said once they were safely in the car and her phone started blowing up as Annabel sent over all the photos, "your mom knows how to handle her lighting."

Rose laughed. It had been nice spending some more time with her mom and dad the last two weeks while she stayed with them. The suite was still being repaired and cleared by the cops for release, but even if it wasn't, she wasn't sure that she wanted to go back. When it was late at night, she often found herself missing the quiet of another home, missing the soft click of claws on wood, even missed—

"Wow," Maia said as they pulled up to a familiar set of gates and found them covered in fairy lights. The house was lit up and Rose felt an odd pang in her chest as she looked up at the window overlooking the driveway. Blake's room.

The party was in full swing by the time they arrived, fashionably late but not rude. The charity auction hadn't yet started, and despite what she'd told Maia, Rose found herself reaching for a glass of champagne as a waiter passed by. One drink wouldn't hurt, after all, and she'd picked out this brand. It was the really good stuff.

People heading in stared as soon as they walked in through the door and made their way to the ballroom. She wished it was because her rose-gold dress was beautiful or because Maia had styled her hair to perfection, but it was something far simpler than admiration – it was awe. Gossip. Like she was a living legend. Because how did a girl like that – blonde? Tall? Rich? – take down a man twice her size? Well, they all knew the answer to that too. In fact, she knew he'd spotted her walk in when a ripple of heads seemed to split down the middle, half watching Rose and the others watching Blake.

She quickly moved in the other direction, the strange feeling of both belonging and being the odd one out prevailing as she swept through the room. It was weird being back here, and she wasn't sure that she'd ever be able to go into the kitchen and not see bloodstains on the floor, even if they had likely already been cleaned up.

She'd woken up in hospital three weeks ago with Noah and her mother at her side. It had been him who had shot Tom before he could kill her – he'd come after all, and Rose had been supremely grateful. She'd actually hired him to be her full-time guard, having now experienced one of the worst-case scenarios personally, it didn't seem so laughable anymore. She'd given him the evening off today, knowing that the gala would have plenty of security. The cops had been all but useless, as predicted, and the list of people she was actively suing had grown unnervingly large.

"I tried to come and see you," a low voice said in her ear as she lurked by the buffet table, making sure everything that was supposed to be there had arrived. Her team was impeccable, but everyone made mistakes sometimes.

"That's nice," she said vaguely and could practically feel the wave of annoyance coming off of Blake at her reply.

"My shoulder's healing well," he tried again. "It was through and through, and I was lucky enough that it didn't damage the muscle too badly."

"I'm glad," she replied, eyes on the room as they all watched her.

"So, luckily for you, that means I can dance tonight." Her reply was cut off in a yelp as Blake snagged her around the waist and tugged her into the middle of the room. There was a band in the corner playing something bland, but they slunk into a waltz as Blake steered her around the room.

"*What* are you doing?" She pasted on a smile and spat the words at him through her teeth and Blake grinned, knocking the breath out of her as she saw him up close for the first time in weeks.

"Oh, so you *can* look at me when you talk. Excellent. I mean, I did nearly die for you."

The words sent a fiery hot rage tunneling through her and she narrowed her eyes. "Of course I can look at you. I'd just prefer not to."

His smile faded, but one dimple remained as the muscle in his jaw flexed. "Really, princess? After everything? You still hate my guts?"

Rose clenched her jaw as she looked past his head and out at the crowd, frowning at a smirking Maia as they breezed past on a turn.

"Or maybe what you're feeling is the opposite of hate," he whispered in her ear, his warm breath stirring the small tendrils of hair there and making her shiver. Lips ghosted over her neck, and she pulled back with a stab of irritation and desire.

"What I do or don't feel is not your concern."

Blake pulled her in closer, his hand warm on the small of her back, his chest solid and firm against hers as they danced.

"Come on, Rose. Tell me why you won't look at me. Tell me why you flinch when I say your name. It's been almost a month! You won't take my calls, you won't let me see you. The only way I even know you're still alive is because your mom told me."

Her face turned sharply to look at him as he steered them around the floor, lone dancers amongst a staring crowd. "Because you nearly *died*. You nearly died for me."

Blake's mouth dropped open slightly, his blue eyes lighting up, and she couldn't help but wish he didn't have the stupid gel in his hair so she could feel how soft it was against her fingers where her hands were locked around the back of his neck. "You're mad."

"Damn right I'm mad," she growled and he laughed, a full belly laugh as he stopped them in the middle of the dance floor and left her staring.

"You care about me," he taunted, and she frowned. Not denying it but definitely not admitting anything either, not while he continued to laugh at her. "Well, princess, that's all I needed to know." Then he dropped her hand and left her standing there as Maia made her way over.

"What was that about?"

"Just Blake being an ass, as usual."

"Darling," her mother chided as she walked up arm in arm with her dad. "That's no way to talk after what Blake did for you."

Maia pinched her as she opened her mouth, and Rose grimaced.

A tinkling sound rang through the air, and they all turned to look at Blake who stood off to the side on the slightly raised stage ready for the bachelor auction.

"Thank you all for coming," he said over the quiet chatter, and Rose glared at a woman across from her who was staring dreamily in his direction. "It's a pleasure to have you here in my home. As you all know, it's been a difficult past few weeks... well, a difficult month or so, really." A few people tittered, and she forced her hands to unclench. "I'm grateful for your support here today, but I do have some news that some of the ladies may find disappointing. Please know my heart does break a little to tell you this."

It felt as if the crowd leaned forward, but maybe it was just her. *What is he doing?*

"I won't be participating in this year's bachelor auction." A few gasps and cries of distress actually sounded out, and Rose shot the offenders a glare. Seriously? They were that desperate? She sniffed dismissively, and Maia chuckled. "However, I do have happier news to share... or rather, confirm."

Rose's heart beat quicker in her chest, and the small sweat she'd worked up spinning around the floor with Blake cooled quickly against her skin.

"I'm engaged!" Blake beamed out at the crowd, and Rose felt sick, like the bottom had been dropped out under her. The room span for a second and Maia gripped her arm tightly, the sensation all that kept her from throwing up. *Her Blake? Engaged?* She could barely hear Blake over the cheers and whooping and even a few catcalls, but then something did stand-out. Her name.

Suddenly the room was turning like a tide and a sea of faces beamed up at her. He hadn't just said what she thought he had, had he?

In case there was any doubt, Blake smirked at her from the stage. "Don't be shy, Rose."

Maia was gaping at her, and Rose's mother looked like she was about to explode from both glee and rage. No. No way had he just told everyone in this room, and therefore by extension the entirety of Cincinnati, that they were engaged. As in, to be *married*.

God, her mom was going to think Rose had kept this from her deliberately. Maia shoved her in the back, and Rose threw Maia a look over her shoulder as she was jostled to the front and stood with her hands on her hips looking up at Blake.

"What are you playing at?" she whispered angrily, and he winked.

"I just didn't want to hide it anymore, princess," Blake said loudly and she groaned. Crap. If her mom wasn't already pissed, then that was about to change.

"You're in for a world of pain," she said in his ear as he walked off the stage and pulled her into an embrace that she tried not to return.

"Thank you, sweetheart, you look fabulous this evening too." Blake winked at the crowd still watching them as the music started up again and Rose stared out at them passively.

"Why did you do that?"

"Do what?"

"Do – Are you *high*?"

"No, but I did get the good stuff while I was in the hospital. Not that you'd know because you never visited." Blake straightened his navy tie, and she looked away awkwardly as he paused. "Oh." A grin tugged at his mouth, and he bit his lip. "You did, didn't you?"

"I–"

"Come on, Rose. What are you fighting, exactly?"

"My mother is going to murder you, and then me, for lying about this and getting her hopes up."

"Lying? I did no such thing." Blake grinned at her, and she wasn't sure if she wanted to kiss or hit him.

"That's funny. I think I'd remember agreeing to marry you."

"Always with the memory..." He tutted and she flushed as she remembered how he'd decided to make things more *memorable* for her on the bathroom floor not so long ago.

"Okay. If not my mom, then my dad will definitely have something to say that you didn't ask his permission first."

"Oh, I imagine he would. Except I did ask his permission."

"You – what?"

Blake smirked. "You wouldn't let me visit you in the hospital, but your dad had no such reservations."

"But that was *weeks* ago!"

He shrugged. "Sad you've been missing out on being my fiancée for even that long? Understandable, I guess."

Rose realized she was breathing hard, the rest of the room having faded away in the way that always happened whenever she was with Blake. At first, she'd just assumed it was her hatred for him consuming all of her thoughts but... she didn't tend to kiss people she hated. Not really. She glanced up and around and saw an awful lot of faces still staring their way and Rose lowered her voice as she folded her arms across her chest and glared at him.

"I'm mad at you."

"For almost leaving?"

She folded her arms tightly across her chest and only dropped them when she watched him notice how much doing so hiked up her breasts. "Yes. And... I miss Bailey."

Blake slid half a step closer and brushed a hand across her cheek gently. "He misses you too. He misses seeing you in bed in the morning or with wet hair when you're fresh out of the shower even though you prefer baths and–" He breathed out shakily, looking down and away from her until she tilted his chin up and was shocked to see blue eyes wet with tears that he blinked away. "I almost lost you too. I'll never forget how cold you were in my arms, or the blood that... God, I didn't think anyone could lose that much and live."

She pressed a kiss to his lips, quick and fleeting, but she knew her mother had seen based on the squeal that erupted from somewhere on her right-hand side. "Yes, well, I couldn't let you out-do me, remember?"

Blake laughed, a deep rumbly sound that filled her with warmth. "Want to get out of here?"

She snickered. "You live here, and I'm living at my parent's place right now." *The Hart* had been home for a long time, but things changed. People changed.

"Upstairs is off-limits to guests," he countered, and she smirked.

"I guess you'll have to make an exception for me then," she said as she leaned in and pressed her hands to his chest before slipping one into his palm and squeezing.

Blake led them out of the ballroom and nodded to Christopher, presumably telling him he was in charge now. "You're not a guest here, princess. This is your home too."

She was so focused on Blake that she didn't have time to

think about the last time she'd been in this house, the photos that had littered the floor and led down the staircase. The truth was that there were too many good memories in this place outweighing the bad and Blake seemed to have a way of focusing her thoughts completely on him whenever they were together anyway.

Blake's hand was hot in hers as he nudged open his bedroom door and pressed her against it as soon as they were inside.

"So does this mean you accept?" He taunted and she murmured in protest when he put an inch of space between their bodies.

"I didn't think I had much choice in the matter."

"You always have a choice, but the heart wants what it wants." He pressed a long kiss to her mouth, stroking her tongue with his before pulling back and leaving her breathing hard. "So what I want to know is, are you mine? Or do you need me to get down on my knees for you again?"

Rose linked her hands behind his neck and let herself look at him, really look. Took in the softness of his eyes, the hopeful curl of his mouth, the locks of unruly hair that brushed his face despite the gel, and she smiled. "Well, I do think you skipped that stage before but... I think there would be very few things sweeter in this world than to be yours, David Blake."

A slow smile spread across his face. "I love you. Have done since I was fifteen and you punched me in the balls for being mean to your best friend."

"Chelsie," she mused, and he smirked.

"The very same."

They kissed again, longer and harder this time until they were both panting when Blake pulled away.

"Must you keep doing that?"

"I'm waiting."

"For what?" She folded her arms across her chest and raised a haughty brow, ignoring the way his eyes heated.

"I told you I loved you."

"Yes."

"You haven't said it back."

"Haven't I?"

"No."

"Oh."

"Rose–"

"Fine. I love you too. Happy?" she growled, and the smile faded from his face as he looked at her hungrily.

"Immensely."

"Fine," she repeated, eyes on his mouth.

"Fine," he agreed, and then they were kissing. Blake's mouth was somehow everywhere at once, tracing her collarbones, licking a path up her neck to nip at her ear, between her breasts as he rucked up the hem of her dress and paused at the bandage covering her thigh. He caressed its edges, his rough hands gentling for a moment as they slid up her inner thighs, making her gasp.

"Blake."

"Hm?"

"Stop teasing me."

He laughed and pressed his fingertips to her bare pussy. "I love it when you forget to put on underwear."

"I didn't forget."

"Oh." His grin turned wicked. "All this for me then? Someone is very sure of themselves."

"Maybe I'd planned on seducing Christopher," she smirked and then moaned as one of his fingers slid inside her.

"And we were having such a lovely time," he chided as he slid in a second finger more roughly, making her pant as she parted her thighs and then wince at the strain on her leg. Blake pulled his hand away and lifted her by the waist, carrying her to the bed and laying her gently in the middle. "Your mouth says such terrible things," he said as he crawled to meet her in the center of the bed. "It's almost like you want to be tortured."

She let out a breathy laugh that turned into a moan as he bent his head and tasted her, licking long up the middle of her pussy before suctioning down on her clit. "Didn't you say something about getting on your knees?"

Blake dragged her to the edge of the bed by her hips and retreated until he was on his knees on the floor looking up at her. "How's this?" he asked before lowering his mouth back to her pussy and sucking hard enough on her clit that she saw stars. "I will get on my knees for you every damn day, Rose. I will worship you until the day I die. Will you marry me?" He breathed the words onto her skin and she gasped for air as pleasure fogged her mind.

"I'll think about it," she rasped out, and he laughed quietly as he tasted her again.

"Wicked woman. Luckily for you," he murmured against her, tongue writing words into the sensitive flesh, "I've missed you far too much to be patient right now. So you're just going to have to wait for your punishment until round two." He pulled back and she shivered at the sound of his zipper opening and whimpered when she felt him nudge at her entrance.

She opened her mouth to reply but could only moan in time with Blake as he smoothly slid into her in one long, luxurious thrust. Her hips flexed automatically and he panted out a breath as she clenched around him. "We really need to stop doing this without a condom."

Blake swore. "Well at least if we have a baby, it won't be born out of wedlock."

"I still don't see a ring," she teased, and he grinned as he moved over and in her.

"Patience is a virtue, princess."

Then she couldn't talk anymore as he made words flee her brain, his fingers joining the rocking motion of his dick as he stroked her clit.

"Rose," he said huskily, and she breathed his name.

"I hate you," she said as he slowed down the movement of his hips before grinding against her and setting her aflame.

"I love you too."

GET

EVEN

REVENGE IS A DISH BEST SERVED HOT

SUN CITY #1

JADE CHURCH

Sometimes, revenge is a
dish best served hot...

Acknowledgments

Firstly, a book is a labour of love and I'm beyond grateful that I get to share my stories with you all. Thanks so much for reading and I hope you enjoyed the time you got to spend with Blake, Rose, Bailey and Co. Carry on past the acknowledgements to read the first chapter of Get Even, a college revenge romance, for free!

A big shoutout to the lovely Helena V Paris who hyped this book up with me while I was drafting and read an early version, your support and insight is always so appreciated. (P.S. I'm sorry about Meredith.)

My ARC team and early readers are the absolute best and I couldn't do this without you, thank you for loving In Too Deep as much as me and for being with me on my writer journey. You're all incredible.

To the book community, thank you for your endless support. I'm sending love to you all.

To my amazing alpha reader, Hannah, thank you for your insight and love for Bailey. And to Katie Wismer, my copy editor, thank you for making sure I spelled everyone's names right – you're the best!

Finally, to my partner in all things, Connor – thank you for cooking me dinner while I went crazy trying to finish my first draft. You are everything.

Chapter One

Enemy - Imagine Dragons, J.I.D.

There were a few things you should probably know. The first was that boys at college were horny. The second was that the girls were horny too. Lastly, I was a firm believer of *Don't get mad, get even* – but I also didn't like to do things in halves. That's how I ended up sandwiched between my ex-boyfriend's brother and best friend.

Brad was moaning in my ear, his breath uncomfortably hot as he pounded away underneath me, wringing small sparks of pleasure from my body. Cody echoed him like this was some kind of pack mating exercise as he moved over me, grunting as he pushed into me shallowly and then harder. The sex wasn't bad, in fact, it was highly satisfying because I knew that Aaron was going to just *die* when he found out about this. Well, maybe next time he promised he loved someone he wouldn't go ahead and fuck their best friend. *Asshole.*

Despite the moral satisfaction, my body was not hugely interested in these guys – mostly because they were idiots and I did generally like to find some sort of intellectual connection in the people I slept with. But... they were pretty, so I focused on the way Cody's golden body flexed in the mirror opposite the bed and the warmth of Brad's hands as they squeezed my breasts. I ran my hands down Brad's abs and gave him a smug smile, there were a lot of them – more than Aaron had for sure. He groaned, tweaking my nipple in one large hand as I sat up and pushed back into Cody's warmth and hardness. His breath stuttered at the change in position and I let out a moan to encourage him on and he began quickly moving again, faster this time. I took the hand Brad still had on my boob and tugged him up so I was sitting in his lap with Cody kneeling behind me, then I directed his hand downwards and pressed his fingers to my clit, giving a loud cry of appreciation. Suddenly they're both scrambling, trying to fuck me harder or faster and I rocked between them with a gasp – *finally*. Whoever said you couldn't have your cake and eat it too was wrong and revenge tasted sweet.

Cody pressed hot little kisses to my neck and heat flooded through me as I reached back and tugged at his blonde curls. I was getting close to the edge as I felt them hit a spot Aaron had never managed to find and suddenly I was shaking through my release, tightening around them until they panted in unison. Brad gripped my waist as they worked themselves to a climax too and Cody slumped against my back as he finished, hair tickling my skin until Brad eased me off them. I was a sweaty mess and I shivered as the cold air rushed over my skin, feeling oddly lonely without them pressed against me. The boys collapsed to the bed on either side of me after ditching their condoms and I smiled at them, kissing one and then the other – now for the *piece de resistance*.

"Say 'fuck me'," I giggled, brushing my dark hair away

from my face and holding up my phone to take a very naked photo of the three of us looking thoroughly fucked with our sweaty, flushed skin and smug smiles. Then I found Aaron's contact and hit send, my finger hesitating for only a second over the button.

"Well, this has been fun boys – I'd say call me but, well, don't." My smile was sweet and they looked bewildered as I stood and searched the floor for my clothes – not that they covered much anyway. I'd come prepared to seduce two guys, thinking they might be a little hesitant about betraying Aaron, but really... it had taken surprisingly little effort. My phone vibrated in my hand and my stomach tightened in anticipation of his response. It had been a scant twenty-four hours since I'd got home early and found my boyfriend in my best friend's bedroom – unbeknownst to them. At first I'd gone straight to my room, sat numbly on my bed and waited for my pulse to stop sounding in my ears quite so loudly. Then I'd stood up and walked to the door, ready to burst in there, cause a scene and humiliate them both. But there was something that would hurt them more – *public spectacle.* Plus I wanted Aaron to know exactly how much he meant to his brother. *His* best friend. I'd spoken barely two words to them, just shown up in my skimpy outfit and gave Brad *fuck me* eyes and suggested he bring Cody along for the ride. That was it. They'd sold him out that quickly.

"You're leaving?" Cody asked, pushing out his full bottom lip into a pout that really was cute but dropped it when I nodded my head. I pulled on the lacy black panties I'd been wearing and Brad sat up, concern starting to muddy those big brown eyes.

"Hey, you're not going to mention this to Aaron, are you?"

Chapter One

My smile was sweet, "Oh no, I don't intend on speaking to him again, but you know how he is with secrets."

Brad looked unsure about whether to be worried about his brother and Cody bit his lip. I walked a little closer and brushed a kiss across his mouth, "Wasn't it worth it though?" I asked and Cody melted, a sleepy grin pulling across his face as he decided it was, in fact, worth betraying his best friend for. I supposed I should be flattered.

A knock sounded at the door and the boys both froze like naughty kids with their hands caught in the proverbial cookie jar. I hadn't foreseen a direct confrontation with Aaron at the scene of the crime, considering he'd still been in Taylor's bedroom when I'd left over an hour ago, but this definitely could be fun.

But when I opened the door it wasn't Aaron staring back at me, it was Ryan, their other housemate. His eyes dropped to my still-bare chest and I leaned against the door frame lazily as his gaze found my see-through panties.

"Do you always open the door in just your panties, Jamie?" he asked with a small smirk and I looked down at myself as if only just remembering my clothes – or lack thereof.

I giggled like he'd just said the funniest thing I'd ever heard, "Oh, no, I don't make a habit of it. I guess my head still isn't back in the real world yet after spending the last hour with these two." I nodded behind me to where Cody and Brad still lay naked on the bed and Ryan's mouth tightened in disapproval.

"I guess I know why Aaron's on the warpath now," he said, waving his cell phone in our direction, and the boys looked at each other in horror.

276

Chapter One

"How the fuck did he find out so fast? My dick's barely dry," Brad said and I bit back a grimace at the imagery.

"Something about a picture? I don't know, but if you don't want an awkward scene then you should probably go," he directed the last at me and I batted my long lashes at him innocently while the boys stared at me in something like shock as they realized what I'd done.

"Oh, of course. I'd hate to be an inconvenience to poor baby Aaron."

Ryan looked like he almost wanted to smile until his gaze dropped to my chest again and he cleared his throat, "You might want to get dressed quickly then."

"Right, yes, it won't take me long. I wasn't wearing much when I got here."

A look of pain crossed his face that only increased as I bent over and stepped into the short black dress crumpled on the floor by the bed and found my shoes. I blew the boys a kiss and they dazedly smiled before frowning, like they weren't quite sure what had just happened and whether they were allowed to have enjoyed it.

"See you later, Ry," I said and he stepped out of the way. He was a complicated one – actually seemed to have a brain rattling around inside his pretty head and a genuine sense of humor, fuck knows why he chose Aaron, Brad and Cody for housemates. I felt Ryan's gaze on me all the way down the hallway until I walked down the stairs and out of sight.

Sometimes, revenge was a dish best served hot. Sure, I could have walked into Taylor's bedroom, found her and Aaron tangled together and had that image burned into my brain – but I'd chosen a messier path because I wanted them to *hurt*. Aaron would hate my public fuck-you and Taylor was about to get what was coming to her too. She'd clung to me since Freshman year and I could admit that I had clung right back – I'd never had real friends before and I'd thought I'd found that with Taylor and Aaron. But the truth was, Taylor needed me more than I needed her. I'd always been independent, never really had much choice in the matter, but she had always had someone willing to bail her out, to wipe her tears or throw money at her problems. Usually her mom.

At the end of the day Taylor was a rich white girl and her mom had taught her the most important rule: *never cause a scene*. If she knew half the shit her precious baby girl got up to... I smirked but shook my head as I closed the front door behind me. I didn't want to involve her mom. I wanted Taylor to know what it felt like to be alone, to have the person she trusted kick her in the teeth. Figuratively, of course. I wasn't going to beat her ass, even if she deserved it, because that would make *her* the victim. I was done giving her chances or excuses. Sometimes you had to cut-off a limb before the poison could spread any further and that's exactly what Aaron and Taylor felt like, poison in my veins, burning me from the inside out until all I felt was white-hot rage. Their mistake, really. The cheating would have pissed me off, but the *lying* was something I couldn't tolerate. Ever. It hit my trigger button like nothing else, probably thanks to my own, sweet mother, and practically ensured that I wouldn't have been able to stop at payback. I didn't need revenge, I needed to *win*. I smiled as my phone vibrated three more times in my hand, Aaron no doubt losing his mind over the photo and the added insult of being ignored. I didn't give a single fuck. There would be time for tears later. For now, I had to go and confront my best friend.

Ingram Content Group UK Ltd.
Milton Keynes UK
UKHW011812120723
425017UK00004B/58